Praise for th

Paul A. Myers

Paris 1935: Destiny's Crossroads

"takes us into the back rooms of high-level officials, writers, and media stars in order to understand why events happened as they did…involved and intriguing, Myers' work definitely is worth reading."

> B.N. Peacock, Historical Novel Society Online Review, Feb. 2012

Paris 1934: Victory in Retreat

"descriptive and thoroughly researched narrative feels true to the era; the "City of Light" shines through the page."

> Gricel Dominguez, Historical Novel Society Online Review, Aug. 2010

Vienna 1934: Betrayal at the Ballplatz

"Myers' characters feel true to the era…an excellent job of making the story real due to his good research and fine storytelling. The interweaving of fact, fiction, real, and fictional people makes this book exciting and romantic."

> Naomi Theye, Historical Novel Society Online Review, May 2009

Also by Paul A. Myers

Novels

Paris 1935: Destiny's Crossroads
Paris 1934: Victory in Retreat
Vienna 1934: Betrayal at the Ballplatz

Cultural profiles

French Sketches: Cap d'Antibes and the Murphys
French Sketches: Cap Ferrat and Somerset Maugham
French Sketches: Monaco, Onassis, and Prince Rainier

History

North to California: The Spanish Discovery of California 1533-1603

Clerk! The Vietnam Memoir of Paul A. Myers

A Farewell in Paris

Paul A. Myers

CreateSpace edition
Imprint: CreateSpace Independent Publishing Platform
Produced by Paul A. Myers Books

ISBN-13: 978-1481100465
ISBN-10: 1481100467

AUTHOR

Paul A. Myers lives in Claremont, California with his wife Minche. When not writing historical fiction and cultural profiles, he works as a sole practitioner CPA. He is a graduate of the University of California, Santa Barbara and has an MBA from the University of Santa Clara. He served as a soldier in Vietnam and later worked in California's Silicon Valley, his last position as chief financial officer of a small public company.

Paul A. Myers on the *terrasse* at Café Les Deux Magots in Saint-Germain-des-Prés on Paris's Left Bank where much of the novel is set.

See author's webpage at **myersbooks.com.**

Email author at **myersbooks@gmail.com**.

Follow on Facebook at myersbooks and Twitter at @myersbooks

Cast of Characters

Fictional

Bill Lawrence – an American literary agent living on Île Saint-Louis in Paris and a veteran of the U.S. Army in World War I.
Kurt Eckhart – an American foreign correspondent in Berlin and a veteran of the U.S. Army in World War I.
Kate Lundberg – an American free-lance writer living on the Left Bank of Paris.

Historical

Djuna Barnes – American magazine journalist, poet, dramatist, and Modernist novelist living on Paris's Left Bank.
Natalie Clifford Barney – wealthy American heiress and salon hostess known as "The Amazon" for her announced and uncompromising lesbianism. Her Friday afternoon salons in her Left Bank garden were famous for the prominence of both the French and American literary and political personalities who attended.
Janet Flanner – American magazine journalist writing the "Letter from Paris" column for *The New Yorker* magazine and living on Paris's Left Bank.
Mina Loy – English poet and artist living in Paris and close to the Dada and Surrealist art movements.
John Maynard Keynes – English economist and British Treasury representative to the Paris Peace Conference in 1919. Wrote the famous book *The Economic Consequences of the Peace* as a dissenting treatise on the Paris Peace Treaty.
Solita Solano – American free-lance critic living on Paris's Left Bank.

Cameo appearances by Margaret Anderson (literary editor), Sylvia Beach (owner of book shop Shakespeare & Company), André Breton (Surrealist writer), Man Ray (Surrealist artist and photographer), Elliot Paul (American journalist), Ford Madox Ford (English novelist), and Morrill Cody (American writer).

This novel is a work of fiction and product of imagination. The historic characters are placed in fictional scenes interacting with fictional characters. The novel attempts to keep historical figures "in character" based on portrayals in biographies and other published sources.

Red lips are not so red
As the stained stones kissed by the English dead.

—Wilfred Owen
Greater Love
Killed in action November 4, 1918
Poem published posthumously

The Treaty includes no provisions for the economic rehabilitation of Europe,—nothing to make the defeated Central Empires into good neighbours, nothing to stabilize the new States of Europe, nothing to reclaim Russia; nor does it promote in any way a compact of economic solidarity amongst the Allies themselves; no arrangement was reached at Paris for restoring the disordered finances of France and Italy, or to adjust the systems of the Old World and the New.

—John Maynard Keynes
The Economic Consequences of the Peace
London, 1919

1. Île Saint-Louis

I walked up the stairs sorting the morning letters one by one. An envelope from Berlin caught my eye. Unusual. There were always a few from New York or London. But Berlin? That was rare. The name "Eckhart" was written on the corner of the envelope above the return address. The name struck a strong chord of remembrance, an uncomfortable echo from the past.

Standing on the landing of the *premiere étage*, the second floor in France, I fumbled with the keys and opened the lock of the thick wooden door. I went over to a long table with the elegantly curved legs of a French antique, pushed some books aside, and cleared a space on one of the polished black walnut inlays that divided the tabletop into quarters. I put the letters down in some sort of rough order and pulled up a chair and sat down.

The letter from Berlin was on top; I opened it and read through several pages of close typescript. I set the letter down and leaned back. I looked out through the rain-misted windows, beyond the gray river flowing past my flat on Île Saint-Louis, to the fog-shrouded buildings lining the Left Bank. The buildings, solid and rectangular, stood like so many battalion squares drawn up for a division review.

The cold grayness of late winter contrasted with the visual warmth of orange-colored curtains curving across the windows of my drawing room, tall and elegant in the French way. Dark brown rugs on the floor and forest-green tapestries on the walls provided a sumptuous feeling of warmth to a room I always kept well-heated. I remembered the cold.

Leaning back in my chair, I took a long sip from a cup of coffee and sat with my thoughts. It would be ten years this summer since that day in July 1918 when it really began. I remembered Eckhart. He had been a lieutenant in Company D of First Battalion where I was adjutant. But that day I commanded the battalion reaction force. Every rifle went into the line that day. All the companies had it tough; hard to say that one had it worse than the others.

I recalled that in Company D the commander and several of the lieutenants went down as they rallied their men to withstand the ferocious German assault coming across the river. Up on the ridge above the battle area, the battalion commander saw the weight of the German assault hit Company D; he saw the company commander fall. He looked over at me and gave the signal. I led my men out of our position and over the top of the ridge—the most harrowing five minutes of my life. I deployed the reaction force behind Company D's position. My men put volley after volley of rifle fire into the onrushing German soldiers until the Germans crumbled and fell back. Our battalion held; our regiment held. Many did not.

After the day's fighting, I went up to regiment to process casualties rearward and replacements forward. Eckhart, I recalled, took command of Company D in the thick of the fighting. The battalion commander spoke approvingly of his blunt, forceful authority under fire.

Later, after the replacements had been hastily put into the line, the regiment crossed the river as part of a multi-division push to the next river. Northeast France was a battle of rivers. Then the regiment was withdrawn into reserve, additional replacements were brought in to top off the rifle companies, and a quick program of training was undertaken. Eckhart organized the training. The regiment went back into the line for the final assault on the Hindenburg Line. For blood-soaked week after blood-soaked week the 3rd Division drove east.

At the beginning of yet another advance late in October, the First Battalion commander went down and Eckhart took over and drove the battalion forward to its objective. The regimental commander came forward and in the blown-out dugout that was the battalion command post he put a major's oak leaves on Eckhart's collar. While rainwater streamed off our wide-brimmed steel helmets, the commander clapped Eckhart on the back while I shook his hand and simply said, "Kurt." Talk, like an unnecessary accoutrement, had been left behind weeks ago.

Several days later, leading one of the assault companies forward in mid-October, Eckhart went down, hit by artillery fire. He was evacuated westwards with thousands of others.

In November, the war was over. An armistice they said. Every army in France had been bled white—German, French, British, and American.

A directive called for all German-speaking officers to be sent to Third Army for occupational duty. I cut the orders sending Eckhart to Koblenz. The paperwork caught up with Eckhart in a hospital outside of Paris.

A couple of days later my own fluency in French got me sent to Paris for duty at the Peace Conference. I saw Eckhart once during the Peace Conference at a meeting in Trier, Germany where arrangements were being hammered out to get food into Germany. At Trier, Eckhart worked with British Treasury representative John Maynard Keynes to remove final obstacles to the agreement.

Later, I heard Eckhart had married a German nurse in Koblenz. A couple of years later I saw Eckhart, with Keynes, at an international conference in Genoa, Italy. He had become a renowned economics correspondent writing from Berlin. After the conference, I lost personal track of Eckhart but saw his name frequently on news dispatches from Berlin.

I glanced down at the letter: Eckhart said he was writing a novel. Could I help with arranging its publication? Well, that was my job. No trouble there.

He would be in Paris for a long weekend in a couple of weeks. Could we meet? I wrote back, "Yes."

2. A Night at the Theater

A couple days later I went out to the Fifteenth Arrondisement to take in a new French play. The theater was a short walk from the Metro stop just west of the Eiffel Tower. An adventurous young drama company, the Comédians de la Croix-Nivert, was putting on a run of modern plays three nights a week in the old theater when it would otherwise be shut down. During the rest of the week the theater presented solid neighborhood fare of melodramas and operettes.

The winter chill was in the building. I saw and watched the first two acts. It was a comedy of amorous repartee finely crafted. Two sisters, one supposedly a prude and the other a coquette, secretly loved a young man. Who got the young man was the turn of the drama.

At the intermission, I pulled my overcoat close and walked out into the lobby of the old playhouse, the carpet more than a little worn, pleased with myself for having come out to see a good evening of theater despite the cold.

Across the lobby I saw friends. I walked up and held out my hand to the woman on the right, Solita Solano. She was wrapped in a big coat with a huge fur collar, a hat closely covered her jet-black hairdo, and spit curls scalloped her cheeks and framed her blue-violet eyes. A beautiful white silk scarf was around her neck, tucked below the fur collar. Her lips were well painted into a bright red cupid's bow. Cute as hell I always told myself, with a tinge of regret. She had a steady girlfriend.

"So you took our advice and came to see the bright young talent," she said in a throaty roar.

"Solita, you know theater." She had been theater critic for the *New York Tribune* back in the States.

Figure 1 Solita Solano and Djuna Barnes in a Paris cafe in 1922. The image continues as a bestselling postcard in Paris today.

"That she does," said the woman standing just to her left, a grand presence with a fine leonine head framed by rich golden hair.

I turned to her and asked, "Will this be in your next *Letter from Paris*, Janet?"

"Probably not. You need to see a lot to write a little," she replied. Janet Flanner was the rising American journalist in Paris with her column in *The New Yorker*. "You know that, Bill. You're the leading prophet on transatlantic literary affairs." Yes, I knew that. I had read it in *The New Yorker.*

I bowed from the waist at the compliment. I was selling both French authors in translation and the American expatriates back into the American market. But well below the level of Hemingway and Fitzgerald—Max Perkins had them sown up for Scribner's. Nevertheless, I was becoming first chair among the second tier.

"Actually, we're here because of Kate. She is doing a round-up feature on drama in Paris for one of the housewifely magazines," and Janet nodded at the third woman standing just to her left.

"Kate, nice to see you again," I said and held out my hand. I had worked with Kate here and there over the past couple of years. A real solid writer.

"You too, Bill."

"Not to talk business, Kate, but I think I have your short story placed," and turned and smirked at Janet, "with one of the housewifely magazines."

Janet let that leonine head fall back and laughed, a big throaty chuckle.

Kate said, with a sense of professional satisfaction, "They're my bread and butter. Short stories, and magazine articles on the war memorials in eastern France."

I hadn't seen any of her articles on war memorials. I wondered about her interest in the subject. For me, Eastern France and its battlefields were mentally off-limits.

Returning to the present, I said, "I admire your work, Kate. Your piece on Natalie Barney setting up her *Académie des Femmes* to honor women writers in France drew some interesting inquiries from New York."

Janet gave me a piercing look of inquiry. I mean riveting.

"I have spoken with Gertrude," mentioning Gertrude Stein, the well-known Left Bank *grande dame*, "that a popular book about her reminiscences in Paris could be a big seller." I paused, "That's what one of the big lights in New York told me."

"With Alice?" Solita shot out.

"With Alice," I replied. Alice B. Toklas was Gertrude's companion, which of course everyone in Paris knew and probably no one in America did. It told you a lot of what you needed to know about Gertrude, though.

Solita and Janet took in this little nugget. I could see them think: was a cultural shift underway? Tolerance in America?

I laughed. They read my mind and smiled.

"I could do more in this area," Kate said softly, her mind turning over ideas.

I turned towards her and said, "Kate Lundberg is becoming a name in New York." I added with a touch of emphasis, "And you know how to tread softly." Writing about independent women of different sexual orientations required sensitivity to middle brow sentiment. The American housewives out in the new suburbs wanted their sexual adventures presented delicately. Poured cream, someone told me, not goo.

Solita and Janet nodded wisely if a bit absently. They were in Paris precisely to avoid daily contact with bourgeois American Puritanism. As were half the other women writers in Paris. Me? I found them all interesting.

Kate nodded her head at my compliment.

"Working on anything else?" I asked.

She looked at Janet, who gave a slight affirmative nod, and turned back to me and said, "Well, yes, I'm working on a fashion piece about the spring openings. Solita and Janet have some magazine leads in New York. Everyone wants to copy the success of *The New Yorker's* Paris fashion column."

"That would be a real foundation." The Paris fashion column in *The New Yorker* had made Paris and fashion a hot topic in all the smart New York cocktail conversations.

"I'm working on a feature about Coco Chanel. She stands in a class by herself; she occupies a distinctive place in the world of couturiers. She has grasped the supreme secret of today's style—simplicity guided by taste."

"A look at what is behind her rise?"

"Yes, exactly."

"That would surely open new horizons."

"Yes, it would. Allow me to pursue some larger projects."

"Have any in mind?"

"No, not really. But I have my eyes open."

"I'll keep my eyes open, too."

"Thanks, Bill."

Janet looked squarely at me, "Bill, Djuna Barnes is the best woman writer working in the Quarter. Way ahead of Gertrude. You should be pushing her work."

"I agree. But Djuna has had problems with the New York Post Office, not to mention the Customs Service. Hard to publish and distribute her work in New York." The common knowledge was that Djuna and her editor had sat in Paris last summer removing passages having to do with bodily fluids from her current novel, which was scheduled for publication this summer.

Janet laughed and added, "Your job is to surmount those problems."

Solita rustled her cape and put that beautiful look on her face and said, “The second half will be starting. Why don’t you join us, Bill?”

Solita had one of the three most gorgeous looks among American women in Paris. Interestingly, all three looks went with women who loved other women. Kate? Well, she had that fresh-faced Midwestern look, a look that was just coming into its maturity at about age thirty. She lived somewhere out in the Sixth, a half dozen blocks west of the residence hotel where Solita and Janet lived.

I nodded and held my hand towards the lobby door. Solita lightly added, “I hear at the end the young man goes free.”

“You mean the two sisters are left in some state of un-freeness?” Janet bantered.

“Spinsterhood. The black void of dread feared by all good Midwestern women,” Solita gaily replied.

I looked at Kate to see if the barb stung.

“I don’t frighten easily,” she said over her shoulder with a laugh as she pushed open the lobby doors, her eyes piercing my gaze in a friendly way.

3. La Closerie des Lilas

It was a cold Saturday morning as I walked under bare trees along the narrow grassy park leading up from Luxembourg Gardens to boulevard du Montparnasse. At the corner was the welcome warmth of La Closerie des Lilas, the always elegant café. Entering, I looked far back to the rear of the room, near a warmth-giving stove, and saw Kurt Eckhart. I nodded a greeting and then turned to hang my overcoat, muffler, and hat on the rack. I walked over as he stood up. He came around the table and shook my hand while clasping me heartily on the shoulder. Yes, old comrades were meeting.

"Nice to see you, Bill."

"It's been a long time, Kurt."

"Yes, it'll be ten years this summer. Oh yes, and Trier…" and his mind searched back in time, "and that time in Genoa for the conference."

"Yes," I said without much enthusiasm.

I nodded for Kurt to take a seat and he stepped back and plopped himself on a chair near the wall. I took the chair across the small round table, my back to the entrance.

"Well, what do you think?" he asked.

"I like it. The storyline has a lot of drive and force."

"So did the AEF when we drove towards Germany in the fall of '18."

We had both been in the 3rd Division of the American Expeditionary Force.

"Yes we did," I said softly. The never-ending stream of ambulances passing by regimental headquarters drove home, for those who cared to look out the window, the terrible cost the American people were paying for being "over there." I presumed Kurt had had his face resolutely facing east towards Germany. His job was to go forward; others reckoned the cost.

"In your outline, the ending is pretty vague," I said, getting at what was the weak point of his planned novel.

"I haven't really finished that. It's a work-in-progress. But it's a tragedy that drives home the point of the failed peace."

I nodded in understanding. I had watched the beginnings of the failure right here in Paris at the Peace Conference in 1919.

"Well, the first couple of sample chapters are a great start."

"Do you mean that?"

"Yes, I do. The book will sell in New York."

"I hear you're the most respected literary agent in Paris."

"Some people say that."

"Will you represent me?"

"Yes. Delighted, in fact." Even from here, I could see this project had real potential.

Kurt looked over my shoulder towards the entrance where something had caught eye. He asked, "Do you know the dame?"

I turned and looked over my shoulder. Kate was just taking off her overcoat and hat and hanging them on the rack. I stood up, remarking to Kurt, "Yes, that's Kate Lundberg, an American freelancer working here in Paris. Building a good name for herself with the glossies in New York." I waved at Kate and beckoned her to come over. Kurt stood as Kate came up smiling.

"Good morning, Bill. You found out my secret weekend workplace. Warm. Away from Montparnasse."

I smiled in agreement and made introductions. "Kurt, this is Kate. Kate, this is Kurt." They shook hands. He almost fell over himself getting a chair for her and holding it while she seated herself.

"Thank you," she responded, a warm smile graciously returning the good manners.

A waiter came over.

"*Café du lait, s'il vous plait,*" she said.

I looked at Kurt, he nodded, and I told the waiter the same for us.

Kate looked at Kurt and then said to the waiter, "*Et du pain.*" Some bread. She looked at Kurt again, "*Et du beurre.*" Some butter.

Kate was right. Kurt looked like a man who liked to eat. Liked to do a lot of hearty things, I guessed.

"*Bien, madame.*" The waiter left.

I quickly put Kate in the picture, "Kurt is writing a novel about the war and the tragedy that came afterwards. We were in the 3rd Division together and…"

Kate seemed a little startled.

"Didn't you know? Most of the people in the Quarter knew," I said.

"I knew Elliott Paul was in a field signals battalion. I didn't know about you."

"Well, Kurt was right up front in the drive east towards Germany. After the Armistice, he was part of the American occupation forces stationed at Koblenz. He speaks German."

"Like half the rest of the American Midwest," shot out Kurt.

"Yes, I know. I'm from there, too." She smiled at him signaling her understanding.

"Anyway," I continued, "the hero marries a German girl amidst the chaos of post-war Germany. Later they go to Berlin where tragedy unfolds." I looked at Kurt, "A doomed romance, I presume?"

"Yes, it was," Kurt replied, an almost hurt puppy dog look coming across his face. Kate noticed and his expression peaked her interest. A man who deeply loved a woman was central to modern fiction, but Kurt's story seemed to grab Kate.

"I haven't finished the last part of the novel. It needs work," Kurt added.

I explained to Kate, "The novel so far has lots of drive and force."

Kate looked appraisingly at Kurt; she could see where the drive and force came from. Like he had said, she knew that people like him had built the American Midwest.

"Kurt's written it in the first person using his name and the name of his dead wife Elsa. The immediacy grabs you by the throat," I added.

Kate looked at Kurt with fascination.

"Here are some sample chapters, Kate. You could read them this afternoon and tomorrow," and I pushed the papers across the little table.

"I want them back tomorrow. I'm returning to Berlin tomorrow night," Kurt interjected. "They're my only copy."

"Yes, of course," replied Kate.

"Kurt, I think Kate could really help us with this project. She could write some feature stories that would come out before publication and then some more afterwards. Fan the public interest."

"Yes, I see."

I looked at Kate; she nodded her head in agreement, "Yes."

"And she could help with the editing. She has a fine light touch. I don't want to disturb the strength of your style. Just a little polish here and there," and I turned and looked at Kate.

"I understand completely."

"That's fine with me. I know I'm a correspondent but I just get the facts on the wire. Chicago tells me I write like a gorilla, but," and he looked at Kate, "my degree was in civil engineering from the University of Wisconsin. This thing in Berlin came up after the war. I do business and economics. Lots of numbers. The people who read my dispatches trade wheat and bonds, they don't count commas."

Kate nodded, enthralled by Kurt's background.

"There's another thing. If we hit publication in the middle of next year, our timing will be perfect."

Both Kurt and Kate looked at me.

"The word is out that Ernest Hemingway has started his second novel. It's about the war."

"The guy who wrote about the bulls in Spain. The guy who couldn't get it on with the English dame," said Kurt. "Damn shame about that," he added with genuine sorrowfulness.

Kate could plainly see where one of Kurt's appetites was.

"Yes, that's him. His new novel will be out next year. We should be coming out at the same time. Piggyback on his publicity when the public takes another look at the war."

"Yeah, I can see you have the angles figured out. Sounds smart," and he looked to Kate for confirmation. She nodded in agreement.

"Do you know what his novel is about? Hemingway was in Italy during the war, I heard."

"Built around his experience on the Italian front during the war."

"That was sideshow," Kurt said a little dismissively. Kurt turned and explained to Kate, "The real showdown was here on the Western Front."

A pained look came across Kate's face, "Yes, I know."

Kate's reaction caught my attention. There was something there. I nodded to myself and then said, "I think I have an idea. Hemingway wrote a short story last year entitled *In Another Country* that suggests some of his themes."

Kate looked at me, her expression making the question.

"The opening line begins, 'In the fall the war was always there, but we did not go to it anymore.'"

Kurt looked a little perplexed.

"Fitzgerald really complimented Hemingway on the opening line," and I looked at Kate by way of explanation. "The line suggests there was something wrong with the war. Something strange."

"It wasn't the war, Bill. It was the peace that came afterwards," Kurt said with real emphasis. "That's the point my book is going to drive home."

Kate was now deeply interested.

"I respect Fitzgerald's opinion," Kurt said. "He knows the score. I liked the *Gatsby* book," referring to F. Scott Fitzgerald's bestseller *The Great Gatsby*. "It really got at the money corruption in New York."

Kurt turned to Kate and again explained with force, "It was the money power that queered the peace."

Kate winced at the words.

"They all wanted to suck it out of Germany like vampires," Kurt continued.

I nodded my head in slow agreement, "I saw it happen right here in Paris in 1919 at the Peace Conference."

"Peace, shit…" Kurt scornfully spat out.

"That's sort of Hemingway's point, I think. I've heard he wants to use as an epigraph the lines from Marlowe: '…but that was in another country, and besides the wench is dead.'"

"The quote would be like the line 'You are all a Lost Generation' on the opening page of his last novel." Kate said by way of explanation to Kurt.

"Yeah, I saw that. It really hit home."

"Exactly," I responded.

"Let me tell you, in my story, the girl's not a wench. She's beautiful," and Kurt looked out into the gray rainy morning and his expression took on a soft faraway look. I could see Kate was captivated by the change in his manner. The woman, whoever she was, had a hold on him, even now after all these years.

"But it was in another country," Kurt said decisively. "Germany." Italy was now on another planet.

"Where does the Hemingway story go?" Kate asked.

"At the end, the worldly wise Italian major, the one with the injured hand standing stoically at the therapy apparatus, loses his beautiful young wife to the influenza. Ever after, the major just comes to therapy everyday and stands at the apparatus and looks vacantly out the window."

Kurt took a long thoughtful sip from his coffee. He looked at both of us, "I know how he feels. It's awful. Worse than the war. The death of a beautiful wife. It takes so much away, the beauty of life itself."

Kate slowly nodded her head up in down in agreement. She seemed to understand the experience somehow. She touched Kurt's hand, "I know." He seemed startled.

"You do?"

Kate murmured, "Yes."

I let the words settle in, Kate's words hinting at something somewhere, it seemed to me. I put a close on the interlude by saying, "I think we're off to a promising start."

Kurt nodded in agreement, then brightened and asked, "Tonight? Are we going to do the town?"

"Why yes. I've made some plans. Dinner over on the Right Bank at a really nice Russian restaurant, the Grand Ermitage Moscovite. It's cabaret style with soft lights and a good band." I could see I had grabbed Kate's interest.

"Then we will go up to Montmartre…"

Kate rolled her eyes.

Not Kurt. At the word "Montmartre," he perked up like a puppy. His appetite for something was raring to go.

Kate said sweetly, "I'll let you boys have your evening. Sort of you own little American Legion reunion. I'm meeting my girlfriends at the Dôme," she said referring to the Café du Dôme on Montparnasse.

I laughed and looked at Kurt, "She doesn't mean that as a compliment."

"Yeah, I heard about the Legion and Paris." Then he looked at Kate, "I heard about girlfriends at the Dôme, too."

Kate made a winsome smile and flashed a come hither look. Kurt was charmed.

"Up in Montmarte, we'll go to Bricktop's. You like American jazz? She has the best. Dukes and earls push and shove to get through the door."

"Yeah, I like jazz. I really do. Worked in Chicago before the war. Hit the joints on the South Side and listened to the Negro bands. Those colored boys can really hit the notes with their trumpets and trombones. Hot Dixieland up from New Orleans."

"Good."

"And after that?" The puppy dog was wagging his tail.

Kate put her chin in the palm of her hand and looked across the table at me waiting for the answer, eyes laughing.

"Send you back to your hotel."

Kurt's face fell.

"But for tonight I have a companion for you. I've invited Madeline to come along. She works as an office girl for a French publishing house here. She's a widow. Young. Seventeen when her husband was killed."

"Some sort of professional?"

"No. She works Monday through Saturday for the publisher. But you show her a good time, she'll show you a good time. At the end, a nice tip maybe. Say a hundred francs. Nicely dressed girls always need clothes. The guys visiting from New York like her. A lot. Be nice."

Kate entered the fray, half seriously, "It's all quite respectable." Yes, I could guess that Kate knew how New York liked to sample the local color. I wasn't so sure about the respectable part.

Kurt turned to her, and with a real leer, said, "Well, someday, Sweets, come to Berlin. One thing I can guarantee you is that it isn't all respectable. What girls do there…and boys…" and then with a salacious emphasis, "and girls with girls…"

"Yes, I've heard," replied Kate nonchalantly.

I looked at Kate, "You could come tonight. I'll take you home after Bricktop's."

"Promise?"

"Promise."

"Okay."

I looked at both of them. "That's all settled. I'll pick you up at around nine. I have a taxi for the night." We all got up and left.

4. Grand Ermitage Moscovite

I watched out the side window as the taxi pulled to a stop on rue Jacob in front of the Hôtel d'Angleterre. Kurt came across the sidewalk, well dressed in an expensive topcoat, opened the rear door of the taxi, and jumped in beside me.

"Kurt, this is Madeleine," and I pointed to the young woman sitting just across on the jump seat.

"Hey, she's some dish," he loudly stage whispered to me. He held out his hand to her, "Kurt Eckhart, and I'm really glad to meet you."

Madeleine was completely vamped for the night: black bobbed hair, a tight crowned hat coming down to a narrow brim below her ears, a touch of black eye shadow—probably to match her underwear—a dark fox fur coat, invitingly open in the front revealing a silvery shimmering dress with tousled flounces in rows up and down in the flapper style. Dark stockings and stylish shoes that could do the dance completed the gig.

"Bill tells me you're in publishing."

"Oui, Monsieur Eckhart."

"Oh, just call me Kurt."

"Oui, Monsieur Kurt," she said. Then she really smiled. Glowed.

"I'm writing a novel."

"So Monsieur Bill tells me," and she reached over and touched his knee and gravely said, "A serious book, he said."

Kurt laughed, "We'll see. And your books?"

"Oh, I help publish books, romances I should call them. The tourists buy them because there are no romance books in America, I'm told. Isn't that so, Bill?"

I nodded in agreement.

"They come in brown paper wrappers?" asked Kurt as he laughed.

"Sometimes," she pouted. Her eyes brightened, "But they are quality." She turned towards me, "*N'est-ce pas*, Bill?"

"Yes, some of the best."

Madeleine tossed her shoulders and said, a cute little pout on her face, "I hear our romances circulate among the best…err, what are the words, Bill?"

"Women's clubs."

"Yes, some of the best women's clubs in America."

Kurt roared.

"Kurt, the profits are quite good. A nice trade," I added.

"I bet."

I looked up and saw Kate's apartment house just ahead. The taxi stopped and as I hopped out I said to Kurt, "Why don't you sit next to Madeleine?"

"You betcha."

I walked across a small courtyard to the front lobby and went in. Kate was waiting in the foyer. She came forward, a wide deeply brimmed hat pulled down over her soft brown hair, a nice overcoat trimmed with fox fur, also open in the front to reveal a glimmering light blue party dress made for doing the Charleston, and light stockings and sturdy high heels for dancing. Simply fetching.

"Hi, Bill."

"Whew, I haven't seen you like this before."

She twirled around in a circle, the hem of the overcoat floating out, and then said to me with light amusement, "The twirl works better without the overcoat on."

"I bet."

"You'll see," she said, and then she smiled in a light fun sort of way that was all Kate.

I held the lobby door open and led her across the sidewalk. Pierre, the driver, held the door open, an appreciative look on his face. Kate ducked her head and slid into the rear seat. I followed.

"Kate, this is Madeleine."

She held out her hand and shook Madeleine's hand. "*Enchantée,*" cooed Madeleine.

"*Enchantée*," Kate replied in a warm manner. She nodded at Kurt, "Good evening."

"We'll start the evening just across the river," I added.

Kate leaned over towards Madeleine and asked, "Didn't I meet you once at Man Ray's?"

"Yes, I was his model for awhile."

"The art or the postcards?" I asked playfully.

"*Tous les deux.*" Both. She batted her eyelashes. Kurt's interest skyrocketed.

"Before Kiki?" asked Kate.

"Yes. Before," and Madeleine turned to me, "and the postcards got me in with the publisher." She turned back and said to Kate, "Now I write, too. It all works out."

"I'm sure it does," answered Kate.

We chatted amongst ourselves as the taxi crossed the bridge, merged with the traffic on place de la Concorde, and flowed up rue Royale. The taxi veered right at the Madeleine and then made a left turn on rue Caumartin and pulled up behind a few other taxis near the door to the restaurant. Pierre jumped out and came around and opened the door. We all tumbled out.

A doorman held the door and we entered Grand Ermitage Moscovite, checked our overcoats, hats, and mufflers with the hatcheck girl and walked over to the maître d', who was decked out in traditional Russian garb with flowing pants stuffed into high boots. He escorted us to a white-satin covered table just off a small dance floor. A large candle glowed with a golden light in a glass bowl in the center of the table. Old silver glistened at each table setting.

"I love the tapestries on the walls," Kate said.

I looked at the sleighs, forests, and the menacing wolves on the winter scenes spread across the faces of the tapestries. A solo gypsy guitarist was playing a soft and mournful tune at the side of the orchestra area. Kurt and I seated the ladies; the maître d' handed over menus.

A young flaxen-haired woman, a kerchief around her head, came out dressed in colorful peasant costume, squares of bright red crisscrossing the flared skirt, and made a deep bow. She whispered to the guitarist, who strummed several chords, and the singer broke into a mournful tale of what surely must have been a lost love on the distant steppes of that now troubled land.

"It's beautiful," whispered Kate.

"I wonder what she says," asked Madeleine.

"I know the story, rather well I'm afraid," said Kurt sadly.

Kate looked at him and said, “So do I. May be we have been to the same place?”

“Not likely,” said Kurt with a note of dismissal.

I reached over and patted Kate on the hand and looked into her eyes, “One’s tragedy is always unique,” and I nodded in Kurt’s direction.

Kate smiled in understanding and nodded lightly. We both understood that, at the end, Kurt’s tragedy would drive the novel he was writing. We were both deeply intrigued by what the details of that tragedy would reveal, how the particular would support the larger truth of a failed peace.

A waiter appeared with a bottle of wine, held it up to me, and I nodded and circled the table with my finger. I whispered a dinner order to the waiter, who nodded. Then he went around filling each wine goblet in turn with thick red wine. Kurt took half of his with a gulp and turned back and stared transfixed at the singer. Madeleine sipped hers, looking over the top of her glass with affection at Kurt, his mixture of sensitiveness and rough-hewn edge really engaging her interest. You could read her thoughts: Kurt was not like the publishing guys from New York. Something more exotic.

Kate lightly sipped her wine, looked at Kurt, and then looked appraisingly at me; she was an artist composing a study in contrasts. I smiled at her. Her eyes twinkled back at me.

Soon waiters brought out a side cart steaming with vegetables and a large bowl of stroganoff. Plates heaped high were whisked under our noses.

Kurt dove right in. “Great stuff. Much better than Berlin.”

Madeleine made a typical French appraisal, “*Pas mal.*” Not bad.

“Better than Chicago,” added Kate.

I simply dug in and then took a long swallow of wine in obvious satisfaction.

The band continued with low mournful gypsy music, the sweet voices of the singers covering the room in a warm glow of melancholy.

Kurt waved off the coffee, “How about a cognac?”

The waiter smiled and headed for the bar.

As the cognac hit the table, the band shifted over to a jazz piece and couples started towards the dance floor. Kurt downed his cognac and looked over at Madeleine, "Dance?"

She was up like a shot with a bright smile across her face and her hand held out, "*Oui.*"

Kurt guided her out, his hands familiarly on her hips. Then he grabbed one of her hands and brought her into a dance embrace and took off.

"He has a smooth light step for such a big guy," marveled Kate.

"Yes, I wouldn't have thought it."

We watched them dance with fascination. The song ended but they stayed out on the dance floor. The band jumped into another foxtrot and I looked at Kate and framed a question with my eyebrows.

"Of course," and she stood up and held out her hand, palm down, a demure smile under inviting eyes.

I took it and guided her out to the dance floor, reached around and put my arm around her lower back, and held her upraised right in my left. We glided around the dance floor; leading Kate was like guiding a perfectly trained feather through a light breeze—simply delightful.

"You're not so bad yourself," she said.

"Thanks. Maybe we have more of a future together than just editing."

She looked up at me; her eyes simply sparkled and she said, "That's the only drawback to the Left Bank. All talk, no dance." She laughed like a southern belle at a cotillion.

"Well, maybe as we work on the book, we can sneak across the river and get a dance or two in."

"Yes, the Right Bank supper clubs are delightful. We could dance our way to our future," and she laughed. Now it was I who was enchanted.

The song ended and we returned to the table. I looked at my watch. It was approaching midnight.

"Time to move on to Bricktop's," I announced.

Madeleine clapped her hands together, "*Bon.*" Good.

"I'm with the lady," said Kurt.

"So am I," impishly added Kate, seeing if Kurt would bite on the double entendre.

But Kurt was all eyes towards Madeleine. He saw a good time up ahead.

I had to say she was dressed to hold a man's interest. And more may have gone on out on the dance floor than I had noticed. Madeleine was good at that, or so I'd heard.

We all stood up and went over to hatcheck and then headed for the sidewalk where Pierre was waiting with the taxi.

5. Bricktop's

Pierre wheeled the taxi around a corner and started up rue Pigalle, smartly swinging the car into the curb just in front of Bricktop's. If you didn't know it was there, you'd miss it.

A doorman came forward and opened the door and I slid out followed by Kurt. We held the ladies' hands as they decamped. We whisked them through the door and checked overcoats and hats. It was just before midnight. The place was starting to fill up.

Kate and Madeleine fitted headbands with something like a star poking up from their foreheads. Sort of a flapper's tiara.

Bricktop was sitting over at her little desk between the entrance and the bar. She lit up a smile at me, whispered to a waiter, and we were escorted over to a table at the far side of the room just off the dance floor. A waiter brought an ice bucket of champagne to the table. I whispered to the waiter and pointed at Kurt. The waiter smiled broadly and turned towards the bar.

"Bricky's is the only place in Paris that serves whiskey at the tables," I said to Kurt.

"Great, we'll chase the whiskey with champagne."

Kate arched her eyebrows in resignation; Madeleine smiled with fascination at the big American. He was going to be her toy tonight. The whiskey would see to that.

I pointed to some tables over to our right and said, "If Cole Porter's in town, he'll sit over there. And over there, the Prince of Wales. Bricky was the one who taught the Prince the Black Bottom. In turn, he hosted the opening party for her first club."

Bricktop strolled over. Kurt gave her an appreciative look-over. She noticed; she always did. Bricky was well made with great dancer's legs.

"Bill, nice to see you again."

She gave Madeleine a friendly smile, "Must be serious. Madeleine's here. Fun tonight." She looked at Madeleine, "Ready for another dance lesson?"

"*Oui, madame*," said Madeleine brightly, and she looked over and smiled invitingly at Kate.

"Dance lesson? What's that all about?" asked Kate.

"Fun," cooed Madeleine.

Bricktop glanced at Kurt and then turned to me, "Got some people in from New York, Bill?"

"Naw, I'm from Berlin," Kurt cut in, answering for me.

Bricky's eyebrows shot up, "Really? Berlin. I was there two years ago. Never saw anything like it. Nightlife? The most exciting I've ever seen. A real circus."

"You must like it wild?" said Kurt.

"Not much I haven't seen," said Bricktop with world-weary panache. "Customers are what drive the action in my experience. So I always like to see what folks like."

Bricktop turned to me and explained, "Anything went in Berlin, and I mean anything. The dope-taking and homosexuality, sort of lighthearted here in Paris, was serious business in Berlin. Some said it was depraved."

"Yeah, there's a raw edge in Berlin," agreed Kurt.

Kate's smile turned down; the seedy side of homosexuality seemed to bother her.

"I think it was just a way the Germans had of forgetting that humiliating war defeat, sort of block out the morning."

"Yeah, you never get too far away from the war in Berlin. Rubbed 'em pretty raw," said Kurt.

Bricktop nodded, "Yeah, in the morning, everything seemed grim and gray and what you would expect a war-torn city to look like. Then you saw the crippled and maimed veterans begging on the street corners." Her eyes took on a faraway look and she glanced at Kate, "and crowds of street children. There was real ugliness in the daytime."

Kate looked at her evenly and nodded in understanding.

"That's why I always preferred the city at night," Bricktop concluded.

Bricktop looked at Kate, "Well, maybe you're in from New York?"

"No, I live in Saint-Germain."

Bricktop chuckled and said, “Yeah, up in those big cafes over on Montparnasse, there’s two types of people. Some have the talent and no money, and the others the money and no talent. Which are you, honey?”

Kate looked flustered and turned to me with a look asking for help.

“She’s got the talent, Bricky. She’s been here five years, working as a writer. Stuff’s published in New York. That’s why you haven’t heard of her.”

Bricktop stroked her jaw and nodded in approval. “Bill, here, he’s helping you place your stuff?”

Kate saw the dig and smoothly answered, “I make my living writing. Everything else I do, I do for fun.”

Bricktop roared with laugher, “We have a lot in common, girl. What goes on in this club never travels across the street to my apartment. Same for you, huh, girl?”

Kate nodded politely to say yes. She was her own deal.

Bricktop looked down at me and said, “She’d make a nice friend for you, Bill,” and she winked. She turned and walked over to another table and the banter started in again fresh.

Some colored guys strolled in and took their place on the bandstand. Pretty soon the latest songs from New York were filling the room, a smoother, more melodic music than the normal American jazz blaring in Paris. The new sound was music from the Harlem renaissance—a much more sophisticated mood than the jump and shout of Dixieland.

“The piano player can really tickle the ivories,” said Kurt.

A large party came in and headed for a table. In the center a dark-haired man guided a statuesque woman to a chair, a lady tall and grand with the sculpted cheekbones of a classic statue. The man held the chair as the woman swept into it.

“Look at those pearls,” said Kate, admiring the three strands hanging around the woman’s neck. “That face would require nothing less.”

“That’s Linda, Cole Porter’s wife,” I said.

“And that must be Cole Porter,” said Kate.

“Correct,” I replied. Kurt looked over, intrigued.

I noticed that Porter's eyes were glued on the musicians. His right hand was softly snapping fingers with the rhythm of the band, coolly appreciating something he had not heard before.

"He really likes the music," Kate whispered.

"Yes. With Cole, it's always the music. He's the founding saint here. He's the one who told her to name the place Bricktop's. Bricky gets the colored boys from New York right off the boat. The latest stuff. He appreciates that. It all starts in New York."

"Yes, it all starts in New York," said Kate knowingly.

As the song closed, the band rolled into another tune and a big handsome colored singer came out and gave a hearty welcome to the crowd.

"He's called Southside," I told our table. "A real stepper and shouter."

Southside launched into a Cole Porter song, a song taking on the contours of a classic, entitled "Let's Do It, Let's Fall in Love." Heads and shoulders in the audience started swaying in time to the beautiful melody of universal love.

Kate looked over at me and made the nicest smile. I was charmed. I simply nodded and said, "Something up the road for you, I hope."

"Maybe."

"He's one of the great poets of our time masquerading as a songwriter."

"He sure is. And I think this band and singer have put a special interpretation on it. Look at Porter; he seems to be in rapture. They're taking his song someplace new."

I looked over and you could see the enthusiasm in Porter's face as he gesticulated to the other people at his table.

Just then another big party came in and headed for the table set aside for royalty. Kurt craned his neck to see. He said, "That doesn't look like the Prince of Wales."

"You're right. That's Prince de Polignac. Bricky taught the Prince of Wales the Blackbottom at his mansion," I explained.

"He's not quite the real thing, though?" Kurt asked.

"Yeah, not quite the real thing. Paris is full of pretension."

"But the royalty's all around us," said Kate, her voice in a state of wonder.

Southside brought the song to a delightful close and half the place stood up and clapped and cheered. Porter looked over at Bricktop with a big smile on his face and gave a thumb's up.

Southside looked over at Bricktop and she nodded with a slight tilt towards our table. He turned around, whispered something to the band, and hit the downbeat with a snapping finger. As a light Charleston tune picked up, he turned and walked over towards our table, a big white toothed grin across his dark face. He held out both hands towards Madeleine and Kate.

"Let me borrow the ladies. Dance lessons."

Madeleine was already up on her feet. Kate looked at me rather startled. I shooed her up, "You'll have great fun. Go with the flow. Madeleine almost set the joint on fire last time."

Kurt pumped his fist into his palm with a loud crack, a big smile on his face.

Kate smiled, stood up, and held her hand out to Southside. The singer took her hand, and Madeleine's, and led the two women out onto the dance floor.

To the audience, the singer said, "Dance lessons." They clapped in knowing expectation.

The band swung up-tempo, loud as can be, with a rousing Charleston tune.

Southside looked at Kate and then at Madeleine, and said, "Follow me." He started to really move his feet, let his knees fly, and crisscross his arms and hands across his knees in classic Charleston fashion.

Kate and Madeleine followed. Kate was superb: flashing heels, flying hands, and the come hither look of a real coquette.

Southside leaned his body well forward and said to the women, "Let's let'em see the show."

Kate and Madeleine leaned forward, chests throbbing to the beat, breasts pumping against the flimsy tops of their dresses as their shoulders rocked violently to and fro. The audience was clapping and hooting.

"They're not wearing much underneath," Kurt said, his face transfixed on the two dancing women, eyes darting from one to the other.

"Silk drawers, I think. Sheer." Kurt was right. I was seeing a lot of Kate. That stab of yearning came right through to me.

Southside eased back and straightened up, admiring the women, letting the audience take the full view. Then he came forward, dancing again, and leaned forward and did a slow three-sixty, his rump sticking out from the end of his spine, bobbing this way and that. He had all the moves of Josephine Baker doing her banana dance in *Danse Sauvage*—without the bananas of course. As he finished the full turn, he said to Kate and Madeleine, "Now giv'em the money shot, honeys. One at a time." He nodded at Madeleine.

She leaned forward, pushed her rear-end out, and started a slow Charleston as she started around, the tempo picking up to full holler as she was half way around, her rear end shaking the tassels on her dress this way and that. The audience was completely focused on one sashaying part of one woman's body as she circled around. Completing her circle she stood a little more erect as the crowd erupted into thunderous applause.

Southside nodded at Kate and she leaned well forward, pushed her rear-end out behind her, and started a madcap Charleston as she slowly turned around. As they say, she really knew how to shake it. As she was half way around, her rear-end a madcap of vibrating sexuality, the audience clapped and cheered.

"She really knows how to shake her rump, imagine what she could do in…" Kurt mumbled in fascination.

"Yes, gets right to the basics, doesn't it?"

Kate slowly came around and completed her circle and straightened up. She quickly held her hands up, palms out, making little circles and shook her shoulders, her breasts jiggling in an exactly opposite syncopated motion, the whole little routine making up a playful goodbye to the audience. The audience stood and clapped and cheered while she made a small bow.

"Are you sure she's part of that women crowd over on the Left Bank?" Kurt said to me over the din. "Such a waste."

I laughed, "She's a good kid." I sensed she was something else, but I wasn't quite sure what.

The band wound down and Southside reached out and took each woman's hand. The three of them gave the audience a deep bow and Southside led Madeleine and Kate back to our table.

"Got 'em all warmed up for you, gentlemen." He smiled wickedly, gave a slight bow, and turned and walked back to the bandstand.

"Oh, such fun. Did you like my dance, Kurt?" Madeleine said with genuine feeling.

"You're top of the line, honey," and Kurt grabbed her hand and kissed it. "May be we'll have a good time tonight."

Madeleine batted her eyelashes and cooed, "*Oui.*"

"Kate, you have talents I wasn't aware of," I said.

"Once upon a time, back in New York, I was something of a dancer, something of an actress for the Provincetown Players."

"In the Village?"

"Yes."

"Did you know Solita or Djuna there?"

"Yes, I knew Djuna. She was part of the Provincetown Players, too."

"And you followed her over to Paris?"

"Something like that. I came over later. She helped me get some writing assignments."

"You were some type of Bohemian?" shot out Kurt, really intrigued.

"Yes, I guess you could say that."

"Djuna Barnes writes those poems and stuff about women with women. I heard about them."

"Over time, Djuna has loved both men and women. It's all a little confusing."

"Were you, sort of," and Kurt stumbled, looking for words, "Bohemian with her?"

Kate gave him a really hard frown, but said nothing.

"Didn't mean to pry," Kurt said sheepishly.

Kate laughed, "Men were born to wondering…especially about that."

"I mean what is it? What do they find in each other?" Kurt was serious, if a little perplexed. It seemed so non-Middle West.

"Passion."

"Passion?"

"Yeah, you know, leg kicking, thigh pumping, head-shaking passion, the sounds that race out of your throat from way down deep inside."

Kurt's eyes were like saucers. "They really get it off, then."

"They really get it off," said Kate flatly.

"What causes that?"

"Djuna has a poem…"

I knew the poem. From Djuna's first book. I cupped my hands over my ears playfully. Kate scowled at me, "Coward."

Kate looked towards the ceiling as she remembered the lines as she recited:

> With cool pale eyes.
> We'd strain to touch those lang'rous
> Length of thighs,
> And hear your short sharp modern
> Babylonic cries.
>
> We see your damp chemise lie
> Pulsing in the beat…
>
> The dappled damp from some vague
> Under lip,
> Your soft saliva, loosed
> With orgy, drip.

Kurt's mouth fell open, "Hot damn."

"Well, in two words, that's it," said Kate and laughed at him with her eyes.

Kurt reached out and squeezed Madeleine's hand, "There's more sides to you dames than I knew." He let her hand go.

Madeleine leaned across the table, her breasts almost pushed out of the top of her dress, and grabbed Kate's hands in hers, "You must write for my publisher. You have the gift of the truth. You are so…" and she fumbled to find words, "yes, authentic."

I leaned over and loudly whispered to Kate, "To write truly from experience..."

She made a playful little snapping bark at me and then turned back to Madeleine and said seriously, "Someday, maybe, in my own novel…" She turned and looked sternly at me, "A product of my imagination."

This little banter went right over Kurt's head. I could see he was stuck on the authenticity part.

"Tomorrow, gentlemen, we were going to do some more with Kurt's book," said Kate and she looked over at Madeleine, "and new friendships need tending tonight…"

"Right you are, Kate. We'd better be off. We'll put Kurt and Madeleine in the Pierre's taxi and I'll take you home in another."

Kurt gulped his whiskey, chased it with the champagne, and leaned over and tenderly held Madeleine's hand and asked, "You're not too tired?"

Madeleine shook her shoulders, jiggling her breasts—it was a good night for that—and with the friskiest eyes I'd seen in a long time, said "*Non*." And she pouted.

Kurt was up in a flash—motivated—helping her out of her chair.

I held Kate's chair as she got up. We walked towards the hatcheck.

"Bill," Bricktop said as we passed, "nice evening." She said to Kate and Madeleine, "You ladies come back again." She smiled broadly and winked at me, "A writer?"

Outside, I waved to Pierre up the street. He brought the taxi down; I held the back door open and ushered Madeleine and Kurt into the rear. "Pierre, take them back to their hotel. The lady and I will get another cab."

I stood back next to Kate and we watched the cab go down the street.

"Why'd you do that? We could have gone with them."

"He'll have his hand up her dress before they hit the river."

"So?"

"Let me get another cab." I didn't want to stand between Kurt and his appetites.

I waved at a taxi waiting for a fare and it came down and pulled up to the curb.

Kate watched the other taxi with Kurt and Madeleine go down the street and disappear into the distance, her gaze more than a little wistful.

I opened the rear door to the taxi and ushered Kate in and jumped in after her. As we went down the dark empty street, she murmured how much fun we had together and wrapped her arms around my left arm. She let her head fall softly onto my shoulder and soon she was purring in a deep sleep.

Later that week Kate agreed—rather eagerly—to go to Berlin with me and work with Kurt on the book.

6. Berlin

The taxi dropped us off on a crowded sidewalk thronging with well-tailored middle-aged men and stylishly dressed younger women. And some well painted older ones. Kurt led us over to the top of a stairway leading down to a cellar nightclub, a bright neon sign above the stairs flashed “The Black Cat” in yellow on a black background.

“Some of the acts are in English. Gets the visiting American and British businessmen,” said Kurt.

“And the Germans,” asked Kate as she surveyed the couples jostling on the sidewalk.

“This is a great place where a couple can pick up a third. Put something extra into Saturday night.”

“Man or woman, boy or girl?” asked Kate with a skeptical glance.

Kurt waggled his shoulders this way and that, and with a shrug said, “Whatever.”

Kate grabbed hold of my arm and looked up at me with laughing eyes, “And for monsieur, *ce soir*? A little of this, a little of that?”

“I was planning on enjoying the floor show. I’m always happy to buy a young woman in need a bottle or two of champagne if it helps ease her way with the establishment.”

“Such a gentleman.”

“You’re the one who wanted to see Berlin and find out what Bricktop meant about anything and everything that goes.”

“Need to develop new experiences for my writing. How else can I become a worldly sophisticate?”

“Especially if you don’t partake,” shot out Kurt.

Kate gave him a friendly frown.

“You can take home whatever you like tonight, Kate.” Kurt leered and said, “There are no inhibitions here.”

"But Kurt, it's going past that forbidden line that puts the real edge to ecstasy," Kate cooed. If nothing else, Kate knew her French poetry.

Kurt rolled right over the riposte, "Forbidden lines went out with the Great Inflation. Ten dollars US bought anything you wanted," he said. Then he took on a thoughtful tone, "And some things you didn't know you wanted, and then some things you probably should not have wanted. Tonight we're going to dance along the rim of the volcano."

We shoved our way to the top of the stairs. Kurt motioned with his arm to descend towards the entrance. We checked overcoats and hats and were escorted over to a large table by a pretty waitress wearing a cute little apron around her waist and nothing else. It was a huge cavernous room; we were two tables or so back from the dance floor. I noticed Kate was wearing a heavier, warmer party dress tonight. And she seemed a little better underdressed than that night in Paris.

"I have some friends coming around to meet us. Actresses."

Kate rolled her eyes.

"Real actresses. For Ufa," he said, referring to the big Berlin movie studio.

"Do any of these movies play in movie houses?"

"Some," said Kurt and he drew his smile into another broad leer.

"Ufa is producing some of the most artistically daring movies in the world today," I said to Kate, helpfully.

"And some that are just plain daring," she bantered back.

Kurt looked over towards the entrance and saw his lady friends and he stood up and waved. Three women, with beautifully waved hair, smiled brightly and waved back. They started to languorously walk across the room, hips swaying this way and that, breasts pumping against loose tops, walking billboards for unashamed sensuality. I guessed they might have had on underwear, but maybe not. I smiled.

We all stood and the one in her mid-twenties took Kurt's arm and possessively held him. Kurt introduced her, "Anita."

Anita smiled warmly at Kurt and then she nodded to the light-haired brunette to sit next to me. "Ingrid," she said to me by way of introduction.

Anita then gave a flick of her hair in the other direction and murmured, "Ilse." The youngest one, something of a waif, moved over and demurely held her hand out to Kate.

The waif said, "My name is Ilse. Kurt has said such nice things about you. Your fine taste. I so want to go to Paris." Kate shook her hand and then the two sat down, the waif pulling her chair up close to Kate's. She put her arm half way around Kate's shoulders familiarly and looked wonderingly into her eyes.

Kate smiled.

Kurt sat and put his arm around his actress and pulled her close, "Anita, what's on the schedule."

"Here, dancing. With whomever you want. Later, oh la la," and her eyes danced with merriment. She looked at me and explained matter-of-factly, "Kurt likes women, but you can have whatever you want."

I reached out and put my arm around the shoulders of the young woman sitting next to me, "Me, too."

Anita continued, "We get paid by the studio, but everyone has to entertain for some extra money these days."

"Yes, Babylon on the Spree," I said referring to the River Spree that ran through beautiful parks just outside the city.

"Yes, Babylon," she agreed, adding, "They say the sexuality is in the air. From the swamplands. Some sort of charge."

"So it would seem."

A waiter came up and put two ice buckets of champagne on the table and set champagne glasses about. He poured champagne for all of us. Then in front of Kurt he put four short schnapps in a row. Kurt ignored the champagne and took the first schnapps in a swallow. Then he chased it with the champagne.

Anita's eyes twinkled as she sipped her champagne. She leaned in front of Kurt and loudly whispered to me, "We'll run up the bill on him later," and laughed.

The band started in. All German, all white. Sort of a clashing and clanging Dixieland sound colliding with the sound from a maudlin German music hall to my ear. Interesting. In the back a tuba gave that distinctive om-pah to the cacophony. Most people continued talking, only occasionally glancing over at the band. The banjo player now and again caught people's interest. Kurt belted back another schnapps.

The next song came up, and a sultry singer came out and a rather nice foxtrot was taken up. Various kinds of couples walked out to the floor and started dancing.

The waif stood up and held her hand down to Kate, "Please dance with me?"

Kate stood up and followed Ilse out on to the dance floor. Ilse took her into embrace, but then Kate, the taller of the two, took Ilse's hand and held it up high and took the lead, if not charge. Ilse looked up and smiled invitingly into Kate's eyes.

Kate led her around the dance floor, some of the other couples, some mixed, some same sexed, gave way and looked on, Kate's expertise clear for all to see.

Anita leaned over to me and grabbed my arm, "Your friend is good. She must lead a lot in Paris. With her friends?" she asked expectantly.

"Probably," I said. Kurt snorted and rolled his eyes.

The tune ended and Ilse and Kate walked back to the table holding hands. Ilse said, "I want you to have fun, too. Let me find someone who can lead you." She looked across the floor and made a wave with her hand and a tall, slim young man, slicked black hair coming straight back from his forehead, came slowly sauntering over, the interested detachment of a true gigolo studying the setup at our table. Ilse motioned him to sit on the other side of Kate. She whispered to him.

Kurt broke in, placing yet another schnapps glass down, "Kate, Joachim's said to have the best fingers in Berlin. Brings the women right off the bed, backs arched to the sky," and he turned to Anita, "right?"

"Yes," cooed Anita and then laughed wickedly as she held her palm out flat to show Kate just how high.

Ingrid giggled.

"Do you know, too?" I asked.

She giggled, "No, he only does the customer. I just get to look."

"That leaves you out?"

"Oh, no, sometimes the customer does me."

Anita said emphatically, "Ingrid really responds."

I flashed my eyebrows in amazement.

Ingrid grabbed my arm and leaned into me with her breasts and looked up me with black sparkling eyes, "Men are best."

Kurt roared, "She's made the sale."

The band started out with a tango and Joachim stood and held his hand out to Kate, who put her hand in his and let him guide her out of her chair and towards the dance floor. Joachim was an accomplished dancer, as was Kate. They went across the floor, then in a blur of elbows and arms turned around and went back in the other direction, both faces seriously looking forward in classic tango style.

At the next turn, Joachim bent her back so that she was parallel to the floor staring at the ceiling. He hovered over her looking intently into her eyes with great seriousness. Kate then gave a high kick with one leg and he brought her back to a standing position in one fluid motion. And off they went gliding across the dance floor in the other direction.

"He's good. One of the ladies' favorites," Kurt chortled.

Anita made a playful frown at Kurt, "He's even better in bed." She looked at Ilse, "Right, Ilse?"

"Yes, Anita."

"Ilse warms them up, Joachim finishes them off," whispered Ingrid into my ear, her tongue playing with the lobe. "The ladies can barely stand it."

The tango finished and Joachim guided Kate back to her chair, then faced her and made a deep bow before taking his chair. Kate thanked him and then leaned over and put her arm around Ilse and said, "Your friend is a quite good dancer."

"He could come with us now and we could have a really good time."

Kate smiled but slowly shook her head no. She looked across the table at Kurt, "Could you explain nicely, Kurt, that I appreciate the offer but I simply don't do boys."

Kurt laughed and leaned across the table and put some US greenbacks in front of Joachim and said, “Sorry, not tonight. But she really did enjoy the dance.”

Joachim snatched the greenbacks off the table and then slowly stood and again bowed to Kate and strode away. Over across the floor three middle-aged women at a table waved greenbacks at him to come over.

Ingrid again whispered in my ear, “Joachim’ll be tired in the morning. Three’s just quantity, so little time for art.”

I nodded in understanding—of course—the art.

Kurt talked right past Ingrid to Kate, “Don’t worry about it. Joachim never wants for tango partners.”

“So I see.”

“Better this way. When you add those gigolo guys, it always seems a little perverted to me,” Kurt said in a moment of reflection. He knocked back the last schnapps; the waiter laid down four more.

Kate smiled and murmured, “Couldn’t agree more.”

Kurt turned to Anita, “See, you and your friends at least make some other money from Ufa. Joachim has to hustle every mark.”

“Oh, yes, but being an actress has many, many demands.”

“You bet,” and Kurt looked at me, “if they pass the screen test, then it’s down on their knees for the so-called interview. Right, *mein leiber*.”

Anita made coquettish eyes at him and batted her eyelashes.

“As they become more accomplished as an actress, why, it’s on their backs and then on their bellies. Whatever the so-called producer wants that day.”

Anita turned and explained to Kate, “During the inflation, it was a cold winter. My mother always encouraged me by saying, ‘Ask them for some coal when you have to do something extra.’ Muti was practical.”

Ingrid added, “For families that did not have daughters or young wives, it was impossibly difficult.”

I watched Kate. She looked on with a fascinated, but distracted, interest. Ilse was gently moving her hand up under Kate’s dress, caressing her thigh. Kate squeezed Ilse a little tighter around the shoulders.

Kurt banged down a schnapps glass and bellowed, “By the time they become stars, they just ask the producer, ‘Which orifice?” And he laughed at his joke and grabbed another schnapps. He noticed Ilse’s hand under Kate’s dress and leaned over to try and get a better look.

Anita quickly pulled her dress up and pulled Kurt clear over sideways and pushed his face down in her lap, “Here’s some, you brute.” I had been right; she wasn’t wearing any underwear. Kurt gave a playful growl and tried to bite her thigh.

Kate turned dreamy and said to Ilse, “In Paris we put some affection, even love, into the relationship before we go up under a lover’s dress. I’m sorry, but this is about as far as I go tonight.” She slowly pulled Ilse’s hand out from under her dress and held it demurely in her lap.

Kate looked across at me and asked, “Could you take me outside and put me in a cab? I can get back to the hotel after that.”

“Yes, of course. Maybe I better go, too,” I said. Then I turned and explained to the table, “I’ve promised Kate a walk in the Tiergarten tomorrow morning. We’ll be taking the night train back to Paris.”

“Oh, you don’t have to do that for me, Bill,” said Kate. “You can have a good time with your new friends tonight. Your own little American Legion reunion. I’ll be fine. I have the passkey to the adjoining doors between our suites. I’ll just put the key in the orifice and turn it to lock.” She smiled sweetly as she stood up.

“Bill, you can go with her. Ingrid will be fine,” said Kurt. He looked at Kate and then turned to me and said, “You’ll do fine tonight.” He knocked back another schnapps and banged the glass down for emphasis. “I’m sure Kate goes both ways. I can tell. I know about things like that,” he said with the sureness of the truly drunk.

Kate bowed at Kurt and gave me a winsome smile and said, “I think tonight’s sex’scapade can best be called as ‘no way.’” She smiled at Kurt. He simply smirked and looked over at me and winked, “She’s just playing hard to get.”

I leaned over and kissed Ingrid on the forehead and turned and looked at Kurt, “Tomorrow afternoon. At the coffeehouse.”

“At the coffeehouse,” he mumbled back.

I walked around the table and put my hand on Kate's waist and pointed her towards the entrance.

Climbing the stairs, I said, "I can't tell if you're a good writer getting better or simply just a great actress."

She looked up at me with a devilish smile. I found it all sort of enchanting. And I had really sort of liked Ingrid. You always do. Oh, well.

7. Romanisches Kaffeehaus

The next day, bundled up against the spring cold, Kate and I walked through the Tiergarten, the vast urban park in the center of Berlin. Despite the chill, spring was in the air; trees were leafing, flowers starting to unfold. We walked past the Reichstag, the German parliament building, and the site of so much news these past ten years.

"If the fighting stays inside the building," I said, nodding at the monumental edifice, "everything will work out. If it spills out into the streets, then who knows where it will go."

"You seem to have a lot of skepticism about Germany," Kate said.

"Bismarck, the famous German chancellor, said you shouldn't see a packing plant make sausage or a parliament make laws. I saw the Peace Treaty being made in Paris in 1919."

"Yes, so much was sacrificed, so little gained."

"Exactly."

We returned to the hotel and checked out while arranging to have our luggage brought to the train station early in the evening. We walked over to the Kurfürstendamm, a broad street running through the most fashionable quarter of Berlin. It was the Champs Élysées of the city. We walked along the wide sidewalk admiring the latest fashions draped on the mannequins in the windows of the many fashionable shops lining the street. Now and again Kate would stop and pay particular attention to some hats or handbags. She stared through the thick plate glass windows at the beautiful clothes and goods on display. I noticed the Jewish names on many of the best shops, possibly more here in Berlin than in the other big capitals of Europe. I said nothing.

We came up to a broad square and crossed over to a huge twin-towered edifice, ugly in its squareness, where the Romanisches Kaffeehaus was located on the ground floor. Entering the vast cavernous coffeehouse full of Sunday afternoon talkers, we walked over towards an area Kurt had mentioned. We saw him sitting at a large wooden table by a window engaged in earnest conversation with two well-dressed middle-aged men with the polished rectitude of well-connected bankers. I had seen such men at international conferences during the 1920s. We started to walk over. Kurt stood up and walked towards us as we approached. He met us at a nearby table and as he shook my hand and nodded at Kate he said, "Could you sit at this table for a moment while I finish my business with *mein herren*?" He waved at a waiter to come over.

"Of course," I said as Kate and I sat down.

A waiter came up and Kurt said to Kate, "Can I recommend the coffee and cream? It is famous."

"Yes, I would be delighted."

Kurt looked at me.

"The same."

"Two," Kurt said to the waiter. Kurt stepped back and returned to his table.

I watched him sit down and take up his pad, which had a couple pages of handwriting on it. He picked up his pencil and queried the two men. They answered in low tones, one making furtive glances around him to see if there were any eavesdroppers. Kurt wrote in his pad.

Kate watched fascinated. "What's all that about?"

"Kurt has a column called 'Berlin Market' in both the New York and Chicago papers every Monday morning describing the coming week in economics in Berlin. He has a reputation for being well connected at the top. Often he datelines it 'a coffeehouse in Berlin.' I guess that's true."

Kate laughed.

As we watched, Kurt finished up the dispatch and pulled an envelope out of his coat pocket. He sealed the dispatch inside it and wrote something on the outside of the envelope. He stood up, as did the two bankers. Kurt waved at a messenger standing over near the waiter captain, who promptly came over and Kurt handed the envelope to him and said, "The telegraph office." The messenger took the envelope and left.

The two bankers held out their hands and Kurt shook them in turn. Heads nodded and *dankes* were exchanged. The two men left and Kurt waved to us to come over and join him at the table by the window.

Kate and I went over and we all sat down. Kurt caught a waiter's eye and circled with his finger for some more coffee.

"You don't look much the worse for the wear," Kate said pleasantly.

"Schnapps can give you a hangover. Women never."

"Plural?" asked Kate with an arched eyebrow.

"We're all friends," replied Kurt, and he gave a long wolfish smile.

Kate smiled understandingly at him but let the subject drop.

"We really like your manuscript, what we've read so far," I said.

Kurt turned and looked at Kate for confirmation. She pulled the manuscript in front of her and said, "I've made some editing changes, and made a couple of suggestions. But I think the changes strengthen your voice, not change it." Kate was succinct and professional.

"Good. I'll look 'em over. You guys are the pros here."

"We're up to the Armistice. You're in a hospital recovering from a wound. We'd like to hear in your own words where the story goes from here," I said.

"At the hospital, once I was back on my feet, I got orders to Koblenz to join the American occupation army. They gave me a small raggedy supply and service battalion. I got it organized, went around to other units and asked for German-speaking soldiers—but only those who wanted to assume responsibility and learn new trades. I got plenty of volunteers. Then we started hiring German workers. So an American corporal might have forty or fifty Germans working for him. A sergeant would be in charge of a company of workers."

"Then I got other Americans that knew the trades to buddy up with a German speaker who wanted to learn. And they found Americans who were willing to learn from the Germans, who are some of the best trades people in the world. So the German workers started teaching the Americans new the trades and skills. Well success built upon success. I soon had almost two thousand American soldiers and thousands and thousands of German workers. All putting Koblenz back together. Getting people fed, distributing supplies."

"I simply didn't know anything about this," said Kate.

"Not many people did. It was a great story, and it wasn't just me, the entire American occupational force turned in a good effort. As a country we should have been proud of it. But of course it was always 'the Hun this' and 'the Hun that" back in the States."

"Just after I arrived in Germany, I went to a German hospital to see what they needed. The army had some supplies but German supplies were in terribly short supply because the British still had the blockade on. I met a German nurse, a widow, just about my age. She was attractive, but you could also see she had had a hard war. Gray was starting to streak her hair at the temples, crows' feet at the eyes. But you could still see the girl behind the woman when she laughed. She was kindly but had a real no-nonsense air about getting things done for her patients. She was the assistant to a much older woman running the hospital. There was an intensity to her effort about caring for the wounded soldiers in her charge. So yeah, Elsa—that was her name—ran the place."

I nodded in slow appreciation. Kurt would go for someone like that in a big way. I looked at Kate; she saw the same thing.

"I put some urgency into getting supplies to this hospital. If nothing else, fresh sheets and blankets, better food. Food was in critical supply that winter. You don't heal if you don't nourish."

Kate nodded her head in understanding.

"We became friends—slowly. American soldiers did not have a reputation, for shall we say romantic love. Sex was just a bargained transaction, something reckoned in pieces of coal. But our friendship warmed—then with a gathering, hungry intensity. She had lost a husband at Verdun…"

Kurt stopped and stared across the room and then he continued, "I remember her saying, 'Verdun, we were so close in 1916…my husband wrote to me…just a few more kilometers…then we will march towards Paris…and peace…and I will come home…' she said this with unbelievable sadness. You know the story; her world went upside down; the telegram from the front...she felt her future was barren. We were each missing something; together we had something."

"What took you to Berlin?" I asked.

"Late in the summer Elsa found she was pregnant. This became a shared joy for us—to make life. I was happy. She was happy." Kurt looked at Kate for corroboration; she nodded her head, smiling with understanding.

"Our army was starting to wind down—way before it should. But Congress wanted to back out of Europe. Bring the boys home. I asked for a discharge and we agreed upon September. I was going to stay in Germany."

Kurt looked at me and said, "Here's where it gets tricky. I've never shared this with anyone else. I had met a German banker that previous winter in hush-hush circumstances through Maynard Keynes. I wrote to him and he put me in touch with the bureau chief of a big newspaper in Chicago. They wanted a finance correspondent and hired me. The banker provided introductions for me and soon I had really good sources all over Berlin."

This explained a lot to me, the easy familiarity Kurt had with Keynes and with Dr. Melchior and other top-drawer German bankers.

Kurt looked at Kate and explained, "What goes on in Central Europe affects worldwide wheat prices. That's a big deal in Chicago. So what happens in Poland and the Ukraine is known first in Berlin, then it's one telegram away from Chicago. My job was to be first with the telegram. Later, New York bought into German bonds in a big way. They couldn't get enough about Berlin."

"Before that, back in 1919. What happened in Berlin?" Kate asked.

"Everything went quite well to start. Nice flat, got a handle on being a reporter and economics correspondent. But in the winter, the politics turned ugly—street fighting, threatened revolutions, then a putsch in Berlin. The putsch failed and the troops behind it—the Freikorps from the recent fighting along the Baltic coast—were formed up and starting to march out while the crowds jeered and catcalled. It was an explosive moment. Elsa and I were watching from the glassed-in terrace of a sidewalk restaurant. There was a volley of gunfire—glass shattered and Elsa was hit. I got her to a hospital, the doctor tried to save her and the baby, but lack of this, lack of that, too little of this," Kurt looked up with a helpless, lost look on his face, "one thing after another and she died on the operating table." His chest heaved.

Kate shrank back, she was ashen. I could see into her mind—to have Elsa's brave sacrifices at the hospital repaid like this by an uncaring fate was cruel and bitter. The madness of the tragedy pulled at your sanity, like so many of the experiences during the war.

I looked at Kurt and said, "I'm sorry."

Kurt looked at me and said, "I think that was when I finally understood what 'sorry' means—just emptiness. Nothing else. Emptiness. I had never really felt that in the war. There had always been a larger purpose, the next objective."

Kate nodded her head in agreement. I sensed she had some personal experience in this area. Maybe that's why she was in Europe. There were currents here I could not see.

I looked down and said, "Yeah, I remember…" I took a sip of coffee, sighed, and looked across the room warm and busy with people, a poignant contrast to the empty, desolate fields I always imagined when recalling the war, the bitter memories of marching under a gray, leaden sky eastwards into the cold of an approaching winter war. For me, particularly after the Paris Conference, my memories of the war always wound up on a gray, bleak street of broken spirits and vanquished hopes. Always. Whoever "they" are, they never understand. Versailles. The Treaty. And before that, the cold. I remembered.

I looked at my watch.

"I better get you two to the train station," said Kurt.

I nodded and stood up. Kate followed.

"Where's your luggage?"

"The porter from the hotel will meet us at the station with it."

Kurt nodded. We walked outside into the cool spring air. Kurt flagged a cab down. As the cab pulled up to the curb, he reached out and grabbed the handle to the rear door and pulled it open and ushered Kate into the rear seat with a sweep of his arm. I followed and Kurt closed the door.

He put his head down next to the open window and said, "I'll get some more of the manuscript to you in the coming weeks. See you in Paris this summer and we can have a mid-course review if it's okay with you?"

"That would be excellent," I said.

"I really enjoyed our visit to Berlin. In some ways it was as I remembered it," Kate added.

"You were here before?" Kurt asked, surprised.

"Yes, but the times were tougher. We saw plays and concerts, but the nightlife was too intimidating for us. Nice to see that it has lightened up since then," Kate said. She smiled through a light little laugh.

Kurt shrugged and made an ironical little snort. He looked at her with real interest. The cab started to move; he stepped back and watched the cab ease into the traffic.

Kate turned around and looked back through the rear window and waved at Kurt. He smiled and waved back.

"I didn't know you had been in Berlin?"

"Oh, on a magazine assignment. Right after I got to Europe; before I settled down in Paris," Kate said. She didn't volunteer anything else. She leaned back in the seat and looked out the other window, alone with her thoughts. Something had caught hold of her thoughts in Berlin this weekend. The war? Berlin? Both?

The night train got us back to Paris early Monday morning. I dropped a drowsy Kate off at her apartment and then went back to Île Saint-Louis and caught up on my sleep. I had set up an appointment with Kate to go over the editing the following week.

8. Café Les Deux Magots

I walked up rue Bonaparte in the May sunshine and came out on a small square. On my left the bell tower of the church of Saint-Germain-des-Prés reached into the sky. On my right the Café Les Deux Magots sat resplendent in the spring sunshine. I was meeting Kate for lunch and afterwards we planned to go over her editing work on Kurt's manuscript. We had plenty to do after our trip to Berlin.

I scanned the crowd; a hand waved from underneath a big spreading hat. I smiled and waved back. I walked over. To my surprise Mina Loy and her daughter Fabienne were seated with Kate. Mina was currently caught between a time-consuming but quite successful career as a designer in Paris and her long-standing reputation as one of the finest of the Modernist poets, a master of short-phrased free verse of striking originality—in my opinion. I kept an eye on poetry; a lot of tomorrow's prose originality came from today's poetry. Besides, translating French poets was an enjoyable sideline with me.

For over ten years, from the time before America had entered the war, Mina had been "new." In 1917, a New York paper said that the "modern woman" looked, talked, and thought like Mina Loy. The paper printed its interview with her on page one. Right next to the interview were the news columns detailing recent sinkings of Allied shipping, the final straws that broke the back of the American camel's resistance to joining the war in early 1917. Besides her undoubted talent as a painter-poetess, both men and women were taken by "her long-legged charms," words used by the actor Bill Williams when he played opposite Mina in a one-acter put on by the Provincetown Players in Greenwich Village. Bill went on to become the poet William Carlos Williams.

Figure 2 Mina Loy and Djuna Barnes in portrait late 1920s in France.

"Hi, Bill," Mina said.

"Hi, Mina. How are you, Fabi?"

"*Très bien,*" replied the little girl, who was about ten-years-old.

"Is Bill representing you, too?" Kate asked Mina.

"No, but he's one of the best customers of my shop. I have done some of the decorating of his flat. Right, Bill?"

"Absolutely," I replied. Mina had a fashionable shop selling lamps and lampshades of her own design in one of the most fashionable districts of the Right Bank. She manufactured the products in a little workshop she called her factory right up the street in Montparnasse. I sat down next to Kate.

"I have two of Mina's illuminated globes sitting across from one another in my drawing room—one a world globe and the other a celestial globe. Perfect symmetry," I said.

"I have added my *Les Etoiles* to Bill's ceiling lights and decorations to his sconces. You should see them, Kate," said Mina.

"Possibly I will some time." Kate seemed guarded with this comment.

Fabi looked at me inquisitively and then leaned over and wrapped herself around Kate's arm and gave her a hug; Kate looked down warmly at the young girl and then smiled at me.

I turned to Kate to explain my interest in Mina's work. "Mina has transposed the images from the pages of her *Lunar Baedecker* to her lamp shades. The starry skies and cosmic reach of her poems now march across the evening shadows of my drawing room," I said. *Lunar Baedecker* was Mina's anthology of poetry published by Bob McAlmon's Contact Publishing Company a few years back. Many felt it was one of the best poetry books of the era.

"The play of light and shadow dramatizes the process of creation and creativity," Mina added. In both her poetry and her designer creations, Mina was fabricating illusions.

"How's your business going, Mina?" I asked.

She rolled her eyes and said, "Imitators are stealing my designs left and right. And my lawsuits don't stop them. You go to the annual Foire de Paris and all you see are designs by Mina," she complained, referring to the annual crafts fair in Paris.

"And then there is the work itself. I've spent three years shut up alone with the lower classes. I'm almost demented."

"Not a revolutionary sentiment," I ventured with a smile.

"My Bolshevik leanings evaporated when I found myself as an employer. In France."

I laughed.

"I have no one to talk to but the accountant. And his only interest is in my ledger." She raised her eyes to heaven.

He must have been a real dried prune since almost every man crossing Mina's path was attracted to her still potent erotic charge. I smiled indulgently.

"You can imagine a poet wanting to learn about accounts!" she lamented.

"Dull," said Kate, and she winked at me.

"Dreary," I added, and winked back.

Mina looked askance at us, her expression a sense of offended *hauteur* in response to our impertinence. She drummed her fingertips on the table impatiently.

"I love your poetry, Mina. You know that," I quickly interjected. Her expression softened, the smiled turned ironical, and she shifted a pointed glance to Kate.

"You know whose work I look to for inspiration in my own work," said Kate, amusement spreading across her face at Mina's acting, a skill perfected in the theaters and drawing rooms of Greenwich Village.

"Friends. Such good friends," she said, gaiety animating her face. Then her expression took a more serious tone; she crossed her hands on the table and said emphatically, "I'm looking to sell the business. It should fetch a good price. I want to buy a small apartment where I could get back to painting and writing. I've lost touch with myself over the past three years running this business."

Kate looked at me and said, "I am on the lookout for an apartment in the building on rue Saint-Romain where I live. Djuna Barnes lives there, too. Mina would be amongst friends."

"That sounds like a grand idea," I agreed.

"Yes, it would," said Mina and she again leaned across the table as if to share a secret, "And my new son-in-law, dear Julien, is setting up a gallery in New York specializing in Dadaist and Surrealist art. He wants me to be his Paris agent."

"Well, no one knows as much about those schools of art as you do, Mina," I said. Her late husband Arthur Cravan had been a founding spirit of Dada. He was a nephew of the great English wit Oscar Wilde. Cravan's untimely death transformed a minor legend into a founding saint of the Dada and Surrealism movements.

"Yes, a return to art," she said solemnly.

"And how about the poem?" I asked. Mina had shared a draft with me of a poem she was writing entitled "The Widow's Jazz." Cravan had died in Mexico in mysterious circumstances in 1918 just after their marriage. She had never really gotten over the loss; their bliss together was Mina's lost happiness. The years did not dim the look in her eye when she spoke of Cravan. Fabienne had been born several months after her father's disappearance.

"It's been almost ten years," I said and glanced at Kate. To my surprise, she had taken on a pained look, the words "ten years" like a sharp unwanted remembrance that had just poked her in the chest. I looked at Kate and wondered.

Mina continued, "Yes, I would like to get together with you and discuss the poem some more. It's almost complete, as complete as it can ever be." She dropped her eyes in a downcast look.

"I remember that day when you recited it at Natalie's salon," I said, referring to the famous literary salon hosted by American heiress Natalie Clifford Barney. Natalie had introduced Mina by saying that through her prismatic poetry Mina had transposed her writing and her person into another dimension. Mina had then risen and stood before the guests and softly intoned by way of introduction that she could only bring herself to speak because so many found beauty in her verse. It was a sweet moment.

Kate nodded her head, caught in her own memory of that afternoon. She leaned forward towards Mina and started to recite the first stanza:

Cravan
Colossal absentee
The substitute dark
Rolls to the incandescent memory

Mina looked at Kate and said, “You remember?”

“I don’t think I could ever forget ‘incandescent memory’.” I looked at Kate again. Mina’s words had hit a chord with Kate.

My thoughts, too, went back to that afternoon in Natalie’s garden and how Mina had recited the poem as if in a dream. Then she hit an impassioned and intense ending; the guests had been rocked back by the starkness of the vision. I now leaned forward towards Mina and recited:

Husband
How secretly
you cuckold me with death

“You, too?” said Mina softly. “To remember a poet’s lines…”

“Yes…” said Kate, and she looked off into the distance, the words having touched something deep in her memory.

Mina watched the two of us caught up in our memories. After a few moments, she said to me, “Kate told me you’re both working on a novel by an American correspondent in Berlin. About the war.”

“Yes, we are.”

“Yes, I remember Berlin,” said Mina. “It was 1922. Everything, and everyone, was for sale. But mostly I remember the fiercely expressive political art. Kate says it hasn’t really changed.”

“Well, yes. The economy is back on its feet. But a lot of people are quite taken with the decadence.”

"Yes, another dimension of Modernism. Decadence of course leads to a loss of cold objective purity, one of the goals of Modernist art."

I nodded my head in agreement.

Mina turned to Kate and asked, "Who was the Russian émigré?"

"Ilya Ehrenberg."

"Yes, he told us one night at the Romanisches Kaffeehaus that Berlin was the city everyone was watching, some with dread, some with hope, because it was in Berlin the fate of Europe for the next several decades was being decided."

I stopped and slowly nodded my head in agreement. "I am exactly in accord with that thought," and I paused and said, "that's a key point in my friend's novel." I looked at Kate; she hadn't said she had been in Berlin with Mina. My expression asked the question.

"I was there on a magazine assignment," she said with a touch of finality.

Mina chimed in, "We tired of the nightlife quickly. Bob McAlmon didn't. He waded right in."

I laughed, "Yes, Bob would." McAlmon, handsome and well set financially, was talented, dissolute, and homosexual. That was Berlin back then.

Mina looked off into the distance—Berlin did that to people. She turned back to the table and said, "This book about the war. Tell me more."

"Yes, it starts with an American infantry officer in the 3rd Division, the division's arrival in France, the training, and then the initiation into battle at Chateau Thierry."

Mina looked past me and said, "I remember as the war fever grew and grew in the spring of 1917 in New York. Cravan had been avoiding conscription so far in the war by leaving one country and going on to the next country as each declared war. He told me that everyone else may allow themselves to be murdered for all he cared, only they need not expect him to follow suit." She looked at me.

"Understandable now. Not so understandable then. We were all for the war."

She nodded her head and then continued, “The war, he predicted, would have devastating consequences—the world would go bankrupt.” Again she looked at me.

“The war loans continue to strangle the economies, poison cooperation between countries with recriminations,” I said. “The reparations issue in Germany is poisonous. It separates Germany from countries that should be its staunchest friends.”

“Cravan was protected by his contempt for so much of bourgeois thinking. He simply roared: ‘I have not fallen for their modern art and I will not fall for their great war.’”

“Well, the art has stood up to time.”

Mina laughed, “Yes, hasn’t it.”

“But the war hasn’t,” I said.

“Cravan came over on the same ship as Trotsky and he struck up a friendship with him,” she said of the famous revolutionary. Leon Trotsky had gone on to command the Red Army and crush the Whites after the 1917 revolution in Russia, consolidating Communist control of the country. “But Cravan was never taken in by the revolutionary fervor; he never chased after ‘isms.’ He told me that after the revolution the red army would be used to protect the red liberty. I guess it always works that way.”

“Yes, the more strident the revolutionary thunder, the more complete the authoritarian aftermath,” I said rather bleakly. Cravan had foreseen that aspect of the future perfectly.

Kate seemed to notice the lost idealism buried somewhere in my answer and said to Mina, “Bill seems to have caught up with Cravan’s pessimism sometime after the war.”

I nodded in agreement. Kate shifted the conversation: “You seem to remember this time with Cravan with fondness, Mina?”

“Yes, our beliefs came into a harmony. I had found the one man with whom my mind could go ‘the whole way.’”

Kate laughed, “American girls use that phrase in a somewhat different way.”

Fabi looked up at Kate with a twinkle in her eye, guessing at the adult meaning.

Mina said, “I was long past my first time but like a young girl,” and she looked lovingly at Fabi, “the formal dream of my life was a marriage of love. I found that with Cravan. To have had that just once…"

I nodded my head in understanding. Yes, the handsome Prince Charming, the marriage for love.

"Yes, it was a brief, bright shining moment for us, those months," Mina said.

Kate looked at Mina warmly, her eyes showing sympathetic understanding for the remembered love of the elegant and beautiful Mina Loy.

Mina set her coffee cup down on the table and said, "I had better get back to the factory. See if I can keep the molds to my newest creations inside the walls." She stood up.

I rose and looked at the little girl, pretty as a flower in the sunshine, "We'll see you again, Fabi." She smiled at me. I looked at Mina and said, "I'll be in touch about the poem."

Mother and daughter said their goodbyes and walked through the tables and out to the sidewalk. The factory was a half dozen blocks away.

I sat back down and turned to Kate, "Yes, Cravan must have been some man. But I think Mina also gives Fabi a cherished memory of her father, a story to help guide her to her own future: the handsome prince, the marriage for love."

"All young girls should have that. It's a tragedy if they don't," Kate said.

She took a sip of coffee and said, "Mina is concerned that both her daughters marry well."

"Well, Joella seems to have done quite well. I watched Julian's courtship of Joella on Île Saint-Louis last summer. They were everywhere—a perfect young couple."

Kate gave a short laugh, "There was more to it than that."

"Yes?"

"Between Joella and Mina, it was quite different from what an American girl would experience with her mother. Mina and Joella went to the receptions at Sylvia Beach's bookstore, the salons and restaurants, everywhere Our Crowd was hanging out and drinking, gossiping and flirting. At home afterwards, Mina told Joella in precise detail what every innuendo and off-color remark meant. It was like a maiden being instructed by a grand courtesan."

I laughed.

"Then for the next reception, Joella was told to pretend innocence but catch every meaning." Kate concluded, "Joella was thoroughly coached on what to look for in a husband. Mina, in her dowager duchess manner, told her to ignore the French and Italians—'seducers all' in her words."

I laughed again and asked, "What was the effect of all that?"

"Joella became wise to the childishness of the adult world, particularly Our Crowd," said Kate as she gave me an accusatory look—I was a charter member of the Left Bank chattering class. Our Crowd was Sylvia Beach's term for the Paris literary crowd; she was the owner of the now famous English language bookshop Shakespeare & Company.

"I plead guilty by way of passing many a pleasant wine-filled conversation."

Kate smiled and continued, "But more important, Joella had her own light. Not necessarily what her mother taught her. She felt strength of character counted, that all of her mother's friends' pretensions to intellectualism and cultivation counted for little. She grew into an organized and businesslike young woman. She organized Mina's business for her, kept it on track. With her gone, that's why Mina wants to sell it."

"I hadn't realized that."

And with a touch of sympathetic concern, Kate said, "Then Joella had to learn that half the time in the game of men she was in competition with her mother. Half the suitors showing up at their door seemed more interested in Mina than Joella. Mina strikes a fire."

"She does do that," I agreed. Mina could kindle sexual interest like almost no woman I had ever met. Kate guessed my thoughts and laughed.

I shifted the conversation to make a serious point. "But you know, Joella might have the right attitude for the future."

"Why?"

"The past is not bequeathing the young a pleasant future. At best, they're going to have to put their shoulders to it."

"That's the second time today your unease has surfaced. You seem troubled by the past and its shadow over the future. Is that why Kurt's novel is so important to you?"

"I think so. We need a story that goes beyond the futility of war and gets at what went wrong."

"Versailles?"

"It started there."

"You were at Versailles, Kurt wasn't."

"Yes, but there was always some missing piece, something we couldn't quite see at Versailles. It remains unsettled in my mind."

"Lot's of people were bothered by Versailles. Didn't the English economist lay down the failures in plain sight in his book? I remember reading about all the controversies in the papers."

"You mean John Maynard Keynes and his book *The Economic Consequences of the Peace*?"

"Yes, I didn't read the book, of course, but the newspaper stories about the book made a big splash even in New York."

"Yes, it was more than just that season's big book," I said, recalling the reviews. "The *Guardian* said that as a piece of literature it was beyond praise."

"Even I could understand that something seemed wrong with all those reparations," said Kate. "You couldn't put Germany in debtor's prison for a generation."

"Yes. That was part of it. Kurt knows Keynes. Rather well. That's why he's the biggest economics correspondent now writing from Berlin. His success is about a lot more than knowing the price of wheat in the Ukraine."

"We're going to have an economics novel?" Kate asked, a wicked sense of fun crossing her face.

"Not if we want it to sell," I laughed. Turning more serious, I said, "I think Kurt has a story to tell which will dramatize the tale, put the political mistake in human terms."

"How?"

"Kurt is going to tell us what it looked like from the other side of the Rhine. What went wrong after the war in Germany. That is where the peace failed."

"He was there. He was in love," Kate said, now sensing the power of the story.

"And that love was shattered. The tragedy will drive the point home to the reader."

"So it was after the war? Not the war itself?"

"Yes, the peace never made up for the sacrifices made in the war. For either side. Hell, for all sides."

"So a love story after the war…tells the story of the war…" and her words trailed off.

"Yes, after the war," and I paused as those months flooded back into my memory, "We were all in love, I think." I looked off across the square at the ancient church, remembering Paris in 1919—the glittering chandeliers, the repartee in the salons, the tinkle of champagne glasses, my fiancée looking at me with those dark, glistening eyes.

"Not all of us," Kate said softly. I came back from my own memories and looked at her, sensing that there was something sad and lost from that time by this beautiful woman sitting across from me in the spring sunshine.

Kate looked up; she saw the waiter and waved him over. "*Deux cafes, s'il vous plait.*" She turned to me, "Maybe we should do a little work. I brought the manuscript with me."

"By all means."

"Kurt writes a lot about training," and she traced her finger down the page and the next page.

"He was a bear for it. Said no one would die because they had not run enough, shot enough," I said.

"Don't the soldiers get tired of the training?"

"No, it actually builds confidence, a willingness to go meet the enemy."

"Did it work out that way? For the soldiers?"

"Yes, at Chateau Thierry, it sure did."

She winced. The words *Chateau Thierry* were like a slap in her face.

"We could go out there and see it. I haven't been there since 1918," I said wistfully. "So much of the novel is set there."

"Yes," she replied in a halting manner, "we should go see it. Together."

"Fine. Maybe after we visit with Natalie." I planned that we should go to Natalie Barney's next salon and arrange for Kurt to speak sometime over the summer.

"Okay," she said, regaining her composure. She looked down and rummaged through some pages of the manuscript, "Let's see, where were we? Oh yes, Kurt then wrote about the regiment receiving its embarkation order. He says something about the 'well connected' getting out. It's all sort of wishy washy."

I laughed, "That's what he thinks about them."

"Who's them?" she asked, perplexed.

"Oh, the sons of the politicians. Kurt's too polite. You might strengthen it."

"What was that all about?"

"Well, sprinkled through the division were officers, the sons of politicians and well-connected businessmen, uniforms from the best New York tailors, the highly shined boots. But the casualty lists in Europe kept growing. It wasn't going to be all over by Christmas. So when the warning order came, other orders came in their wake, sending these darlings off hither and yon.

"Where'd they go?

"Oh, you know. Distant National Guard units in upper Michigan and outer Alabama."

Kate laughed, "What did Kurt say?"

"It was fine with him. He said they'd just get in the way. To Kurt, politicians are just the guys who fix county paving contracts."

She laughed. "I hadn't heard that line before. Now I know how to edit that part of the novel."

Smiling, she made some penciled notes on the manuscript. She looked up, "Then you all left for France?"

"We had pre-embarkation leave…"

She nodded her head in some knowing form of understanding and then dropped her glance and murmured, "Yes…" She kept her eyes down.

"And then we boarded the troopship and headed for France."

"Yes…" she said absently as she kept on writing. She took a sip of her coffee, and with her head down and her eyes scanning the sheet of notebook paper, scribbled some notes. She looked up, businesslike, and said, “Let me work on this. We can go over it at our next meeting.”

“That’ll be fine,” I said.

She set her pencil down and looked at me, a faint smile crossing her face, her eyes looking at me with interest.

9. Rue Jacob

As I walked up the narrow street on the Left Bank late Friday morning, I looked up ahead as well-dressed women and men walked through an arched entranceway—two large, dark green double doors stood open—into the cobblestoned courtyard at 20 rue Jacob, the residence of wealthy salon hostess Natalie Clifford Barney.

Earlier in her life Natalie had been the great friend of French poet Remy de Gourmont. It was he who christened her *l'Amazone*, the nickname she had carried proudly ever since. Gourmont published a series of essays entitled *Letters to the Amazon* celebrating his many intellectual conversations with Natalie, really a series of intellectual intercourses, which he published in a leading French literary journal in the years before the war. The letters burnished his public renown while stamping Natalie as a leading intellectual. Many said Gourmont was her major intellectual conquest. Natalie, with her pure, unapologetic pursuit of lesbianism at every level, was said to do conquests where other women might be simply described as seducing.

After the war, I worked with Natalie translating some of the now deceased Gourmont's poetry and getting the poems published in New York and London. She was grateful and I became a regular at "her Fridays," as she called her salons. Here I met most of the American women writing in Paris and came to represent many of them to the New York market, which of course was the big time next to the piddling money to be made in Paris.

But the salon was not just women. Important male authors attended and there were always French and American men of distinction if not talent in attendance. The food was exquisite, cocktails at the bar, and champagne in abundance. Natalie knew what men liked. She was good at oiling a conversation.

Today I wanted to see if it would be possible in a couple of weeks to have Kurt give a presentation on his great American war novel at one of Natalie's salons. Everyone in Paris knew that

Hemingway had returned to America and that he was working on his war novel. Everyone also wanted to see if Hemingway's second novel could equal the success of his first novel, the best-selling *The Sun Also Rises*. Hemingway was on people's minds.

My idea was that I could give a little talk on what we knew about Hemingway's coming novel from his short story *In Another Country* published last year. The story was about Hemingway's experience in Italy during the war while recovering from a wound. More importantly, broad themes were set forth, ideas we might see developed in a novel. Everyone knew Hemingway was a boxer—he'd knocked down quite a few guys in Paris—and I could say that Hemingway telegraphed his punches. Everyone would get the hook.

Then Kurt could give a brief summary of his novel and how his story, unlike say *All Quiet on the Western Front*, would show how it was the peace that failed, not the war—despite its many miseries. That would get people talking. Some of that talk would drift across the Atlantic to New York. I would be able to sell Kurt's book with one, possibly two, telegrams. I had a good idea of who wanted to go up against Max Perkins and Scribner's in the next round.

Today, the trick would be not to drink the champagne before I had earned it. I laughed to myself as I headed through the entranceway.

In the garden under a large spreading chestnut tree I saw Kate talking with a young American writer. I sauntered up and nodded at Kate and said to the young man, "How's it going, Morrill?" He was staring straight ahead.

"I'm looking at Margaret Anderson."

"Yes, so I see." Margaret Anderson was the founder of the avant-garde literary magazine *The Little Review*. Her longtime companion and former lover Jane Heap edited the review back in New York. Margaret had been living for some time with artist Georgette Leblanc in France. Nevertheless Margaret would be a good gateway to get some of Kurt's novel excerpted and published in *The Little Review*. It would really build interest. Margaret had been the first to publish chapters from James Joyce's *Ulysses* in the United States; she had the New York court conviction on obscenity to prove it. Kate could work the *Little Review* angle.

"I first saw her in 1915 in Michigan," Morrill said. He had the dreamy look of a fond recollection on his face.

"Did you talk with her?"

"No, I was just fifteen. I just looked at her. She was the most beautiful woman in the world…the golden blond hair like a halo…the fine figure…the tailored blue suit."

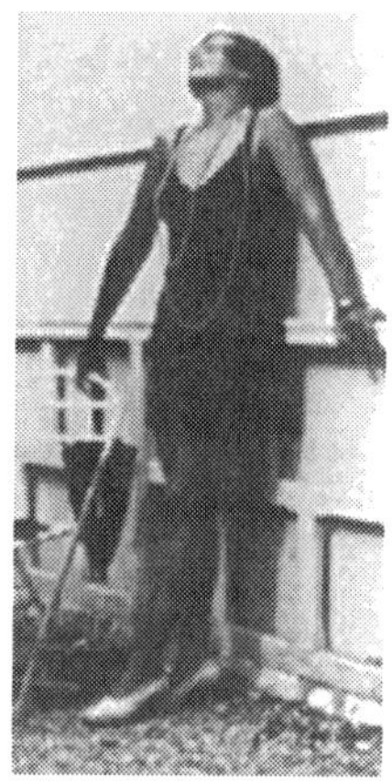

Figure 3 Margaret Anderson.

Kate watched the star-struck young man with interest. Well, yes, Margaret was, even now, a real showstopper.

"She's one of my Three Graces," I humorously added.

"Three Graces? Who are they?"

"Oh, the three most beautiful women in expatriate Paris."

"Who are the other two?"

Kate also looked at me with inquisitiveness, an eyebrow arched in expectation.

"Solita Solano and Djuna Barnes."

Kate broke into a smile and gave a slight nod of approval. Good choices.

Morrill's face fell. "Your three women all like other women."

"Like goddesses, they are beyond our reach. Their unattainableness adds to their allure."

Kate laughed.

Morrill's face twisted in consternation as he added, "That's sort of what leaves you wondering at these Fridays. Are the women here because they're lesbians or because they're literary talents in their own right?"

"Some of both I would venture," I replied. Kate kept an even expression, not so much as a flicker.

Morrill looked thoughtful for a moment while he reconsidered and then said, "With Djuna you never know. When Thelma wanders, possibly she wanders. You sure find her in the cafes looking for Thelma."

"I don't think that's true," contradicted Kate. "Fidelity, not promiscuity, is Djuna's star. Thelma can be something of a disappointment in that regard."

"Boy, you can sure say that," said Morrill.

Everything the two of them said was true. But I never tried to understand Djuna. She was the wild rose. There were so many contradictions, but I loved her writing; she was the best writer among the women in Paris. That's why Gertrude Stein wouldn't give her the time of day.

Kate continued explaining to Morrill, "She had a long running affair with Courtenay Lemon in New York and an affair with Laurence Vail before he married Peggy Guggenheim. Or should I say Peggy Guggenheim married him. Or acquired him." I laughed. Then I looked at Kate but I could see that her mind was now off into the distance of her own memories. "There were others," she mumbled. Kate seemed to know a lot about Djuna.

"You were in New York with Djuna?" I asked.

"We were in the Provincetown Players together in Greenwich Village. She was a writer. I was a part-time dancer and publicity writer. And I worked in an advertising agency during the week. You know, rent."

"Yes, I know rent. And you came to Paris with Djuna?"

"Sort of."

"And the rent?"

Kate gave me a sharp glance at the impertinence of my question and then decided to answer it: "She got me a magazine gig for a Paris story. And some other stuff. I worked for the rent," she said with sharp finality.

Margaret walked over, her face breaking into a big smile of welcome, and shook Morrill's hand, "How's your mother and your sister? Your family was so nice to me up in Michigan."

"They're fine. They ask after you."

Margaret beamed, looked at Kate inquiringly and said, "Did you know Morrill back in the States, too?"

"No. We were just talking about Djuna Barnes."

Margaret rolled her eyes, "That woman's mind is as complex and winding as a labyrinth. She's not even on speaking terms with her own psyche. Did I say dark?" But she added lightly, "She is amusing and the wit can be devastating. I try to stand out of the way."

"She has been helpful to me," said Kate quietly.

"Yes, she has," Margaret said sympathetically.

"Margaret, *The Little Review* published quite a bit of Djuna's stuff," I added.

"Yes, we published a lot of the best of what might be called 'the early Djuna,'" said Margaret.

"Yes, *Night Among the Horses*," added Morrill.

"Yes, that was back almost ten years now," recalled Margaret.

"December, 1918. I remember exactly," said Kate.

"Exactly?" I asked.

"Exactly. We all lived in a big house on Greenwich Avenue…"

"You lived in that cavernous old house?" asked Margaret. She obviously knew the house. Margaret had been in the center of literary New York in those years.

"Well almost everyone with Provincetown Players lived there. I was young and new and so I lived down that long hallway near the kitchen. Djuna and Courtenay Lemon lived in the front in a small flat strewn with newspapers. They were quiet, orderly—except for the newspapers. In those years, Djuna was one of the highest paid journalists in New York. Always fashionably dressed. We all wanted to be like her."

"Yes, I'm sure you did," said Margaret. "Did you know that Georges Clemenceau lived in that same flat when he lived in New York?"

"Yes, I had heard that. But that was a long time ago," said Kate.

I laughed and added, "But you're right, Margaret, a regular wasps' nest." Clemenceau had been the French premier during the Versailles Peace Conference, the statesman who famously said that war was too important to be left to generals. Kate frowned at me and then she turned back to Margaret.

"I understand your tension with Djuna, Margaret," said Kate apologetically.

I had been in Paris right after the war, but I had heard the gossip from New York that Djuna had had an affair with Jane Heap, Margaret's longtime companion and editor of *The Little Review*.

"Yes, but that wound up being liberating," said Margaret. "Other things have blossomed here in Paris as a result."

Margaret had come to France and found the love of her life, artist Georgette Leblanc. But it was not necessarily an exclusive relationship; Margaret now lived outside Paris with Georgette and a French woman. And something was brewing between Margaret and Solita Solano to everyone's common knowledge. Interestingly, I never heard about anything brewing with Kate Lundberg. She must be more than just discreet. She couldn't have been living in that big house in Greenwich Village and not done something with someone. But what? With whom?

Turning to me, Margaret asked, "And what is Bill Lawrence up to?"

"I have a talented guy writing the great American war novel. He's a correspondent in Berlin. Maybe later this year *The Little Review* might like to run an excerpt. Hemingway's writing his big American war novel for publication next year. Might be a lot of interest."

"Hemingway!" She exclaimed and laughed.

Morrill looked at her, perplexity across his face, "You and Hemingway?"

Margaret gave him a playful frown, the one teachers give to a slow student, and said to him, "Me and Hemingway?" She laughed at the idea.

"When I first came to Paris," Margaret explained, "he said I was the prettiest legend he had ever seen. That big lopsided grin. Constantly running into me. All the time. He was in love with me," and Margaret laughed a big smiling laugh.

"But I found him," and she looked at Kate and smiled impishly, "gooey."

Kate arched an eyebrow and looked at me and stifled a laugh.

"What about Hemingway the writer?" I asked.

Margaret stood still for a moment, then looked at me with those wide eyes, and said, "Simple."

I slowly nodded my head in agreement. Astute. Kate nodded in agreement.

Margaret turned to Morrill, "Let's get a glass of champagne."

Then as an aside, Margaret said to Kate, "We'll get together on an article to go with the excerpt from this great big novel for *The Little Review*." Margaret grabbed Morrill's elbow and guided him towards the table where champagne was being poured. He looked like he had won the lottery.

Kate sidled up next to me, amusement across her face, "Well, I guess we know how Pauline Pfeiffer became the second Mrs. Hemingway. The door was wide open!"

"Margaret does that to people. Pauline probably had to scheme."

Kate laughed.

Just then Sylvia Beach walked over, holding out her hand: "Bill, what a pleasant surprise." She turned and smiled at Kate and said, "Djuna tells me you're working with Bill on editing a war novel by an American living in Berlin. Well, that ought to be a different perspective."

Figure 4 James Joyce, Sylvia Beach, and Adrienne Monnier in the book shop Shakespeare & Company.

"Yes, I am—a doomed romance becomes a metaphor for the failed peace."

"That sounds intriguing. Hemingway's doing something with his experiences in Italy during the war. He told me before he went back to America that he was optimistic about his coming novel; that it was really coming together."

"We hope to publish about the same time. Hemingway will provoke a lot of interest in the war," I said.

Sylvia's expression sharpened and she looked at Kate and asked, "You said 'the failed peace,' not the war." Her expression framed the statement as a question.

"Yes, a German perspective from the other side of the Rhine. That's where the peace failed. That's why the rest of the world looks at Germany with anxiety and fear," said Kate.

"Yes, the voice that can illuminate that story should be heard. The peace…" and Sylvia sighed as if peace were a long-lost youthful illusion. "I remember. I was one of the thronging thousands cheering Wilson's procession down the Champs Élysées just after the Armistice. We were all so hopeful." You could hear the wistfulness of those now distant cheers in her voice.

"What were you doing in Paris, Sylvia?" I asked.

"My sister and I were finishing secretarial training; then we took jobs with the American Red Cross in Serbia. We left Paris just after Wilson's arrival. From Rome we rode in a train carriage with no windowpanes for five days through a blinding snowstorm to Belgrade. Once there we learned that women had no voice in the decisions. The men, the doctors, held the highest rank but these creatures were in the dark ages as regards women. Women corrected their errors and did all the work," and she looked at Kate with an ironical gaze. "But what can you expect?"

Kate nodded in understanding.

"That experience made a regular feminist out of me," Sylvia said, a trace of that long ago anger still in her voice.

"You were there in the aftermath of the war?" I said, shifting the conversation.

"The aftermath of the war was worse than war. Thousands died in the epidemics that swept the country. The insanity on display was beyond what even literature could prepare you for, the pitiful condition of the returning prisoners, the utter desolation of the country…the entire experience was the end of innocence," she said.

"So you came back to Paris?" I asked.

"Eventually, yes. Six months in Serbia was a long time." She looked at me and said, "While in Serbia, I kept in touch with Adrienne—we shared a love of literature and of independence," mentioning Sylvia's longtime companion, Adrienne Monnier, a French bookseller.

Sylvia turned towards Kate and explained, "During the war, one of my great friends from my days in Florence had gone back to America and married a successful lawyer. She had just had her first child while I was training in Paris. But that wasn't for me." She stared intently at Kate, almost asking the question about roads not taken.

"Yes, the first child. I remember the delight at the very thought of having a child…once…" said Kate softly.

"Yes, was that to be my destiny also I asked?" Sylvia looked off into the distance. She turned to Kate, "Or our destiny?"

"I remember," sighed Kate, "when that alternative was in front of me." Sadness colored her expression; I hadn't heard this before.

Sylvia saw Kate come to her understanding and she continued her story, "Once I got back from Serbia, I looked at my options. I decided to stay on this side and make something or other work out. I wanted a little book business of my own. Adrienne found a shop for me. Paris was full of Americans and these pilgrims were going to need books they could read in their own language. I told my family I couldn't go back; America seemed only interested in sports and business."

"Yes, I know," said Kate, the sadness still enveloping her expression.

Sylvia took on a reflective air and continued to address Kate, "Adrienne's gentle friendship let me cultivate my true career, our lives started to flow together, my wanderings found me a true home in Paris."

"I understand," said Kate, looking into Sylvia's eyes with a frankness I hadn't seen before.

"Yes, I'm sure you do," said Sylvia.

I listened as the two women talked. I asked myself if in Sylvia's discussion of roads taken and not taken, had there been a choice? Or had some natural destiny just called? I wondered.

Sylvia turned to me, breaking into my reverie, and said, "When your book comes out, we'll have a reading by your friend at Shakespeare and Company," the name of her famous bookshop. "Tout Paris will be there."

"We will look forward to it," I replied.

Sylvia smiled and said, "I better get back to the shop." She looked at Kate, a shared understanding between them. She turned and headed towards the arched entranceway.

Kate watched her go and said softly with admiration, "Six months of true experience lets you get at the truth of things. To discover yourself."

"Yes, if you survive the war, the war holds up a mirror to you. The inner feelings come out," I said.

"In Serbia, Sylvia had first-hand experience with the devastating aftermath of the war. She will be able to provide a powerful testament to Kurt's message when he speaks at her book shop," said Kate.

"Yes, she will. Undoubtedly she will get a lot of writers buzzing about this book long before it's published."

Kate glanced over at the departing figure of Sylvia Beach and murmured, "There's so much more there than I had realized."

"Yes, the war…the desolation of peace…" I mumbled.

Kate looked at me with glistening eyes, her thoughts obviously back on the war. I watched for a few moments and then I changed my tone and said to Kate, "If nothing else, we're lining up one book promotion opportunity after another this afternoon."

Her expression came back to the present and she said to me in a businesslike tone, "Yes, we are. What are you going to do now?"

"I'm going to go talk to the Amazon herself. I think Kurt requires a careful presentation, but I also think she will be intrigued. Natalie hated the war and never thought much of the peace."

I turned and walked up the steps into the two-story *pavillon* that was Natalie's residence. Going through the small entry hall I went into the spacious dining room and saw at the other end Natalie talking with friends and acquaintances. I caught her eye and her face brightened in welcome. She whispered to the man sitting to her left and he vacated the chair and headed for the refreshment table. Natalie patted the chair indicating I should come over for a talk. I grabbed a glass of champagne and hurried over. You didn't keep the Amazon waiting.

Figure 5 Natalie Clifford Barney as a young woman in a portrait painted by her mother.

"Well, Bill, what have you for us today? I saw you chatting in the garden with Margaret and Sylvia. You must be plotting something."

"Oh, I am. I have a new client. I knew him in the war. We were in the same regiment at the Marne in 1918."

"Yes," she sighed, "I remember the stupidity and uselessness of the whole ordeal. It brought a beautiful age, my age really, to an ugly end. And by 1918 the political errors which prolonged it were unpardonable."

I nodded in solemn agreement. I now believed that, too. I said, "Anyway, he is writing his version of the great American war novel."

"Well, I never want to be seen as supporting the concept of war at all. I hate the fact that women raise children only to see them die in war."

"That is really his story. He was in Germany after the war in the occupation army. He saw the opportunity to rebuild Europe that was missed. He met a German girl, married her, and went to Berlin as a correspondent. Some sort of tragedy followed—I'm not sure on the particulars—but it was a doomed romance. It was a crushing and unforgivable event for him. The story drives a powerful message. And Kurt is a bold and driving personality. He powers the words in front of him like an autumn wind blowing leaves down a country lane. Raw talent. He would be a very interesting speaker."

"If you say so..." I could see she was weighing the words, making an appraisal.

Just then Kate came into the room. Natalie brightened and waved her over to the chair next to mine while she politely asked the lady sitting there if Kate could take her seat "for just a few minutes."

As Kate walked over, Natalie watched her with a deeply appraising gaze and whispered to me, "She's one of the bright talents among the beautiful new things. Djuna says so." Kate sat down.

"I was just telling Natalie the outlines of Kurt's book," I said to Kate.

Natalie nodded. I continued, "The other dimension is that Hemingway has started his second novel, which is to be his great novel of the war. Or at least that's what he's saying."

At the sound of Hemingway's name, Natalie's face fell into a small frown and she whispered a drawn out, "Yes." Skepticism lifted her eyebrows.

"The war and its disillusion will be a major public topic," I explained. "Hemingway's new novel guarantees that. A chance to again talk about the war and try to salvage something from its horrors for the future."

Natalie nodded in passive agreement and then looked past me and said to Kate, "Hemingway. You know Ezra and I set up the Bel Esprit project to give promising young artists monetary stipends to support quality in the arts." Ezra was of course the poet Ezra Pound, who had done so much to bring Margaret's *Little Review* to the forefront a decade earlier. Coming to Paris, Ezra had helped promote Hemingway and other young writers. He, too, had translated some of Remy de Gourmont's writings and promoted them to publishers and literary magazines. That cemented a relationship with Natalie.

Natalie continued, “Ezra urged Hemingway to apply for funds, and I of course was pleased to oblige.” Natalie matter-of-factly explained her little story, “He and his wife took the money out to the racetrack and put it all on one horse. The horse lost.”

Natalie made a hard look, “Hemingway, *il est mal élevé*.” He is badly brought up. Nothing matter-of-fact about that judgment at all. The Amazon had spoken.

Kate’s eyebrows shot up in shock and she nodded her head in acknowledgement. In French circles, to be badly brought up was a damning phrase since it visited the sins of the child on the shortcomings of the parents, or vice versa as the case demanded. It consigned someone to the other side of the social railroad tracks.

Natalie watched Kate’s reaction. I think she saw the response she wanted. Then Natalie looked at me, turning to the business at hand, “Yes, it is coming on ten years since the end of the war.”

She looked off into the distance, “Time for art to speak.”

Natalie stood up, Kate and I followed. Natalie said, “Yes, we would be pleased to have your friend speak at one of our little gatherings. Only new thinking can hope to avoid this endless legacy of war given to mankind.” She held her hand out to Kate, each of us getting our own smile and thank you in turn. Dropping my hand, Natalie turned and headed over towards another circle of guests.

Kate walked alongside me as we headed outside into the courtyard, Kate whispering in an undertone, “You seem to know just the right time to say the word ‘Hemingway’ to the right woman.”

I smiled. He was a big target.

We ambled across the courtyard, nodding greetings at the clusters of guests chatting away in the courtyard. Near the Temple of Friendship, a small Greek temple Natalie had rebuilt and sat in her garden, I spotted a tall woman in animated conversation with several men and women in a small circle. I whispered to Kate, “There’s Djuna. I am working on a project with her and Thelma,” mentioning Djuna Barnes’ long-time companion Thelma Wood, the brilliant silverpoint artist. “I think Djuna should be able to write some profiles about Kurt and the novel that would get wide circulation back in the States. She has a big readership for her European features among millions of American women."

Kate nodded in agreement, "I know."

I caught Djuna's eye, and she politely broke off her conversation and started walking over. The dark raven colored hair was swept back in a chignon, the cheekbones framed a beautiful face, the long dark fashionable dress moved over supple hips to an almost narcotic effect—I always felt the spell. There were the big earrings, the elegant bracelets, and a figure that the French called "well made."

Djuna came up and hugged Kate like a big sister; I guessed their friendship was somewhat closer than I had thought.

Djuna held her hand out to me and said, "Kate told me about the trip you and her took to Berlin. Is it still the wild town it was?"

"With our friend Kurt it sure is."

"She said he's an American original."

"Well, with Kurt, if one woman is good, two or three must be better."

Djuna gave a short, bitter laugh. "Yes, Berlin's that sort of place."

By way of explanation I added, "Kate and I didn't really partake. We went back to the hotel early. We wanted to work on the manuscript the following day before returning to Paris."

"Well, she didn't partake the last time either," replied Djuna.

"You were there?"

"Why, yes. Kate and I were in Berlin in 1921. Had a room in a house next door to Bob McAlmon. He was of course wild. Partake? My God! But Kate and I were working. I had a bunch of assignments from *McCall's*."

"What did you think of Berlin?"

"Full of buggers from America who bought boys cheap," and she laughed. She must have been thinking about McAlmon and his friends. She lightly added, "The only thing I bought was a blouse."

Kate and I laughed.

"Kate and I went to the cinema a lot; it was ahead of everything else in those years. And lots of good theater. And we worked. *McCall's* couldn't get enough about Europe in those years."

A look of surprise came over my face. Kate had not shared anything with me about Berlin other than having been there with Mina Loy in 1922. She had not said anything about being there with Djuna; just that she was in Berlin on a magazine assignment. Before that, they had been in the Village together. I hadn't realized Kate had been so close to Djuna for so long.

Djuna looked at me and continued, "We did a grand tour. After Berlin, it was off to England. An interview with a duchess, I think," and she looked at Kate for confirmation.

"Yes, a duchess."

"Well, you had a good look at Berlin right after the tragedies of 1919 and 1920," I said.

Djuna gave me a penetrating look, "Bill, that's what intrigues me about the novel your friend is writing—to see that a good peace just does not flow from the end of war. A completely different story arc was possible."

"Yes, the road not taken."

"The dramatic potential is huge; the contrasts and paradoxes are startling," said Djuna with cocktail party insistence. She smiled at me—she could put the weakness in a man's knees—and said, "If I can be of any help with your project, just let Kate know. We're in touch."

"I will."

Djuna turned and started walking back to her circle of friends. Now I was like Morrill. I just stood and watched that fetching figure move across the courtyard, the sway ever so seductive.

Kate laughed, "She does that to all men. And some women."

"I've never quite understood that."

Kate turned towards me, her eyes twinkling, and she paused and pondered. A small indiscretion was back there somewhere. She took a sip of champagne and said, "When I first settled in Paris, after Djuna and I finished the European tour, I got to know Mina much better than I had in New York. There she was the *grande dame* and I was a young lady-in-waiting among the Village social set. Even then Mina and Djuna were best friends, a bond that has only gotten stronger."

I made a quizzical look. Mina was considered the goddess of heterosexuality incarnate. Kate laughed.

"They are alike; they have lived for the sensual. Mina told me that when Djuna first arrived in Paris she told her that she had had nineteen lovers and that women were better in bed than men."

Kate laughed and then added, "Of course that's a proposition Mina is unlikely to test."

There was a casual open-mindedness about Kate that appealed to me.

"You know Natalie wrote in one of her poems about a 'brow of genius and a lonely heart.' I've always felt that fit Djuna," I said.

"There's a lot of truth to that, Bill."

"Djuna's not looking for Prince Charming?" I asked.

"Prince or princess, I would think. Perhaps the right one has not come along." She smiled enigmatically and murmured, *"Peut-être."* Perhaps.

I stood back and looked at Kate with a sense of appraisal, wondering what she was all about. As that mystery deepened, my fascination strengthened.

She laughed, "I wouldn't bark up any wrong trees, Mr. Lawrence."

"I'm interested in you."

She was a little taken aback by my frankness. "Fine, Bill," she said, a bit shaken. Then her face took on a dispassionate expression, almost like a schoolteacher, and she said, "I think we have a journey to make—together."

"You mean that trip to Chateau Thierry?"

She nodded yes. Then she looked over my shoulder out into the distance. "Yes, Chateau Thierry," she said with a deeply felt sense of significance.

Yes, by all means, let's go to Chateau Thierry. I sensed there was more out there than just my memories, some sort of rendezvous with roads not taken.

I broke the spell and said to Kate, "This has been a good afternoon for us. Let's go to the Deux Magots and I'll buy you a cup of coffee."

"Why, yes. I would be delighted. May be we could talk about Chateau Thierry?"

Now it was my turn to stare off into the distance. The war. Yes, Kurt's novel was about the war. My war, too.

"Yes, let's. Maybe a brandy or two with that coffee?"

She laughed again and looked at me with playful interest. I felt mostly confused.

10. Late Lunch at Les Deux Magots

Kate and I walked up the sidewalk into the bright afternoon sunshine, the glare washing back down the polished surface of the well-worn stones. The *terrasse* of Les Deux Magots was ahead.

"Look. There's Janet and Solita," I said, pointing to the two women sitting at a small table in the shade. We walked over and they smiled and made room at the table. I pulled up two chairs and held one for Kate. She sat down.

"Been to Natalie's?"

"Yes," I replied.

"We got a late start and missed it," Solita added.

"See anyone interesting?" Janet asked with a deadpan expression. The whole crowd was always interesting.

I laughed, "Saw Djuna. She told me something about her and Kate's trip to Berlin way back when."

Solita turned to Kate, "You're working on editing that war novel for Bill's friend, the Berlin correspondent."

"Yes."

"So you get to re-visit Berlin again," Solita said, "and of course, the war…"

Kate nodded in agreement.

"The war…" and Janet looked off into the distance, distracted by an unwelcome memory. The war was doing that to everybody today.

"I was thinking that Kurt might speak about his novel at one of Natalie's Fridays," I said. "I planted the seed with Natalie. She's interested."

"She is?"

"Yes."

"Wonder why?"

"It's coming up on ten years this November."

"Oh, yes," Janet sighed. "The eleventh hour of the eleventh day of the eleventh month." Janet recited the famous phrase about the end of the war and the start of the Armistice with practiced monotony. We all knew it by heart.

Solita broke in, "We see the war the same way as Natalie. Simply put, war is a natural outgrowth of men's militant nature, and because they are drawn to war, they are unable to fully love the art of living." She plumped her glass down and drove home her point, "So they settle their political quarrels with war."

I nodded my head in agreement. The vehemence of Solita's words was emphatic. She had taken men's measure.

Janet picked up the cudgel and came at the subject of men and war with sarcastic disdain, "Men can make war, and they are absurd enough to believe they are superior for doing so."

"Something personal, Janet?" I asked.

She took the last sip from her wine glass and waved at the waiter. She made a circle with her finger indicating something for all of us.

Figure 6 Janet Flanner at costume ball in Paris during the 1920s.

"Yes, the war. That was when we decided to get married," she said. I knew she meant to Lane, her now divorced husband. Kate told me they were still great friends. He was a successful banker back in New York. I had never been able to arrange that kind of armistice with an ex. It had always been simple defeat for me.

"We thought he might be called up for military service. Visions of heroic men nobly marching off to the front danced in my imagination. Passion and patriotism come together in one wave," she said in recollection, apparently in disbelief that she had ever been so naive.

"We were in love and he was to go to war," she said with an intonation as if the line were poetry.

"Did he?"

"No. He couldn't pass the physical. He tried. He believed."

"I think we all did, back then," I said.

Solita leaned towards Janet, "Got you out of Indianapolis, didn't he?"

Janet flung her head back and laughed, "Sure did."

I looked at Kate. She had sat quiet through the whole conversation. I looked at her again, my face framing the question.

"I was still at Vassar."

I nodded in understanding.

We chatted deep into the afternoon, the sun falling in the western sky, the shadows lengthening across the square in front of us. We spoke about Janet's current commission to translate Colette's *Chéri*, one of the great novels by France's premier novelist, a beautiful tale of the power of the sensual and the sexual pulling a young man and an older woman beyond the boundaries of accepted convention. Very French.

11. Chateau Thierry

The morning sun shone brightly at the far end of the barn-like Gare de l'Est train station. The hiss of escaping steam transformed itself into billowing clouds of glistening white moisture that rose towards the glass-topped rafters. Soon the locomotives would pull their carriages away from the long concrete piers. I walked over to a coffee cart and saw Kate holding a paper box containing some steaming cups of coffee along with several brioches.

"Good morning. Ready for Chateau Thierry?" I asked.

"Yes, the train is right over there on platform five," she said.

We went over to the platform and walked out against the rush of morning commuters pouring out of the carriages. Coming to a second-class car, we waited as the last of the passengers disembarked and then mounted the steps and went into the carriage. We settled across from one another next to a big square window on what would be the shady side of the carriage as the train headed east to Chateau Thierry, not quite an hour away on the track to Reims. She handed me a cup of coffee.

"Cream?"

"No thank you."

"You come out here often?" I asked as I sipped the strong black brew.

"About twice a year. Before Decoration Day and Armistice Day. I write feature articles for the magazines back home about the war cemeteries and memorials. There's a lot of interest in where the boys are. The ones who didn't come home."

I sighed. It was always a painful memory. Those young men marching forward under the broad-brimmed steel helmets, the jaunty confidence on their faces. And then the ordeals that led to their not coming back. Memories of hellish artillery fire always seared my mind. "Yes," I said absently. The train lurched and started forward.

"Last fall I wrote about the Marines and the 2nd Division at Belleau Wood. Before that the 26th Division." She continued on, speaking of that battle and this division. She didn't mention the 3rd Division or Chateau Thierry.

She paused and sipped her coffee.

"What was it like?" she asked.

"The war?"

I leaned back in the seat and watched the rolling French farmland stream by the window, here and there punctuated by a small wood. The small woods had been hell during the war, particularly in that final push east towards Germany. I collected my thoughts.

"We trained a lot. At the beginning, Kurt was executive officer of Company D. He was also the assistant battalion training officer. Very focused on what he called 'deliberately aimed rifle fire.' That's something more than just marksmanship. It was about an entire platoon or rifle company laying down a tight band of aimed rifle fire right along the top of the enemy trench. Make it a killing zone, he said."

"Did it work?"

"Yes, if the enemy artillery fire lifted in time."

She nodded and shifted the conversation with a question: "The Americans held where the others fell back. Why?"

"The frontline leadership, the lieutenants and sergeants," I replied.

"Why?"

I leaned back and remembered, "We held a division review in the spring. General Pershing came. The entire division, battalion by battalion, was drawn up facing west. Pershing inspected the battalions, walking slowly by each one, letting the men see him. Then he stood on the reviewing stand facing east towards the Germans. That stern visage, the visor of his cap pulled down in front, like the beak of a hawk. He was a symbol of stern steadfastness. And he would look east, the direction from which the Germans would come. He seemed to know it was his spirit that would make the men hold."

Again I paused and then said reflectively, "There was something else. The Americans were here to finish the fight. That was Pershing."

Kate looked at me with interest, her eyes beckoning me to continue.

"The lieutenants really soaked it up. They spoke of it afterwards. Pershing had transferred this rock-solid determination to the junior officers watching him that day. It was like what we would call today a transfusion—his spirit into them. They all wanted to live up to his example."

"And Kurt?"

"Kurt? Well, yes and no. Kurt was completely inner-directed; he didn't need an outside example to stiffen his determination. But he instantly saw what Pershing had done. He would speak in the future about 'what the command expects' as a motivation tool. You knew he wasn't talking about the battalion commander," and I gave a brittle little laugh.

I sipped my coffee and looked at Kate. You could see she had a fascination with Kurt.

I continued, "You see, Kurt was a little older. He had an engineering degree. He had worked on big construction projects. He knew how to lead men in building things. Big things. He knew just what to tell men to get them to go forward. Never a bully. But real insistent about results."

"So you went into the line?"

"Yes, in mid-June. The Germans had pushed the French right back to the Marne River. The 3rd Division's machine gun battalion had held the Marne bridge at Chateau Thierry in early June. A really heroic action. Set a fine example to the rest of the division."

She nodded her head in acknowledgement; she knew the story. It was a good one.

"The rest of the division came forward in mid-June. We marched up the dusty roads, the tired and bedraggled French soldiers resting along the sides of the roads under the plane trees. They would stand up and cheer us, and then cheer us some more. Real sincerity. They knew what it was like."

"We strung out along the south side of the river, just in front of the railroad tracks. And dug in. Then we dug in some more. Kurt knew a lot about digging in. He was up and down the whole regiment. We practiced against a German river crossing. Everyone knew they were going to make a big push."

“What was your job?” she asked.

“I was the battalion adjutant. Paperwork. I also commanded the battalion reserve force. That’s the headquarters clerks and cooks and orderlies—clerks and jerks! Our job was to fill in any holes. We were positioned behind the railroad tracks. We would go over the top to counterattack any breaks in our line.”

“Sounds scary.”

“Harrowing yes. But you fight the way you train.”

“You trained?”

“Oh yes. Kurt rehearsed us. We practiced going across the tracks and coming into fighting positions at the top of the slope. Again and again. Kurt had pre-dug foxholes just where he wanted us; we just had to dive in. The positions were always slotted between two of the rifle companies. The Germans liked to hit the seams between units. So it was just a question of which slot we were going to fill that awaited the commander’s decision.”

“What were you going to do then?”

“Kurt said not to worry about the Germans in the river or any on our side; the line companies would take care of ‘em. Instead, we were to put down deliberately aimed rifle fire on the far bank. That is where the Germans would be staging the second and third waves. Turn it into a killing zone, he said.”

“Did it work?”

“When the time came, beautifully. Almost.”

“Almost?”

“I stood up too soon. I was hit in the arm and had to go to the rear.”

“Badly?”

“No, I got bandaged up and was called back to regiment that night. They consolidated all the adjutants at regiment. I stayed at regiment the rest of the war. Probably saved my life.”

Kate leaned back and took this in. “I have heard a lot of accounts of the war while writing my magazine articles. Valor, courage—yes. But rarely this type of applied thinking. Smart.”

“Well, that was Kurt.” It was the truth. Kate seemed quite taken by it. My heart sank a little.

The train pulled into the little farm town of Chateau Thierry. It was mostly rebuilt. There was a small square with a café under a veranda. A taxi waited at the station. We stepped off the steps of the carriage onto the long concrete slab under a shingled roof that kept the rain off waiting commuters. We walked down the slab and descended some stairs and walked towards the cab.

The driver was heavily mustachioed; he was missing his left hand. There was a metal apparatus in its place. He seemed to recognize Kate.

"Bill, I have used Didier before. Maybe we should go see the memorial on Hill 204 first?" Her question had the directness of a command.

"Of course."

Didier held the rear door open and Kate got in the back seat; I followed. Didier, closed the door, and walked around the front and got in. We drove out the west side of town and up a long slope to a big circular memorial surrounded by upright marble slabs. Didier parked in a small parking lot and Kate and I got out and walked out into the center of the memorial.

Then we walked over to the eastern edge of the circle offering a broad panoramic view of the Marne River valley and the flatlands lying to the north and east of Chateau Thierry. The River Marne was a silvery thread winding east along the south side of the little village. I had never seen a view of the terrain; it had always just been space on a map—deadly space filled with Germans. I was almost fascinated.

Kate pointed to the wood-covered hill to the northeast and said, "There's Belleau Wood. The cemetery is just in front of it. Maybe we can see it last."

"Yes," I said absently. Undoubtedly there were names I would recognize. The sting was gone, but the sadness stayed with me. I looked out at Chateau Thierry and pointed with my arm, "There's the river. And the bridge over it. Up that slope, just past the ridge, are the railroad tracks. You can still see them there. The regiment was dug in on this side of the ridge all along the river to the east. My men and I were on the back side of the slope, on the other side of the railroad tracks."

Kate stood and stared intently as I pointed out each landmark. It was almost like she had already been there. She murmured

"Yes" in turn as I pointed out the features of the terrain where that long ago baptism in fire occurred.

"Maybe we should go over there and I can show you what happened."

"Yes, I would like that."

We turned and walked over to the cab and Kate gave Didier some directions. We drove back down the country road, then turned at Chateau Thierry and crossed the bridge, the river lazily flowing beneath. Poplars, dense with summer leaves, lined both sides of the river. Didier guided the cab up the slope and pulled over just before the railroad tracks. Kate and I got out.

We walked east along the track bed. I explained, "In 1918, we felled almost all the trees. We used the timbers to build our bunkers. Kurt was really expert—we dug deep, double timbered the roofs, and then put a couple of feet of rocks from the riverbed on top of the timbers. Covered that with dirt. Indestructible."

Kate's eyes were glued to the riverbank. She glanced at the other features of the slope. I stopped and pointed over to the other side of the train tracks, "My men and I were dug in over there. The initial barrage was terrific. Anything out in the open would have been killed. A German artillery barrage is a thorough and frightening thing—a storm of steel. Deadly."

She looked at me and her expression registered the trueness of my description. She had not heard this before.

"The barrage lifted and at first light, it was the middle of July so it was around four in the morning, the Germans started across in assault boats. Other Germans shoved hastily assembled pontoon bridges out into the river. Our boys came out of their bunkers and took up fighting positions along the shore and put up a terrible fire. The Germans were surprised. Those that made it ashore were tracked down and killed. Some hid and were later captured."

"So the Germans were driven back?"

I sighed, "No, the Germans are nothing but tenacious. They got a foothold between Company D and Company C. The battalion commander ordered me to take my men to the boundary seam between the two companies. We came over the top of the hill, took to the foxholes, and started putting down a line of fire on the far bank. I watched as the commander of Company D took some men and moved to attack the Germans on the riverbank. Nearby, one of our platoon leaders led his men out of their holes and met the Germans coming across the river in the assault boats at the river bank, the lieutenant throwing hand grenades into the German boats as they approached the shore, his men shouting and firing and killing the Germans in the water. As the assault floundered, one German got a shot off and killed the lieutenant. He was dead before he hit the ground." I turned and looked at Kate; it was like the battle had just happened minutes before.

Kate simply looked sad and nodded.

I continued, "Then the company commander was killed. Kurt moved forward and took command. He systematically maneuvered the remaining platoons to eliminate the last German pockets of resistance. I had my men keep up fire on the far bank. The Germans melted away back up the north slope of the river."

"Do you remember the lieutenant's name?"

"Why yes. Lieutenant Jones. I wrote the letter to his family."

"Can we go down and see?"

"Yes, of course." I held out my hand and we started down a rabbit track towards the poplars lining the riverbank. At the top of a small escarpment just along the river we stopped. I pointed down the river to the bridge, stepped to the right a half dozen paces, and then held out my arm to the church steeple. I looked down at my feet, triangulating my position back to where the lieutenant had turned back the German river assault ten years before.

I looked at Kate, "About here."

She looked up the river, then down the river. She stared across the river at the village. You could see her imagining the German boats coming across the river in the gray darkness. She turned and faced me.

"Lieutenant Jones was my fiancé."

I looked at her. I simply nodded. We stood there for several minutes looking this way and that, alone with our thoughts.

"We had better go. We can go to the memorial cemetery."

"Are you sure?" I asked.

"Oh, I have been there many times. I have been here, too, not exactly at this spot. But others pointed out where they thought he fell from accounts of the battle. But you were here. A real witness. I will write his parents. He was their only son."

I could only nod. We walked up the hill and then down the train tracks to the cab.

The cab took the same country road out west of Chateau Thierry and then continued northwest a couple more miles and turned off. Large metal gates hinged to twin rock piers stood open. A long wide drive extended west towards what appeared to be a rock tower undergoing construction. On either side of the drive rows of white crosses stood in eternal formation on the shimmering green grass. Didier stopped the cab near what I could see was a limestone tower. We got out.

Kate swept her arm past the uncompleted tower, "It is going to be a chapel modeled on a Romanesque church. Beautiful like an ancient image. There are architect's drawings down at the superintendent's house by the entrance. We can see them later if you like?"

"That won't be necessary."

"I've been to all the American memorials in eastern France. They are going to be some of the finest work ever done by the American government. Truly beautiful and magnificent in their sorrow."

"Do you think Congress is feeling remorse?"

"No, melancholy I would think."

I sighed, "Yes." Sadness is what I always felt when I looked back at the war.

We walked over between the rows of crosses. Kate seemed to know where she was going. Presently we stopped before a white cross. Inscribed in the stone was "Thomas Jones, First Lieutenant, 3rd Division."

"I used to come here often. But not so much anymore. My life has gone in other directions. The future that awaited me in 1918 is gone."

"And what was that future?"

"Oh, I suppose that of a married woman living in a Connecticut suburb with a husband working in the city. He was working on Wall Street when I met him—I was down from Vassar for a weekend." She paused and looked off into the distance, possibly recalling long ago "what if's" of that vanished future. Then she said with a certain finality, "I am sure I would have loved my children deeply." I could see that part of our conversation was over.

"And today?"

"Oh, I am pleased with how Paris has worked out. I had never imagined such a life." She paused and looked at me, "Possibly there's some guilt at my current success having to originate in someone else's tragedy."

"Yes, anything that is good after the war always comes tinged with what happened in the war."

"Yes," she said, wistfully looking into the distance. "You understand," she intoned softly; I barely heard her. She turned and took a long sweeping glance at the entire cemetery, possibly another in what had been a long series of farewells over the years.

I stood silent. After a moment her gaze swung back at me and she smiled like giving a benediction. I said, "We better be getting back. Maybe a late lunch in Chateau Thierry before catching the train?"

"Yes, I would like that."

We walked over to the cab.

In Chateau Thierry, Didier brought the cab to a halt in front of a café with several tables sitting in the shade of a big spreading tree heavy with summer leaves. I paid him off and graciously thanked him. He put his hand to his cap in salute and left. Kate and I went up onto the veranda and Madame pointed us towards a table with a red and white checked tablecloth.

"*Du vin rouge, s'il vous plait, madame.*" Some red wine, please.

Kate scanned the menu and then suggested a roasted rabbit dish. Eyeing the rather stout build of the lady of the establishment, I said, "I trust she eats her own cooking."

Madame put a carafe and two glasses on the table. I poured wine into our glasses. I took a sip and then looked at Kate, seriousness in my expression I hoped.

"Was it unfulfilled love that sent you off in new directions?"

She looked at me evenly. I had pried. She turned deeply thoughtful, thinking inwards almost as if I were not there. Her expression softened. She took a long sip of wine and then set her glass down. She folded her hands in front of her on the table.

"It was not an unfulfilled love."

"I did not mean to pry."

"That's quite all right. I had hoped to tell you anyway—eventually." She smiled at me lightly.

Then she looked away into the distance of her memories, composed her thoughts, and turned back to me.

"I went and spent the last week with Tom before he went overseas. My mother said I should go to him as a wife or I would regret it for the rest of my life. I did."

She paused for a moment.

"It was a beautiful week. A sensuous rapture of first love in beautiful bedrooms along the sunny Connecticut shore. Velvety nights, clean sparkling mornings. A honeymoon tinged with the melancholy of the coming departure."

She looked at me and said, "Djuna opens one of her poems—'This night I've been one hour in paradise.'" Kate's eyes glistened with the memory and she murmured, "I don't think it can be said better."

"Yes, the poem was in her first anthology." I had found the poem powerfully original and had asked around about the romance behind it. Djuna had had an intensely passionate affair with Mary Pyne, a beautiful redheaded actress and poet with Provincetown Players. Mary had died in New York of tuberculosis, attended by Djuna to the end.

Kate watched me, guessing that maybe I knew the story behind the poem. She said simply, "Djuna told me that before Mary there were men and women, but that after Mary there was just love." I nodded; that would explain a lot.

Kate looked out across the square, alone with her thoughts, possibly savoring one more time those now distant pleasures of first love along the Connecticut shore.

I waited a few moments and then picked up the narrative, asking her, "I remember boarding the troop ship at Hoboken. Were you one of the many waving young women on the dock?"

"Yes, I was so fulfilled by the week, so hopeful about the future. How could he not come back? His physical presence was so real. It did not seem possible."

I looked at her with wonder and sorrow.

"Then…too soon…came the telegram from the War Department. I was simply devastated."

One tear came to the corner of her eye. She wiped it away.

"I went to the small town in Connecticut where his parents lived for the Memorial Service. It was intensely moving. And by then casualty reports were coming in daily to towns large and small. The other side of 'Over There' was brought home to us 'Over Here'."

"Yes, I wrote many letters for the commander's signature in those weeks. Right up to the end of the war. It never let up."

She looked at me and gave a weak smile. "I was in New York after the Armistice and saw the victory parades. The experience mostly separated me from all the rapturously happy people lining the sidewalks. But it also tells you to set this aside and move on. I did—eventually."

She lifted her glass and took another sip of wine. She put her glass down in a little ritual of finality.

I lifted up the carafe and refilled her glass, and then mine. I held mine out to her for a toast, "To the past? To the present? To the future? I don't know which?"

"How about the present," she answered.

"Excellent," I replied and clinked her glass. "Are you happy with the present?"

"Happy?" She looked at me quizzically, like a strange word had entered the conversation uninvited.

"I don't really think that way, now. I think more about personal liberty, the ability to pursue my dreams. So I guess I am more like Djuna and Janet," and she paused and smiled, "and they say I am like Mina." She gave a small laugh at what must have been an inside joke. Mina was a strikingly handsome woman with a romantic past with some of the really talented men of the avant-garde. What did this mean? I wondered. Again, my heart sank a little.

"Mina?" I asked, my turn to be puzzled. I didn't know whether the reference to Mina was some 'just us girls' allusion to Kate writing poetry or about her engaging in affairs with wildly romantic men. Djuna had a little chap book *The Ladies Almanack* coming out soon. The page proofs I had seen were almost impenetrable to outsiders due to all the little inside jokes about the women of the Left Bank. But Kate wasn't in it as far as I could tell. No clues there.

"Yes, I live just downstairs from Djuna. A nice new apartment building out on Rue Saint-Romain. Mina lives nearby. We're looking for an apartment in our building for Mina. Then we'll be all together."

"I didn't know that."

"The wonderful thing here on the Left Bank is the way women support each other. The support allows a degree of personal liberty not possible anywhere else."

"I agree." I worked with most of the woman writers on the Left Bank. A remarkable group. Fun, but with a hawk-like watchfulness for any encroachment on their personal liberty. Heterosexual or lesbian, they would partner but that was sort of it—they were wedded to independence, the bracelets jangling on their wrists saying they were a different kind of woman. They would rarely submit to what they felt was matrimonial-style domination. And no word could gnash teeth like "patriarchal." Their society was a web of often overlapping fidelities sustained by an overarching commitment to personal honesty—as contradictory as this sounds.

Where did Kate's fidelities lie today? Down what path was her personal liberty leading her?

I asked, "Just what dream are you pursuing with your liberty?"

"Writing. What else?" she said. Then she smiled at me, almost seductively.

"You mentioned editing in New York. Anything to that?"

"I get nibbles. But I'm going to stick with this for a while longer."

"Good," I said with conviction.

She smiled at me warmly; I think she saw what she had wanted to see.

"I mean…"
"We better go catch that train to Paris," she said.
I motioned for the bill.

12. La Quatrième République

Early Friday afternoon, I walked up the shady side of rue Bonaparte towards Saint-Germain-des-Prés and turned onto rue Jacob. Up ahead I saw the sign "La Quatrième République," the little bistro where I was meeting Kate. I ducked inside a low doorway into the narrow downstairs bar and caught the waitress's attention and asked, "Mademoiselle Lundberg?"

"Upstairs."

I started up the restaurant's narrow circular staircase that wound around a big wooden post. A series of false steps in a Cubist design were painted along the walls of the stairwell and were an intriguing introduction to the avant-garde décor of the upstairs dining room. Reaching the top of the stairs, I saw Kate sitting near the window speaking with Janet Flanner, who was standing next to the table and getting ready to depart. I walked over and said, "Hello, Janet."

"Hi, Bill," Janet replied, "I was just speaking with Kate about the fashion piece she's working on." She gave me a long skeptical look and asked, "Business or pleasure today?"

"We're working on our book project," I said in a businesslike tone and then added cheerfully, "but time with Kate is always a pleasure."

"Yes, of course," Janet replied, a somewhat knowing smile on her face. "By the way, the stew's excellent today. My compliments."

"The Fourth Republic? Does the owner know something we don't?" I asked.

"Monsieur Chuzeville thinks that the way the Third Republic is going, a fourth will be unavoidable," Janet replied.

"Bill, look on the bright side, the next regime will be a republic, too," Kate added.

"On that happy note, let me leave you two to your lunch," Janet said as she stepped around me and headed for the staircase.

"And any other pleasures you two have in mind," she said over her shoulder.

I gave Janet a warm smile and then sat down across from Kate and said, "Hello. Charming place."

"Yes," Kate replied, her eyes warm and welcoming. "Janet has lunch here every day. I'm working on a second fashion piece. I'm going to discuss it tomorrow afternoon with Djuna and Janet. At the Café de Flore."

"Really? I was going to bring it up after we finished our work today, but maybe now would be appropriate." I sort of fidgeted as I collected my words and then got them out, "I was wondering if we could have dinner tomorrow night together. No work, all social. Maybe continue where we left off at the café in Chateau Thierry?"

"I would really like that, Bill. Could we meet at the Flore around six?"

"Yes." I felt relieved and a lightness of expectation came over me. She noticed and laughed.

"I sort of feel that way, too, Bill." Her smile was both winsome and seductive. I was floating.

"Janet was right. You have added a pleasant pleasure to our lunch."

Kate smiled at my little sally and then waved to Yvonne, the waitress.

"We'll have the *prix fix*," and she winked at me, "That's all they have, but you'll like it anyway."

Yvonne brought over a carafe of a light tawny red wine and two glasses. She filled the glasses.

"Onionskin wine. From the mountains of Jura, the owner's home province. It's quite good," said Kate.

I sipped some and nodded approval.

Kate moved the conversation to business: "I read Kurt's manuscript about the regiment's advance from Chateau Thierry to the next river and then on to the end of the war. I hadn't realized it was so tough."

"Not so bad at the beginning, but worse as it went along. A couple of days after the German river assault, the Germans hit us with another massive bombardment. The regiment held. That was where the 'Rock of the Marne' nickname came from. The following day we were relieved."

"So you went into reserve?"

"Yes, we were resupplied with new men and equipment. Kurt drove the battalion's replacements hard with three days of intense training. Very effective."

"In his letters Tom wrote a lot about Kurt being a real driver. The lieutenants didn't know whether to hate him or love him."

"Yes, real hard, insistent, but also at the end of the day encouraging. Kurt knew how far to go."

She nodded her head for me to continue.

"Less than a week after coming out of the line, we went in at night and relieved another regiment north of the Marne River. The entire corps was advancing towards the Vesle River. We drove forward for five days incurring heavy casualties from well-placed machine gun fire and murderous artillery barrages. Attacking the Germans was to march into hell. Constant casualties. We got a brief respite when we were pulled back into an area just behind the line for a couple of days. Too brief."

Yvonne came up to the table and put down a plate of hors d'oeuvres and a big slice Jura paté. I dug in to Kate's delight. "Are we at the right place?" she asked.

"Yes," and I put another piece in my mouth, "and with the right person." She beamed.

Then she said, "Continue."

I swallowed, took a sip of wine, and said, "At the end of the first week of August, we moved up to the Vesle River. Our first assault across the river was turned back by heavy artillery fire and lots of machine gun fire."

"Two days later the regiment was to assault the river again. One battalion was to try to force a crossing on a narrow bridge at one end of the line, but our artillery preparation was weak and our supporting fire not good. The regimental commander called the attack off."

"What happened?"

"Kurt said it best. He was with me at the regimental observation post as we watched the attack go in and then falter. Afterwards we walked outside together. He simply said, 'Failure to plan. Artillery was not concentrated. There should have been lots of supporting rifle fire on either side of the bridge to suppress the German machine guns. The assault on the bridge should have been supported by river crossings downstream and upstream to divide the enemy. Looks like some officers were polishing their Sam Browne belts rather than sweating the plans. You plan right up to when the soldiers jump off.'"

"Kurt always seems to understand, doesn't he?" Kate said.

"Yes, he does."

"What happened next?"

"We went into reserve, received and trained replacements. We trained for almost seven weeks. We had learned a lot. Kurt drove the lessons home during training."

"When did you go back into the line?"

"We went into the line at the end of September for the really big allied offensive, what later came to be called the Meuse-Argonne Offensive. We didn't know it, but this was the one that ended the war."

"Any more rivers?"

"No rivers. Forests were the obstacles this time. At the end of the first week of October the regiment was ordered to assault the Bois de Cunel. On the morning of the attack, a heavy fog hung over the engagement area. Our artillery put in smoke and our infantry advanced on the Bois. Just before reaching the wood they were discovered and the Germans put up heavy machine gun fire. The First Battalion commander went down. Kurt took over and kept the companies moving into the wood and then cleared the wood and took up a line on the north side, the regiment's objective. That's when the regimental commander went to the battalion command post that night and pinned major's leaves on Kurt's collar."

"Were you there?"

"Yes, I went with the regimental commander everywhere in those days. He really relied on Kurt. It was really tough driving into the Germans day after day while incurring these mind-numbing casualties. Keeping a level head was not easy. Kurt was steady."

"Did the regiment get any rest?"

"Yes, for a couple of days. Then the regiment was ordered to advance. Kurt gave the briefing. Told the officers to wait for the German artillery to lift before trying to get the men to advance. He said that officers and sergeants had to set the example, to stand above the trenches and wave the men forward. He said it was a time for example, not for missionary work. Most of the men would advance. He was dismissive of exhortation, what he called missionary work."

"Did it work out that way?"

"Yes, almost all the men not wounded would follow their leaders forward. The memory of the gallantry of our Civil War burned brightly in our men's memories."

"How did the advance go?"

"We got into the next wood, the Bois de Pultiere. Same story: heavy resistance, lots of German artillery—you started to wonder where all the shells came from. We dug in at the forward edge of the Bois de Pultiere. The next day the Germans poured in a murderous artillery barrage. Kurt was wounded and evacuated. The regiment was just used up."

"Did the regiment go on?"

"No, we held our position. A couple of days later the regiment was withdrawn and marched to a rear area. A muster of the regiment was held on a grassy field near a temporary bivouac."

"I keep asking about Kurt. But what was your role?"

"I was now the adjutant. So I was responsible for forming up what was left of the regiment. There were four hundred men spread across fourteen rifle companies. Full strength was three thousand men. One company was under the command of a corporal, another under a sergeant, ten were commanded by second lieutenants, and two by first lieutenants. There were no majors, no captains."

I took a sip of wine and looked bleakly at Kate.

"I called the regiment to attention, turned and saluted the regimental commander, and stepped aside. The regimental commander stepped forward in front of the regimental color and regimental flag, battle streamers hanging limply down from the tops of the staffs."

"He said, 'At ease.' The men came to parade rest."

I paused and looked at Kate, "Then the regimental commander just stood there silently. Presently he looked over at me and made a small wave. I called the men to attention. The commander saluted the men, then turned and walked back to the rear of the ceremony. I dismissed the men. Very solemn, very sad, but quite moving."

Kate asked, "Was that the end of the war for the regiment?"

"Yes, a couple days later we were trucked back to a replacement camp. Then the war ended. Everyone was insanely happy, but also bitterly sad."

"Did you see Kurt?"

"No, a couple days after the end of the war, a circular came from army headquarters asking for German speaking officers to be assigned to Third Army at Koblenz. I cut the orders and sent them off. The orders caught up with Kurt at a General Hospital where he was recuperating. Later I heard he was in charge of a big supply and service organization in Koblenz, a real mover and doer."

Kate nodded at this but her thoughts were back with the fighting. "I just didn't know," she said.

"No one does until you go into it. And when you're in it, you half believe it can't be real."

"The manuscript I have ends in the hospital just after the war; it doesn't go on to Germany. It ends with his receiving the orders for the transfer."

"Yes, going to Germany would be the next chapter."

Yvonne brought lunch, two big bowls of steaming stew. As we ate, I asked, "What do you think of the manuscript?"

"I've made a few small changes, typical editing. But the straight ahead, driving style is intact. It's Kurt, not Kate."

"Good."

"You will meet me at the Flore at six tomorrow evening? I am meeting with my mentors."

"Mentors? On writing or on life?"

"Writing," said Kate, and then she made a smile, "and some on life, too."

"I look forward to it."

"Do you have a place picked out?"

"Yes, I nice little place under the trees down by the river. Cool on a summer's night."

“Good.” She raised her wine glass in salute and took a sip.

13. Three Fates

The sun was shining on the Saturday afternoon crowd hurrying along boulevard Saint-Germain, men's hats bobbing in a sea of people, women's broad-brimmed hats gliding through a tide of afternoon strollers, like schooners toward a harbor.

I turned into the Café de Flore and immediately saw the black-clad Janet Flanner, Solita Solano, and Djuna Barnes sitting like the Three Fates behind a table along the wall. White ruffled shirtwaists broke the sharply tailored black broadcloth suits, sort of like whipped cream floating on black coffee. White satin scarves complemented white gloves. A waiter was clearing away coffee cups.

Kate was sitting across the table on a wicker chair. I heard her say "thank you" to the three women as she was putting a manuscript away in her handbag. Kate wore a light gray skirt and a broad-collared white blouse with a sky blue sweater—somewhat like a schoolgirl sitting across from the mistresses at some private-school inquiry, if not inquisition.

Kate saw me and waved me over to an empty chair next to her. As I sat down, Djuna said, "Kate was just going over her ideas for a fashion article on the summer openings at the couturiers."

Janet added, "*McCall's* picked up her last piece on Coco Chanel. Now we're looking at *The New Yorker*."

"With some help from you?" and I raised my eyebrows to frame the question.

"Not much. You know Djuna has done more to set the tone for a so-called *New Yorker* article than I have. Djuna was there first. I'm still new."

Solita broke in from down the table, "Kate is moving to put light criticism into the fashion pieces. That's why the Chanel piece is so important. There's a revolution in style and design accompanying the change in taste." Solita Solano, a former drama critic on a New York daily, had a sharp eye for changes in culture.

In my opinion, she was the leading freelance critic on the Left Bank.

A waiter brought up three big martini glasses brimming with ice-cold gin, images of large olives magnifying through the sides of the long-stemmed glasses. He set them down in front of the three black-suited ladies. I could see that business was over, the evening about to begin.

"Join us, Bill?" asked Djuna.

"No thank you, we're having wine for dinner and I want to savor its flavor when I get there."

Janet snorted, "Candlelight, too? Sounds like seduction," and she looked directly at Kate, "I told you he was up to no good."

"Seduction?" Djuna asked rhetorically. "Where there's attraction isn't that the desired outcome?"

"Yes, isn't that why we're all in Paris," said Solita, and added impishly, "Even for some of the men."

"Are you saying Bill is normal?" asked Djuna.

"Never," bantered Solita, "but possibly red blooded."

"Whoa, ladies, you're racing ahead of yourselves. Kate and I are just following up on some of our memories from the war, which we discovered last Tuesday on our visit to Chateau Thierry. We had more in common than we had thought."

"And a nice *tête-à-tête* over lunch at *La Quatrième République* yesterday," added Janet.

"If Bill could drink that coffee, maybe he deserves the prize," added Djuna.

"Were you ever a prize, Kate?" asked Solita with feigned innocence.

"Once, yes, I believe," answered Kate.

"Once?" queried Djuna skeptically. Once was a concept almost unknown to Djuna in any romantic pursuit. "When we were in the Village, Kate, you didn't leave all those beau holding their trousers up, did you?"

Kate batted eyelashes and said demurely, "Mostly."

I listened without seeming to be overly interested. But the admission was electrifying. Janet's look drilled right into me; she saw my interest. She had an eye for the male calculation behind an adventure. She had come to her conclusion about me yesterday afternoon and was not going to let go. Mostly, I was hoping she was right.

"We were reviewing a manuscript," I replied.

Three sets of eyebrows were raised in disbelief. Three martini glasses went up to open lips in judgment.

Kate laughed, "Yes, I am working on the manuscript."

"Yes, the great American novel about the war," Djuna dryly observed. She looked at Solita and Janet and said, "Kate told me about the trip to Berlin to work with Bill's friend, the author. Berlin hasn't changed. When Kate and I were there in 1921—*McCall's* sent me—things were so cheap that you felt almost ashamed to be there. McAlmon was in his heaven."

We all laughed. Djuna wrote that way, too.

Djuna continued, "Your German friend…"

"He's American."

"Milwaukee's a German province somewhere west of civilization," Djuna replied. "Anyway, he's quite a handful. Let me see, talking with Kate the word 'appetites' came up."

"Margaret said Hemingway was a handful. More than that?" asked Solita.

"Kurt Eckhart is a force of nature," said Kate.

"A force of nature? Hmm," murmured Djuna. "Well, I like my tea strong."

"He's certainly that," said Kate.

Djuna tilted her head, and thought some more, "Well, a little sweetness in the brew is okay, too."

"Sweetness? Kurt?" said Kate in a perplexed sort of way. Then she thought better of it, "Yes, I think there was a bit of sweetness—once. I think that is one of the themes in his novel."

"Lost sweetness?" snorted Djuna. "Well, sometimes I find devils more interesting," she added as if running down a list of what she found attractive in a man. Maybe she was casting about for something new; I had heard things were a little thin between her and Thelma. I watched as Djuna took a sip from her martini, her mind contemplating Kurt Eckhart.

"Fodder for that marvelous writing machine of yours?" I asked.

"Well, yes, Bill," replied Djuna. "Of course, when sex is simply recreational, that leaves one free for more important matters, such as art." Djuna liked to say things like that. She took another sip from her martini to nail down the conclusion.

"In Paris, I think sex is always a bridge to somewhere new," added Janet.

"Somewhere new? Yes, why ever come to the Left Bank if not for the journey," said Solita, "to somewhere new."

Djuna looked at Solita with approving eyes and raised her glass in agreement, "To somewhere new." The other two raised their glasses. All took a sip.

"Well, Kate and I are off to dinner, if not on our journey," I said lightly.

"Sounds serious," shot out Janet.

Kate smiled demurely at her and then said reflectively, "Chateau Thierry was."

I stood up and held Kate's chair as she arose. By way of goodbye I said, "When you get up to Montparnasse, give my regards to the chaps."

"And may the sun rise on you two," said Djuna. She drained the martini and waved to the waiter for another round. Montparnasse was going to have its hands full tonight.

14. Dinner by the River Seine

Kate and I walked down rue Bonaparte towards the river in the late afternoon sunshine. We turned and walked along the *quai* past the park in front of the ancient stone church of Saint-Julien-le-Pauvre. We came up to a broad *terrasse* bordered by elm trees and spotted with some tables; a little half-basement restaurant was down some steps. We walked in and I spoke to a waiter I knew. He guided us over to a table at the side of the *terrasse* and held the chair as Kate sat down. She smiled a polite thanks to the waiter; he grinned and made an approving glance at me. I felt great.

"Well, Bill, a charming place. Come here often?" She arched an eyebrow.

"Not so much anymore. I've been busy. Also thoughtful."

"Thoughtful?"

"Yes, Kurt's book has opened up a flood of memories."

"Yes, it has," said Kate with a touch of sadness.

The waiter came up with a bottle of red wine and I simply nodded my head in approval. He poured two full glasses of wine. I whispered a dinner order to him.

I took a sip and collected my thoughts, "Yes, I can see looking back that you, Kurt, and I were all at Chateau Thierry that day. Together in a sense."

"Yes, I suppose so," said Kate. She moved to change the subject, "What did you do after the war?"

"Another circular came down from army headquarters transferring French-speaking officers to Paris to support the Peace Conference."

"So you went to Paris."

"Yes. Straight to the Hotel Crillon," and I nodded my head down the river towards Place Concorde where the magnificent Hotel Crillon sat like a Greek temple overlooking the great public square of Paris. The grandest hotel in Paris was of course where the Americans were quartered for the Peace Conference.

"Promoted to major so I could dine with my French and British peers. Little different from Kurt's promotion."

"Speaking of dinner," she said and nodded at the approaching waiter. He came up and placed steaming seafood dinners before us. He presented a bottle of white wine; I gave another perfunctory nod—he knew I didn't like my dinner conversations interrupted—and he poured.

Kate dug into the seafood, "Uhm, good. You have an eye for a fine dinner." She took a sip of wine and asked, "What did you do at the conference?"

"Worked with our British and French colleagues on drawing new borders and maps as the leaders debated and adopted provisions of the Treaty."

"Where?"

"That's what was surprising. Almost all over the world. Central Europe, the Balkans, the Middle East, South Asia, the Far East, the Pacific—there are all kinds of little islands out there."

"So they remade the world?"

"They tried."

"You seem skeptical."

"The new borders seem a recipe for friction, if not wars, for decades to come."

"Wasn't the League of Nations the big problem, at least for the United States?"

"Yes, that's true for the United States. Killed Wilson. But the big problem for everyone else was that the question of Germany was not settled. The biggest country in Central Europe was not put back on a positive road to the future."

"Yes, Djuna and I were there in 1921. Germany was left a mess."

"Yes."

"Didn't the people at the Peace Conference realize that?"

"One did. That was John Maynard Keynes, the British financial diplomat. He understood."

"He wrote a best-selling book about it, didn't he?"

"Yes, *The Economic Consequences of the Peace*. I heard a lot of the arguments from British colleagues during the conference."

The waiter came and cleared away the dinner plates. He returned and asked, "Monsieur?"

I looked at Kate and asked, "How about a cognac?"

"Why yes," and her eyes twinkled with merriment.

The waiter returned with two large snifters, the golden liquid bright in the candlelight of the tabletop.

Kate lifted her glass up, looked across the top of the rim, her eyes bristling with inquisitiveness and asked, "And your fiancée? Did you meet her at the Peace Conference?"

I laughed. "You checked up on me?"

"My friends say they know all about you." Her eyes sparkled and she made a knowing smile.

"Yes, Jenny," and I took a breath as I remembered my biggest romantic disappointment—so far. There had been the disappointment in New York before the war and then the disappointment in Paris after the war. My life had been well balanced with regard to disappointments. I shrugged.

"My friends don't know why your romance broke up? You seem to have been quiet about that."

"She was the daughter of a French cabinet minister. Distinguished political family. In 1919, Americans were the toast of Europe. We were the new thing. We were invited to all the best parties, entertained at the most exclusive salons."

"What happened?"

"Well, as the Peace Conference wound down, I told her I would stay on in Paris and start a literary agency. I was in that business before the war in New York. So, now rather than the dashing major, I was just a middle class guy having to make a living."

"Not so distinguished," Kate tossed out.

"*Exactamente,*" and I laughed.

"Then?"

"Well, after the middle of 1919, the Americans went home. Something of a bitter taste was left behind."

"And?"

"I think Jenny was politely nudged towards someone in the French political world," I said softly trying to keep any trace of bitterness out of my voice.

"Yes, family considerations count large at the top of French society," said Kate.

"Yes they do," I said with a touch of finality.

"But your literary agency has prospered?" Kate said sweetly.

"Yes, it has," I said. "I was from New York. Knew New York. Then Paris took off. I was at the right place," and I looked at Kate, "and so were you."

"Yes, Paris is working out for me."

Now it was my turn to change the subject. "And so after your fiancé died in the war, you went down to New York. What did you do?"

"Oh, I got a job in an advertising agency and then started in as a volunteer with the Provincetown Players. That's where I wound up living down the hall from Djuna. And I struck up a friendship with Mina Loy. Her poetry really spoke to me," and she hesitated, "after my doomed love affair."

She took a sip of her cognac and looked into the flame of the flickering candle in the center of the table, "At Vassar, we were all girls, captivated by Edna Saint-Vincent Millay, but later," and she paused again and picked her words, "after becoming a woman, then Mina's poetry gives you a whole new dimension, the dimension you need. At some point you have to see life," and she paused, "see it real."

"You mean romance?"

"No, love. When you're young, romance hides love under a bedspread of rose petals. Loy has a more adult view."

"Rather graphic."

"Real I would say. Women live with more reality than men think."

"Yes, Djuna keeps pointing that out."

Kate laughed, "Yes she does. The bed gets wet."

I nodded not quite knowing where to go with that comment. I continued, "So you go from Millay to Loy?"

"Yes, I think that's the journey. At least for me."

The journey? The word struck a chord with me. I would like to make the journey—with her. But then I'd known that for months. I took a sip of cognac and shifted the conversation, "Speaking of

Djuna. Living down the hall from her, that sounds pretty Bohemian." I was trolling for something.

"A little bit," said Kate. Her eyes twinkled with remembered delight and a smile that said she wasn't going to say much more.

"From there?"

"I started freelancing. Then Djuna got some big commissions to come to Europe and she asked if I wanted to come along. Said there was plenty of work to go around and that I could write secondary pieces for the other magazines. She was pretty well locked up with *McCall's*."

"Yes, I remember."

"So we came to Paris and then traveled around Europe, interviewing and writing. We circled back to Paris. She of course had met Thelma Wood by then."

"You had your friends?"

"Yes, I always had friends. Mina, then Janet, the others. You need contacts to survive as a writer. And some friends for warmth."

I smiled.

"Then I found a good literary agent in Paris," and she looked at me, eyes laughing.

"Yes, I remember. For warmth?" and I laughed.

"You never know," she said and batted an eyelash with mock coyness.

I was intrigued—and more than a little warmed up. I decided to dig further, "I have known Edna Saint-Vincent Millay off and on here in Paris. Did you know her at Vassar?"

"Well, yes. We all did. She was a couple of years ahead of me," and Kate looked at me evenly, "but I wasn't in her circle."

"Circle?"

"You know," and she again leveled her stare at me, "some of the girls were intensely interested in each other." Kate paused and took a sip of cognac, looked off into the distance and then returned, "On the other hand, my friends and I were interested in meeting boys, going down to New York and having a good time, hoping to find a proper young man to love that would meet our parents' expectations—I mean that was why they sent you to Vassar. Maybe you could have both, we thought. The dream."

"Of course. The dream, its realization and its troubles, drives the short story market."

Kate nodded in agreement and then said, "Edna? We all loved her poetry. She had the gift."

"Yes, I have always loved those lines from *Recuerdo*," and I searched my memory, remembering the lines, and started to recite:

We were very tired, we were very merry –
We had gone back and forth all night upon the ferry.

Kate laughed and said, "Those nights in New York."

"Yes," I laughed. "And the mornings." And I started reciting again:

And the sky went wan, and the wind came cold,
And the sun rose dripping, a bucketful of gold.

Then I said, with some excitement in my voice, "I think of those lines in the mornings when I look out my bedroom window as the sun turns the buildings across the river into a golden façade, the water into a shimmering pool, a golden rainbow of color."

Kate's eyes glistened with delight, "Yes, I remember. Those nights, then the mornings, we were all so grown up in New York. Sophisticated." She sighed, "We were so young." She laughed at the memory.

She sat quiet for a moment. Then she looked off across the river and remembered something. She said, "Yes..." and the word hung in the air. Then she recited, "*Now the golden-sandaled Dawn.*"

"Sappho, I believe."

Surprised by my attribution, she looked at me and said, "Yes, from *A Hymn to Aphrodite*." Aphrodite was the Greek goddess of love.

"An enchantress, I recall."

Kate's eyes blazed and she reached across the table and took my hands in both of hers, "Let's see it together. Again. This morning. The golden-sandaled Dawn."

I squeezed her hands in warm agreement. Her eyes were lustrous, her smile inviting.

"Yes, let's."

I stood up and came around the table and held her chair as she stood up. I left some franc notes on the table and we left. We walked across the street to the wall along the *quai* above the river and then walked along the sidewalk towards the bridge that crossed over to Île Saint-Louis. As we walked, we came to a point just opposite from where my flat was. I turned to her and took her in my arms, held her close, and deeply kissed her, the warmth of her invitation coursing through my body, her slenderness inviting. Then I turned her around and stood behind her and pointed with my arm towards the far shore, "There's where my flat is. On the second floor. Overlooking Quai d'Orléans. Home of the beautiful sunrises."

"I so want to go, to see the beautiful sunrise." She turned around and put her arms around my neck and looked up into my face, "With you." She kissed me, a flame-like intensity coming over me.

15. Ce Soir, Madame?

I opened the door and extended my arm to usher Kate into my drawing room. She walked into the middle of the room, looked through the tall windows out across the river, and then spun around and said, “What a magnificent view!”

“Can I get you a drink?”

“Some wine maybe.”

I went over to the sideboard and poured two glasses of wine and walked over to Kate, who was now standing by the window.

“Yes, it’s beautiful,” she murmured as I came up. She took the glass of wine and took a sip. She looked out the window again and then turned around and faced me.

“You said you were wounded?”

“Yes, in the arm.”

“Let me see,” and she set her glass down. She reached over and took my glass and set it down beside hers. She stood in front of me and started to unbutton my shirt while pulling the tails out of my pants.

“Which arm?”

“The left.”

She pulled the shirt and shirtsleeve down exposing my left arm. There was a scar, somewhat jagged running across the bicep between the elbow and the shoulder. She ran her finger along it.

“I see. That would have put you out of action for a while.”

“Yes.”

“What happened?”

“That day, on the hill at Chateau Thierry, just as we turned the Germans back at the river, a sharpshooter on the other side of the river must have gotten a bead on me. I was standing up in the trench, trying to see what the next move should be.”

“Did it hurt?”

“The bullet spun me around. I was surprised and shocked. Then I crumpled into the trench. Some of my men got me up and put a field dressing on the wound. I said I could get back to the aid station on my own. One of them helped me back to the aid station."

"What was that like?"

"Dreadful. A charnel house. There were a lot of wounded laid out on litters. The orderlies arrange them in order of the severity of the wounds. They line up those thought to benefit the most from surgery near the entrance to the operating theater. Triage. Those away from the entrance most likely will die before being seen by the surgeon."

"What did they do for you?"

"Oh, an orderly looked at the wound, applied antiseptic, and bandaged it up. Said a surgeon could look at it tomorrow."

"What did you do?"

"I made myself useful. I went around giving the wounded water where possible. You can't do that for stomach wounds. You hold their hands as life ebbs away."

"Sad."

"Very. They mostly call for their mothers. Sometimes a wife. They know it's the end of the line. You just can't imagine that war is worth the human suffering. You feel deep down that if people saw the suffering firsthand they would somehow stop wars from happening."

"But the wars keep coming."

"Yes they do."

"So what we're doing with this book—bearing witness—does it work?"

"I don't know. At the end of the day, books build understanding and insight. That has to have some effect."

"But only a limited effect. There's always a large group for war."

"Yes, sometimes I wish I could write the book that would describe the whole experience in its singular awfulness. Change the world, or at least the outlook of the majority."

"The majority? Who are they?"

"A shifting group of people who enable the war makers."

"How do we reach them?"

"I think somehow their empathy must be engaged so that they see themselves as part of the future devastation of war. Then they might ask 'Why?' in advance."

"That sounds like a hard emotion to activate."

"Yes. Nevertheless, I keep wondering if some writer might walk in the door with such a manuscript."

"Is that Kurt and his book?"

"No, he's doing something different. I think what we are reading now is Kurt showing us the horrible cost paid for the victory. He's putting a high price on the victory so later he can show the even higher price of the failure."

"So Kurt was disillusioned by the peace, not the war," Kate said, a look of understanding coming over her face.

"Yes, that's it."

"Nevertheless, it is a book that confronts the reader with some hard questions."

"Yes it is. That's its strength."

Kate looked thoughtful, "I have been reading the manuscript trying to understand where he's going with his story. What you said explains a lot."

"Yes, well neither of us has really seen the second half of the book, the German part. He told me he wants to paint a picture of the failure as it looked from Berlin. He wants people in the Allied countries to understand just how bad the failure was."

Kate nodded her head and then pulled the shirt back up onto my shoulder. She handed my wine glass back to me and took up her own. I took a sip and said, "I'm sorry if I am breaking the romantic spell."

She took a sip of wine and looked directly into my eyes, "Not at all. I want love with a man of his times," and she reached over and touched my arm.

She quickly brightened, "Do you have a bathroom? Something I could wear? *Ce soir?*"

"Let me get you a dressing gown. Down the hall."

We walked down the hall; I opened a closet and rummaged around and took out a silk gown on a hanger and held it out to her, "This ought to do."

"It's lovely," and she twisted her head around and looked down the hall, "There?"

"Yes, I'll wait in the bedroom." *Ce soir, madame?* The words danced in my imagination.

I watched her walk down the hall, the swaying hips, a feeling of physical expectation coming over me, a warmth of anticipation that soon she would be in my arms. Maybe she had a reason to gently remind me of my past disappointments. Maybe she had a different view of our future.

In the bedroom, I went over and opened the windows letting the warm velvety breeze into the room, the light swirl of humid air caressing my skin. In the closet I found pajama bottoms and put them on. I went over to the bed and tossed back the covers and fluffed the pillows. I climbed in and pulled the sheet up halfway. I lay back and stared up at the darkened ceiling. The water ran in the bathroom; I heard the fumbling sound of clothes being hanged. I waited. A vague image of Kate's undressed beauty glided around in my imagination.

A door opened. She came in and slid into the bed beside me. "There. Fresh."

She smelled like a dream. I reached over and caressed her along her flank, my fingers tapping out a tattoo here and there. I opened her dressing gown, light and silky, and moved my palm along the top of her hip, feeling the smoothness of that long delicious curve. "You're like some kind of dream. Promise you won't go away."

"No, I have come to love."

"Good. I have waited for love. Too long, I think."

"It comes when it does. Like the fog. On little cat feet."

I laughed, "Chicago speaks."

"A Swedish daughter of the Midwest."

I pulled the gown back off her shoulder and pulled her close, kissing her deeply, caressing her breast, feeling her arms go around me, the fingers dig into my back, her back arch to push herself against me. My fingers explored her body, pushed a leg away, the warmth pleasing to my touch.

She burrowed into my neck, kissed my ear lobe, pushed her tongue into my ear, drew fingernails across my back with one hand, grabbed my flank with the other and squeezed.

I gently rolled her onto her back, kissed an upturned breast, and squeezed her inner thigh with my hand, then ran a finger nail along her inner thigh, listening to her softly respond—a drawn out *uhmm* sound ending in a gasp. Her fingers grabbed into my back. I started with my lips down her body and then pushed her leg far out.

Her fingers were in my hair, her back arched and fell, her body in a slow gallop, and we went along the trail together in growing waves of rapture. She let a long sound out, flinched, then trembled and her whole body eased. Her fingers played with the curls in my hair.

She murmured, "I love the imagery of Sappho, the warm summer air across the velvety darkness, the lover between love's thighs." She stayed quiet a moment. "But it takes a man's kiss to put the fire to the metaphor."

"My sentiments exactly." She laughed.

"You're a dream," she said.

I caressed her cheek with my hand and kissed her deeply, listening to a warm sound of contentment come up from deep inside her.

She pushed against me, but I pushed back and rolled her over onto her back. I moved over on top of her and leaned down and kissed her on the lips, "My lady." Her hands squeezed the flesh of my back. She turned her head for a moment as I slowly pushed forward, the warmth enveloping, the sexual pleasure rising up from my loins to meet the love in my heart. We came into our rhythm, then I felt her legs around me, her legs clasped behind my back and we shivered and shuddered in some haphazard fashion, one then the other, she seemed to be both before me and after me.

Then she was off by herself for a while. I simply let my head hang limp against her ear, smelling the warmth of her hair. I rolled over and lay beside her, marveling at my enchantment with her, the physical beauty so nicely giving expression to the many-splendored personality inside. My mind lingered with the hope and deep desire to go the distance with her, to travel down time to the end of our days together. God keep me from disappointment.

I woke in the morning with fingers exploring me this way and that, a soft wall of brown hair lay across my chest, moist lips on my neck. Fingers played, hair swished across my skin. I just lay there with a building sense of rapture. I wondered just which god had put his daughter into my bed this morning.

She kissed me and then nuzzled against my neck and whispered in my ear, "You are my delight. Oh… you're fun." She reached around me and hugged me, pushing her breasts into my chest, "I think you really like me."

"Yes, I do."

She ran her fingers around, dug a nail in and said, "See, you and Djuna agree. Women make the best lovers."

I stared at the ceiling and gave a laugh.

"I hadn't ever quite thought of it that way," I replied.

"Most likely you had never thought of it at all."

"Caught. You're quite right." I reached over and grabbed her under her armpits with my hands and lifted her face up towards mine. She swung her leg over me and sat astride my stomach, her breasts hanging down above my face and stared down at me with dark laughing eyes. She moved her pelvic region over my stomach, light moisture rubbing across my skin. She craned her neck down and kissed me, rocking her pelvis across my stomach, and then she slid down and she was upon me.

She began a slow rocking motion, her back arched. She continued slowly, off in her own world. Her breath started to come in gasps and she increased her rhythm. She grabbed my pectoral muscles in her hands and squeezed as she moved towards her climax, her head dropped and her eyes burned fiercely into mine. She bumped hard against me and then broke into her release as she rocked back above me. Then she fell forward and collapsed on top of me as I felt my own ecstasy release from myself. I was happy as hell, and lay there quietly, my fingers running up and down Kate's back. This was a separate room in the house of human existence.

I lay there enjoying my early morning laziness, my face buried in her brown hair, and said, "I wonder what they're doing in America today?" She sort of bit my neck.

Then she pushed herself up and looked down in my face, her hair falling down from her head so that her face looked like she was peering down at me from the end of a tunnel. In a mischievous tone, she said, "That's not a question you're supposed to ask in Paris, little boy."

I smiled.

"A penny for your thoughts?"

"Don't edit out the bodily fluids."

She laughed and I felt the moist rubbing of dewy hair back and forth against my lower belly. "We'll continue another time—the editing that is." And she pressed down on me, pushing me into the mattress.

I laughed.

Eventually, we got up and went out into the drawing room, the French windows open to the river, a light breeze rustling the curtains. Kate brought a pot of coffee over to the small breakfast table in front of the windows and poured cups of coffee for both her and me. She went back to the kitchen and brought back a baguette and a dish of butter and set these on the table. Then she sat down across from me, leaned across the table and blew me a kiss, a big smile of happiness on her face. She looked out over the wrought iron balustrade of the balcony to the river slowly flowing by and said, "Simply beautiful. I could stare at it forever."

"You could come live here," I said.

She looked at me and tilted her head and gazed at me with a light touch of skepticism, "*Peut-être*." Perhaps.

I ran my fingers through my hair and looked at her, "I love you. I want to live with you."

She looked at me and smiled lightly. She seemed to be where she wanted to be. "Well, now, my future?" She took a sip of coffee and then let an ironic smile spread across her face as she contemplated what I hoped was now a new future—with me.

I asked a question with my eyebrows and waited. She twisted her head this way, then that way. She was cute as hell doing this.

"Let me see. Mina's going to New York in the fall to visit her daughter. When she gets back, I could sublease my apartment to her."

"Yes, that would be very sensible."

"Sensible? To whom? A girl has to think about herself."

"That's what I want you to do."

"I know you do. That's one of the things I love about you."

"Well, then?"

"You know 'lover' is a spring-summer fashion, winter begs for the heavy tweeds of permanence. Mistress is an arrangement, but it lacks permanence, the pledge of commitment."

"Yes, so in the fall, then. A better arrangement, something permanent—a commitment, words chanted under candlelight in a stone chamber, *peut-etre?*" Perhaps.

"Permanent," and she bore in on me with a stare direct in its intensity.

"Something with a ring, *peut-etre*?" I said.

"Something with a diamond, *peut-etre*?"

I nodded my head in agreement.

"That would make me very happy."

Then I laughed and looked at her, "The red rose hiding among the carnations."

She laughed. "We'll see."

16. Ladies Almanack

I walked up rue de Sèvres past the Bon Marché where well-dressed ladies were coming out after an afternoon of shopping at the fashionable department store. A block past the Vaneau Metro entrance I turned left onto rue Saint-Romain and walked down to the entrance of the new six-story apartment building. Yes, it was nice. I had only seen it in the dark. I rode the *ascenseur* up to Djuna Barnes' apartment on the fifth floor and knocked on the door.

"Come in."

I entered and saw Djuna, Mina, and Kate gathered around the oak dining table with colored pencils and open copies of Djuna's newest creation, the little chap booklet *Ladies Almanack*. Mina's daughter Fabi didn't look up; she continued drawing with single-minded purpose, filling in the spaces on one of the drawings in the book. Then she would set a colored pencil down and take up another, industrious and methodical in the way of ten-year-olds.

A little more than a thousand copies had been printed by Bob McAlmon's press and today the women were coloring the illustrations in fifty of these copies. These would become a special deluxe edition. I really wanted to see the book, get a chance to take it all in with one grand sweep. Djuna was an exceptionally original talent and the buzz on the Left Bank for weeks had been about this book, a lampoon of the mostly lesbian ladies of the Left Bank. The gossips chattered away about which woman on the Left Bank was represented by which one of the gaudily named characters in the book. Glasses clinked in delight as correspondences between a fictional "lady" and her real life counterpart were made. Well-thumbed page proofs had been circulating around Paris for weeks; I had seen a couple.

"Hi," said Djuna. "Welcome to my lair." It was a beautifully appointed apartment, the afternoon sun streaming through the windows and illuminating the brightly colored furnishings.

“Some one told me that I might be able to buy a couple of books here.”

“Well, right you are.”

“The price better be right, mister,” chimed in Kate.

“Can the price live up to the lofty reputation? May I glance through a copy?”

“If you’re looking for mention of your ladyship, well, there are no betrothed in this testament’s sacred scroll, marriage not being one of our sacraments,” Djuna said.

Kate smiled.

Djuna looked at Kate, “It is written in the book: ‘He be one Man who does not brag.’ Do you think we might be in the presence of another?”

“Not today,” Kate gaily replied.

Djuna turned to me, “There. You must pay for your copies of the book.”

“My pleasure. I shall brag often of the purchase.”

Djuna smiled. She handed me a copy from a stack. I went over and sat down on the large comfortably stuffed sofa. I thumbed through the nicely printed book, a little less than a hundred pages, and admired the many pen-and-ink drawings illustrating the book. There was an introduction and then twelve chapters for the twelve months of the almanac. The book was written in an embroidered old English style as if it were another *Canterbury Tales*, the bawdy classic from the beginning age of English literature.

Figure 7 Cover art by Djuna Barnes for *Ladies Almanack*.

The first sentence was extraordinarily memorable and had the stamp of a classic: "Now this be a Tale of as fine a Wench as ever wet Bed, she who was called Evangeline Musset…" Everyone knew the reference was to Natalie Barney and that the book was a satire of the Left Bank lesbian society loosely centered on Barney's salon. The opening paragraph goes on to describe the sacred mission "for the Pursuance, the Relief and the Distraction, of such Girls as in their Hinder Parts, and their Fore Parts, and in whatever Parts did suffer them most, lament Cruelly, be it itch of Palm, or Quarters most horribly burning, which they do oft occur in the Spring of the Year…" Nothing demure about this catalogue of sexual fevers.

If there was any doubt that lesbianism was being celebrated, the introduction went on to describe Dame Musset as "so much in Demand, and so wide famed for her Genius at bringing up by Hand, and so noted and esteemed for her Slips of the Tongue that it finally brought her into the Hall of Fame, where she stood by a Statue of Venus…" A real good time girl, if you were a girl.

For other women not within reach of the famed Wench, there was "the consolation every Woman has at her Finger Tips…" Well, the message didn't lack for universality.

The other sexuality was represented by the character Patience Scalpel, the token heterosexual who "could not understand Women and their Ways…" even though "she heard them pinch and moan within the Gloom of many a stately Mansion…"

Shortly after Miss Scalpel speaks in her own voice, "In my time…Women came to enough trouble by lying abed with the Father of their Children." Then speaking of the lesbian tribe, she asks, "What then in this good Year of our Lord has paired them like to like, with never a Beard between them?" She concludes, "My Daughters shall go amarrying!"

Everyone knew that Patience Scalpel was the beautiful and talented Mina Loy, who just now was sitting across the room from me. She was Djuna Barnes' best friend in Paris and one of Natalie Barney's favorites, possibly because she was such an exemplar of the beauty and talent of the ideal woman.

"Well, what do you think Bill?" Djuna asked.

"It's going to be a classic. Janet asked a good question the other day—who is going to read James Joyce in fifty years?" I paused, "I don't know the answer to that. But fifty years from now people will be reading *Ladies Almanack*."

"Why?"

"It's short, to start with. And the originality of phrase after phrase is striking. A lot of people are going to talk about it. It's one of a kind. Anything similar published in the future will be dismissed as derivative. You own the real estate."

"And *Ryder*?" she asked, mentioning her soon-to-be-published Modernist novel.

"It's complicated. Readers are unsure what the message is. And it is angry."

Djuna nodded her head.

"*Ladies Almanack* is fun. It's amusing. That's why you get away with the subject matter." I looked over at Kate and said, "But it may be impossible to comprehend."

Kate laughed, "For you, yes."

I turned back to Djuna, "This is a book that will get passed around in the women's clubs of America—if it ever gets there."

We all laughed. Mina cut in, "Yes, Djuna's language is a delight. She's the best of the poets working in prose today."

"I agree."

"Fresh originality, a new joinery of words, that is just one of the gifts that women bring to Modernism," Mina said.

"I agree, Mina. It's a masterpiece."

Djuna shifted subjects, "When do I get to meet your new author, the next Hemingway?"

"Tomorrow at Natalie's. He's speaking."

"Kate's showed me some of his manuscript. Interesting. I think Kate is trying to shift the tone in the right direction. His woman protagonist seems too goddess-like, not real enough. Doll-like, not woman-like."

"That was his real wife Elsa."

Kate looked at me and then turned and explained to Djuna and Mina, "When Kurt described Elsa to us in Berlin, she had gray streaks in her hair, lines at her eyes from work and stress." An almost dreamy look came over Kate's face as she remembered

Kurt's words, "It was a beautiful portrait, pained and poignant. I want to go back to that." She shifted to a tone of disappointment, "In the current manuscript the heroine becomes a flaxen-haired young nymph."

"I agree. You should work with Kurt to get back to his original description. It's bittersweet and tender, like an autumn day," I said.

I looked at Djuna, nodding her head in agreement and collecting her thoughts. I continued, "That's the opportunity here. Kurt has a clear voice, an eye for the vivid if we keep him from wondering off onto a cloud of sentimentality."

Djuna looked at me and said, "No one stands more in favor of original voice than me. And sentimentality..." Everyone around the table laughed except Fabi, who kept diligently coloring her illustrations. "The narrative should move from a woman rooted in the difficulties of life during the war to—I gather she's doomed—to something goddess like—but only after leaving this earth."

"Yes, that should be the trajectory," I said.

"So, he's speaking at Natalie's tomorrow."

I nodded in agreement.

"Maybe Natalie will invite him to stay for dinner?" Mina added.

"Yes, that would be interesting," said Djuna. "Normally, Natalie's not real interested in men's explanations about war."

I picked up an extra copy of *Ladies Almanack*, one of the colored ones. "I'll give Kurt a copy. He'll like it." I stood up. "Kate, we better go. We're having dinner with Kurt at eight." I turned to the others, "See you tomorrow at Natalie's."

"Bye, Bill," they said in unison.

Fabi stopped coloring and looked up, "Bye, Bill." She looked at Kate with affectionate interest and said, "Aunt Kate."

Kate and I departed.

17. Hôtel Lutetia

I looked at the candlelight dancing on the surface of Kate's lustrous brown eyes—pools of crystalline sparkle framed by cheek bones glowing softly white from reflections off the white tablecloth. We sat in the darkened dining room of Hotel Lutetia. Her face floated above a triangular shaped martini glass. I stared at her a lot now. She simply charmed me, all the more so because she seemed to take such delight in me.

"Kurt said he'd be here about eight," I said.

Kate looked over at the entrance to the dining room. "Here he comes. And you won't guess who's with him."

I looked over and saw a dark-haired well-dressed woman.

"You're right. I don't know," I said—while laughing to myself that the elegantly sheathed rear-end did seem a little familiar.

"That's Madeleine."

How could I have forgotten?

"Right you are," I said as I stood up to greet our approaching guests.

I reached out and shook Kurt's hand and turned to Madeleine, "My, you're looking nice tonight." She was dressed in one of the new Chanel black dresses, a single strand of pearls beautifully set off against the black cloth. A nice mink stole was around her shoulders. The stole looked New York, everything else stylishly Parisian.

"Yeah, Madeleine's on her way to New York. Leaves on the boat train tomorrow morning. Promised to get her to the station on time," Kurt explained.

"Yes, you have to be at Natalie Barney's at noon."

"Don't worry, pal. Madeleine's train leaves at nine." He looked admiringly at her and said, "She wouldn't miss it for the world. I'm strictly second place."

Kurt looked at the approaching waiter and circled his hand above the martinis on the table, "Two of the same."

Kate leaned across the table towards Madeleine and took one of Madeleine's hands in hers with girlish enthusiasm, "New York? I got my start as a writer there. You have to tell me everything about it."

"Oh, I'm so excited. I'm going to be a translator. For six months."

"You seem to be doing well, Madeleine," said Kate, eyeing the mink stole, taking in the strand of pearls.

Madeleine beamed and reached up and stroked the fur with her hand, "Yes, I've made many friends in New York. They come visit me in Paris all the time. They like my *joie de vivre*, my sense of girlish enthusiasm, so they say."

"Ah, yes, the girlish enthusiasm," said Kate and smiled somewhat wickedly at me. "And now they want you in New York?"

"Yes, they say it's time for me to improve my street English, develop a closer feel for the vernacular."

"Yes, New York is the world capital of vernacular."

"For the translations, they want me to be naughty without being, how do you say, too Anglo-Saxon."

I laughed, "The Post Office wouldn't approve. For most American writers, they can only be Anglo-Saxon in Paris."

Madeleine's eyes twinkled, "They want me to translate the memoirs of the great courtesans. They want me to suggest the many aspects of love using English words in French-style phrases."

I nodded my head in appreciation. Shrewd. Someone in New York was onto something.

"That would be art," said Kate.

Madeleine beamed. "*Merci, madame.*"

Kate looked sidewise at me and then said to Madeleine, "I was being offered an editorship in New York earlier this year." Kate eyed me mischievously. "We might have been neighbors."

"Might require lots of enthusiasm," I ventured. Kurt chuckled.

Kate leaned back and glanced between Madeleine's pearls and her mink stole, "The right pearls, a nice stole, easy to get enthusiastic." Kate took a sip of her drink and set her martini glass down and with a real smoky look at me said in a husky undertone, "We're all shopping something, aren't we, Mister Literary Agent?"

"That's the highest art," said Madeleine with a completely charming insouciance that would carry her far at the Manhattan cocktail parties. She took a sip from her martini to seal the witticism. Yes, all the right moves.

Kurt roared, "Told you she was a natural."

We all laughed and Kate and I held up our glasses, "To Madeleine."

Kurt tossed a glance in my direction and then leered at Kate, "Imagine me thinking you went both ways?"

Kate leaned over and hugged my arm possessively and looked across at Kurt and purred, "I still keep," and she lovingly drew out the next word, "*in touch* with my girlfriends."

Kurt rolled his eyes and said, "You can put the woman in Paris but you can't take the Midwest out of the girl."

I laughed and said to Kate, "He's got your number."

Madeleine chimed in, "She's such fun," and smiled at Kate. Kate's buoyant acceptance was providing her just the right send-off to New York.

"Oh, before I forget. Here's a copy of Djuna Barnes' little book *The Ladies Almanack*. Dame Musset is a satirical portrayal of Natalie Barney, the hostess of tomorrow's reception. It's a romp about the ladies of the Left Bank." I pushed the book across the table at Kurt.

"Oh, I've heard all about them. Read articles about Gertrude Stein and Hemingway. Don't quite see what he saw in her. She looks like a well-dressed fire plug."

Kate laughed. "Well, after Hemingway's book, a word from Gertrude is gold in New York."

"Gotcha," Kurt said. "Your friend Djuna's going to be some sort of fire plug for us?"

"She has been known to put people on fire."

Kurt gave Kate a throwaway smile—he wasn't much interested in tomorrow morning while Madeleine was company tonight. He took a long sip from his martini and said, "Madeleine and I got to get up early tomorrow. We better call it a night." He stood up and then held Madeleine's chair.

"Can I meet you at the station tomorrow morning?" asked Kate as she rose. "After the boat-train leaves we could have a cup of coffee and go over the manuscript before going to Natalie's."

"Sure, fine," Kurt said.

Madeleine stepped around the table and held her hand out to me and smiled with self-assured elegance, lightly saying, "*Bon soir, Bill.*" She held out her hand to Kate and made a playful curtsey. She was perfect for New York. The American women would think she was a marquise.

18. Temple Steps

Over a hundred guests milled about in the warm summer sun in Natalie Barney's garden at 20 rue Jacob. It was another one of Natalie's famous "Fridays." Kurt and Kate had not yet arrived; they were rehearsing his talk over at the train station this morning.

I surveyed the scene. Over to one side of the courtyard was a small Greek temple, named the Temple of Friendship. There were four steps leading up to the stone portico from where Kurt would give his talk.

On the other side of the courtyard, in the shade of a large chestnut tree, was a long table spread with ham, chicken, cucumber, and roast beef sandwiches. Guests were two deep around the table jostling to get at least one long arm into the table. Sandwiches were surrounded by cakes and pastries with vanilla, chocolate and meringue as fillings. Champagne and cocktails were flowing to the guests in copious amounts.

Glancing over at the entrance, I saw Kurt come in dressed like a banker on holiday. Kate was at his side, sprightly in a light summer dress. She waved and they walked over and Kate said, "We made it. He's all rehearsed."

A dozen steps away, Natalie gave a look of recognition, broke off from her guests, and came over extending her hand towards Kurt, "You must be our speaker today. Natalie Barney."

"Yes, I am."

"So pleased you could come. There's been a buzz about this for days. And a horse race with Hemingway really grabs people's attention."

"I think I'm saying something different, if what Bill says is true."

Natalie nodded her head acknowledging Kurt's point.

"I am telling a story of a brave war and a failed peace."

"A brave war?" said Natalie rather skeptically.

"Yes, the sacrifices of the war put the failure of the peace in sharp relief."

"Yes, the sacrifices I can agree with. And the benefits of the peace have been rather thin."

"It has been the failure of the peace that makes the war seem so futile in retrospect."

"Retrospect? I felt that way during the war."

"You had rare perception."

Natalie smiled. I was relieved at Kurt's compliment.

Suddenly, a mischievous schoolboy smile spread across Kurt's face as he pulled a book out of his pocket. It was a copy of Djuna Barnes' *Ladies Almanack* that Kate had given him. Kurt held it out towards Natalie, "I was wondering if I could get you to autograph it?"

Natalie was taken aback and she mumbled, "It's really Djuna's book."

Kurt looked directly at her, "You're the book."

Natalie, again taken aback by Kurt's directness, fidgeted and then brightened and nodded agreement. Her own mischievous smile spread across her face and she asked me for my fountain pen. She held the book and wrote a big signature across the title page and then handed the book back to Kurt with a triumphant look of satisfaction.

Kurt turned the book around, smiled broadly in recognition, and showed the book to Kate. The big bold signature read "Evangeline Musset." We all laughed in good-hearted approval.

Natalie looked across the sea of guests and nodded her head at Djuna Barnes, who was in earnest conversation with some other guests.

"Speaking of Djuna, there she is," said Natalie.

Kate whispered to Kurt and held her hand out, pointing, "That's Djuna Barnes."

Djuna, seeing Kate's outstretched arm, excused herself from the conversation and started walking over. She was once again tall, elegant, and beautiful. I felt that the reason Paris was Djuna's favorite city was because she knew how well she looked in it. The one complemented the other.

Kurt stood transfixed watching her approach, completely captivated. He turned to Kate and mumbled in pleased disbelief, "That's Djuna Barnes?"

Kate smiled and nodded her head.

"She wrote the book you gave me?"

"Yes."

"I never would have thought—she's arresting."

As Djuna approached, she smiled warmly at Kurt while she put an arm around Kate and gave her a big hug. Then she said to Kurt, "Kate has told me so much about you. We are all fascinated about your take on the war and the peace. Seeing the peace from the German side of the Rhine River will be a fresh experience for most of us."

Kurt was impressed with the way Djuna articulated her point. He held his hand out, "Kurt Eckhart."

Djuna gave his hand a firm shake and then held it while she looked at him warmly and said, "*Enchantée*."

Natalie spoke before Kurt could say more, "Djuna, our guest is collecting signatures on his copy of your book."

"Oh yes, Bill said he was going to give you a copy of my book." She laughed, "You're liable to get an accurate impression of me."

"If that's so, then I look forward to learning more. You're something new to my experience."

Djuna flashed her eyebrows playfully and looked at Kate. She turned back to Kurt, "Did you read my little gem?"

"Just got it last night. Read parts of it, beginning and end. I've got some questions, though."

"Well, then you're right in line with Patience Scalpel, my friend Mina Loy," and Djuna batted eyelashes at Mina Loy, who had just come up and was standing beside me. I had a hard time believing that Mina Loy ever had to pose any questions about women and sexuality; she was that rare woman of a certain age who beautifully radiated finely captured experience. It was hard to imagine a gentleman who would not want to turn back the covers and stretch himself alongside the exquisite figure and elegant personality of Mina Loy.

Kurt turned to Mina and held out his hand, "Pleased to meet you."

Kurt turned back to Djuna and said, "I had never imagined so many kinds of itch bringing women to a yelping pitch as you catalogue in that first paragraph of your book."

"Women aren't climbing into someone's bed to do missionary work," Djuna answered.

"But you're saying the only consolation every woman has is at her finger tips or at the hang of her tongue. Men don't have any part to play?"

"Not at rue Jacob," said Djuna, holding her palm above her eyes and scanning the crowd in the garden like a sea captain on the ocean. We all laughed.

"Yes, and at the end of the book the *grande dame* is consumed by fire on the great funeral pyre. All that is left is the tongue, worshipped by a hundred women followers. And it was the tongue that was placed on the altar in the Temple of Love where it flickers to this day." Kurt glanced up at the Temple of Love just steps away from us as if the tongue were actually in there.

Djuna nodded her head agreeably as Kurt was reciting the thrust and substance of her ladies' tale. Such a good student her expression seemed to be saying.

Kurt pushed in with his point, "You're saying the tongue is the object of a woman's sexual fulfillment. You've replaced the phallic symbol of ancient cults with the tongue."

"*Peut-être*," said Djuna with a humorous shrug. The women in our little circle were smiling, almost wickedly, keepers of some inner secret of their cult.

"Men have no role?" Kurt asked. You could almost sense the hurt feelings, the disappointment.

Mina's eyebrows arched up and she laughed, "That was my question, too? You have to lie with the father of your children."

Kate laughed.

"Look at those last sentences again. It is a disembodied tongue," said Djuna.

Yes, the disembodied tongue—now I saw it. I hadn't caught that distinction before. I had read the passage the same way as Kurt. Kurt brightened.

"Yes, I see. You are not limiting yourself." Kurt said.

Djuna looked at Kate with a laugh, "Me? Limit myself?"

"Her?" said Mina.

"Never," added Natalie. "Sugar and spice and not very nice."

Kate laughed in sympathetic response. She looked at Kurt, "New York was different for Djuna."

"Yeah, she was with some guy. How about you sweets? Were you with some woman then?"

"She was with me," Mina said quickly, winking at Kate.

Djuna's eyes darted from person to person as the repartee bantered around the circle, smiling in warm remembrance of old memories. Then she turned and faced Kurt. She looked up into the sky collecting her thoughts and said, "As to ladies and gentlemen, when there's a storm over Paris, there's thunder and lightening over both the Left and Right Banks. Zeus hurls the bolts in all directions."

Kurt smiled and rocked back on his feet, a sense of smugness coming over his face, as he struck a pose almost as if he were Zeus standing like a big marble statue in Natalie's garden. Kate and Mina laughed. Djuna smiled and leaned over and said softly to Kate, "When they realize it can be their tongue, why, we're almost there..." and she dipped her head and whispered words into Kate's ear.

Kate's face lit up, the eyes laughing, and her head nodding in agreement. Kurt looked on in singular fascination, captivated by Djuna Barnes.

"Ladies," I said and stepped forward and handed Djuna my fountain pen. She signed Kurt's copy of the book and handed it back to Kurt. Djuna turned to me and said, "I like your friend. He thinks. And it's always so nice to bump into someone who has read your book for meaning. Looks like you're running a good horse in the book derby."

"Yes I am."

Natalie broke in. "I think we better start. I will go and make the introduction. Bill, you're going first, correct?"

"Yes."

Natalie walked over and mounted the steps of the Temple of Friendship. Kurt and I followed and stood to one side at the bottom of the steps as Natalie went up to the fourth and highest step, the

Doric columns framing her like a picture in some long ago Elysian field.

"Good afternoon." Natalie waited while the crowd quieted down. "We are going to have a fresh look at the war that broke our hopes and the peace that has curdled our dreams. Bill Lawrence, whom many of you know so well, will give an introduction to Kurt Eckhart, today's speaker." She stepped down and walked over to some friends who handed her a champagne glass of apple juice.

I walked up to the top step and turned and faced the guests and started in, "I see many friends here today. And many of you are friends or acquaintances of Ernest Hemingway. As many of you know, he's returned to America where he's writing his second novel. Before he left Paris, he told many of you that it was about the war and that he was really feeling good about it—the book that is, not the war." There was some light laughter.

Other heads in the audience nodded in agreement. The Hemingway story and the trainload of gossip trailing behind it was freshened up every morning in the Left Bank cafes with the coffee.

"So, what do we know about what some of Hemingway's big themes might be?" I let the question settle in.

"And what was it that happened to Jake Barnes in the war?" The cause of Jake's impotence in *The Sun Also Rises* was an enigma of perpetual speculation in Paris cafes.

I turned and shot out, "Djuna, is it true Jake is supposed to be your brother?"

Startled, heads turned towards Djuna. She didn't miss a beat, "No, I think Gertrude suggested it so that Jake could play the part of my husband in the sequel—out of envy for my love life of course."

A roar of laughter went up from the guests. Djuna knew how to bite.

I let the laughter die down and continued, "Seriously, I think we have some pretty good ideas about what those themes might be. Last year Hemingway published the short story *In Another Country*. It's a good story. He opened with the line 'In the fall the war was always there, but we did not go to it any more.' Scott Fitzgerald told Hemingway that he loved the line. The line carries with it the theme of separation from the war, a putting of personal distance between the narrator and the war. Dare I say, possibly a separate peace." I had the audience's rapt attention.

"The climax of the story is the Italian major with the crippled hand who has survived the war just to have his beautiful young wife die of pneumonia. He is totally disillusioned. He just stands in front of the therapy machine in which he has no faith and looks out the window."

"So we have the death of someone young and beautiful, someone who is not expected to die. This theme is reinforced by the title of the story, which echoes Christopher Marlowe's line, 'Besides she's dead and it was long ago and in another country.' Some people think that may wind up being the epigraph for the new novel Hemingway's writing."

I let that sink in. "Now let me introduce Kurt Eckhart. Kurt and I were in the same infantry regiment in the war, from Chateau Thierry through the Meuse-Argonne campaign."

Some of the people gasped. They remembered what those words meant.

I held out my arm towards Kurt, who bounded up the steps, shook my hand and turned and faced the audience. I stepped down and walked over and stood next to Kate.

"Thank you, Bill." Kurt settled in and began.

"The beginning of the novel covers those hard months of fighting in 1918 because it establishes the terrible price paid for the Armistice. Normally, the price paid would be compared to the benefits won. But the aftermath of this war was different. It was the opportunities lost, not the benefits gained, that has come down to us."

Heads nodded in solemn agreement. Life was nice in Paris, particularly for most of this audience. But behind this façade was a great unease, a sense of the future shifting out from under our feet.

"The English economist John Maynard Keynes brilliantly laid out the case in his book *The Economic Consequences of the Peace,* published just months after the Peace Conference." Many heads nodded. It had been a hot topic of conversation in the years just after the war, so prophetic, so disturbing.

A lady towards the back exclaimed, "I saw his wife dance with the Ballets Russes. She dances like an angel. Of course his economics must be divine."

People around her laughed. Kurt laughed and asked the lady, "Do you know how he came to like Lydia?"

"No," the woman stammered.

Kurt smiled broadly and said, "As many of you know, before the war Keynes' taste in partners ran to young men in his famous Bloomsbury circle."

I looked at Natalie; her expression had clouded over, concern spread across her brow. My anxiety went straight up—oh no, not now, Kurt.

Kurt continued, "Keynes and others in his circle held important jobs in London as the war went on. But the war swept away all the handsome young men, apparently to Keynes' and his fellows' consternation. The war also brought many young women to the London offices, some of them smartly dressed up in uniforms. Some of them cajoled Keynes and his friends into taking them out. To their great surprise, the men found new delights that they had not previously imagined."

The guests laughed in appreciation. Kurt continued, "Keynes became captivated by femininity, and what is the most captivating example of femininity? Why a ballerina of course. Keynes was completely taken by Lydia when he first saw her perform."

Kurt took a breath and went for the punch line, "Now this is a fascinating example of supply and demand at work. It remains to be seen whether or not the economists put this example in their books!"

The guests laughed. I looked over at Natalie, laughing with a radiant glow about her. Kurt had the audience in his grip.

He turned back to the lady standing in the rear and said, "Returning to the *Economic Consequences of the Peace,* let me reassure you, madame, that not only is his economics divine but it has the double advantage of being quite correct."

People smiled.

"After the book was published, Keynes went on to advocate strongly for a two billion dollar reconstruction loan to rebuild the

German economy and get central Europe back on its economic feet. That would have been of immense benefit to everyone."

Kurt let the silence build, "But of course the politicians went back to the sterile argument about reparations and the slogan 'Let the Hun pay.'"

Someone in the audience shouted, "Squeeze them till their pips squeak!"

People laughed as they remembered the famous line made by a British cabinet minister on his way to the Versailles Peace Conference.

The guests looked at Kurt. He changed his tone, "I was with the American army that entered Germany that November. Because I was German speaking, I was assigned to the occupation army headquartered at Koblenz on the Rhine. Up the river was the French army, down the river the British."

"What we found was a country deranged; the defeat had unleashed demonic forces. The civilians faced starvation with winter setting in."

"I was given a small support battalion. We went to work. We put Germans to work. First hundreds, then thousands. Headquarters asked if I could do this, if I could do that. I said yes. Pretty soon I had a regiment at work."

He took a breath, "Now I want to say something. After the American Civil War there were about twenty-three million Americans. Sixty years later, in 1920, there were over one hundred and twenty million Americans. That is a five-fold increase in less than sixty years. We built a country, a big successful country."

Kurt let that sink in. He continued, "Now I don't want to insult anyone more than I have to, but look at Ireland. The British have had it for four hundred years and done nothing. In contrast millions of Irish came to America and we put 'em to work. They built railroads across the country, skyscrapers in New York, and everything in between."

Kurt stopped and eased back, his eyes twinkling, "You keep the Irish off the whiskey and their backs to the work, and you can get a lot done." The guests erupted in laughter. But Kurt had made a telling point.

"That's the American way. That's what a lot of us wanted to do in Germany in 1919."

With disgust on his face, Kurt spat out, "But that's not what the government wanted. They wanted us to do less and less as the year went on. Then we all went home. Job undone."

Turning philosophical, Kurt said, "In the novel, the hero meets a German girl, a beautiful young woman working as a nurse taking care of some of the many wounded soldiers. He helps her, they fall in love, she gets pregnant. He picks up his discharge from the army and they go to Berlin."

Kurt stared off into the distance, a certain wistfulness spreading across his face. The guests watched enthralled; they sensed the personal story. "Not to give it all away, but the beautiful young woman dies in childbirth. Not because of the war, but because of the peace." Scorn drenched Kurt's words. "The British kept Germany blockaded halfway through 1919. Crucial supplies were denied the German people. The German people's noses were rubbed in the sins of Kaiser's Germany, even though that regime was long gone."

Just then behind us, an elderly British gentleman exclaimed, "My God, if King George were here, I dare say the American would run him through with a bayonet!"

Kurt chuckled and said, "That's half of it. But I saw the other half. I got to see John Maynard Keynes work with all the parties at Trier and later Spa to get the political logjam unblocked so Mr. Hoover could move the American food into Germany. Keynes, able to operate on his own initiative, was an exemplary example of leadership, never afraid to help people in deep need."

The old man broke into a big smile and raised his cane and gave it a couple pumps. Everyone else laughed. Kate grabbed a big breath and then smiled, a sense of gratification coming over her face.

Kurt, sensing the triumph, brought himself to a stop; he took a deep breath and relaxed. He looked out over the audience, "So that's the driving point of the novel: the road not taken and how that led to the peace failing. Thank you for your attention."

Kurt stepped down and walked over towards Kate and me, asking, "How'd I do?"

"Quite good," said Kate and gave him a big hug.

Djuna came over and clapped Kurt on the back, saying, "Hemingway will out art you, but you will bowl them over with driving force. You have the big story. People need to hear this."

Natalie came up, smiling at Kurt, "You are sending the public discussion off in a new direction, the road not taken. A beautiful hope crushed." She looked wistful for a moment and then turned to me, "Bill, could all of you stay for dinner. I would like to discuss this further. Is it really too late to rebuild? If we could stop all of these armaments, we could build a more prosperous Europe." Her voice trailed off.

"Yes, of course, we would be delighted to stay."

Natalie's face lit up. She turned to Djuna, "You, too, dear." Djuna nodded her head in agreement.

Natalie said playfully to Kurt, "Steel sharpens steel. So it is between Djuna and everyone else!"

19. Dinner at Natalie's

As the last guests departed through the arched entrance to rue Jacob, Natalie came over to where I was standing with Mina, Kate, Kurt, and Djuna. She said, "We can go inside to the dining room."

We trooped through the small entry hall and into the big drawing room, now set up as a dining room, the soft afternoon light came through the spacious windows looking out onto the garden. Kurt walked over and into the alcove and looked up at the domed ceiling gazing at the paintings of the four nymphs. He nodded his head in appreciation. He came back and Natalie pointed him to a chair on her left. Djuna sat down beside him. Kate and I took chairs across, Mina at the other end. Wine was served.

"I am much taken about your thoughts about building and rebuilding…if the men could be put to useful work…" and Natalie's words trailed off.

"Men build or they fall into apathy. Idle hands are the devil's workshop," Kurt replied.

"Yes, but first things first," said Natalie. "I believe love, the province of women, demands far greater heroism than war, the creature of men."

"What you are saying is that more love would mean less war. I don't believe that," replied Kurt. "Something else is the problem."

"Well, for all these centuries of patriarchal rule, we have been afflicted with this war curse," Natalie countered. "The patriarchal rule has not averted bloodshed by war, but rather increased it and made it more terrible."

Kurt nodded his head in agreement. Kate looked on fascinated.

Natalie moved smoothly to her conclusion, "So is it indeed not madness to hope that women might stop this slaughter of what in the end are their children?"

"That is a good argument," replied Kurt. Natalie dipped her head in salute. "If giving women the vote helps even the balance in the political scales, then this would be a great step forward."

"Yes, the vote," said Djuna. Kate vigorously nodded her head in approval.

Kurt continued, "If women can tip the balance towards building, rather than engaging in the destructiveness, then a better world can be had with the social materials at hand."

"So you see some sort of salvation in building?" asked Natalie.

"I think it is where you start," replied Kurt. "If Keynes were here now having dinner with us, he would be in broad agreement with you. He said that the war had been fought in the name of nation, state, and emperor. These, he said, were false gods, efforts by the old politics to divert attention from the great tasks of work."

"Yes, false gods," said Natalie, "I have felt that in my bones. My sensibility screams against them."

"My generation has wanted to move past them, towards something better," Kate said, "but I can see…if the economic foundations are rotten…the political structure of the peace will fail." Kate's mind moved from point to point but she did not follow the chain to its hopeless conclusion.

"Keynes said that the intellectual's duty was to tell the truth in face of necessary political lying," I said. "To add a literary dimension to his criticism."

"An economist said that?" asked Djuna.

"Keynes relaxes with artists and writers; he's in that circle," said Kurt.

"Why yes," replied Djuna and she waggled her shoulders nonchalantly, "some of my best friends are economists."

We all laughed.

Natalie broke back in and looked at Kurt, "And the motives for war?"

"Vengeance and vindictiveness are two of the horsemen," said Kurt. "If you can slip building—or more generally the constructive—into the chain of events, then you might head off war by the pursuit of a larger, more noble goal."

"Nobly said," pronounced Natalie. Kate smiled in relief.

"Thank you," said Kurt, and he took a solid draught from his wine glass. "That is Keynes' argument in his book and he has remade it every year since. The Allies need to turn away from vengeance and focus on rebuilding Central Europe around a prosperous Germany."

Natalie nodded her head, "I despair of progress." She looked down the table, "Perhaps a reign of powerful women is necessary to unmake the mistakes of powerful men…" and her voice trailed off. She added, "If the voices of women are hushed up like children's…"

Kate nodded her head in approval, her spirit now in thrall to the voice of the older woman.

"Our voices will not be heard until our literature roars," said Djuna.

"Yes, our literature must speak," added Kate.

Mina nodded her head in agreement and said, "Our poetry, too."

Kurt nodded his head in turn to the three women and said, "In general, true. It would be doubly true if all society were guilty of starting wars. But when you look at how real wars start, the chain of mistakes that set off the slaughter, you see that broadly speaking men are not the problem. The high hat crowd is, the men that run the banks and the ministries."

Kate was struck by the wisdom of Kurt's words, "I hadn't looked at it that way."

Natalie looked at Kate and shook her head in disagreement, "There's a deep psychology at work. The masculine need for battle extends to every aspect of human life, resulting in the conquering of women and the destruction of women's work—children, love, and hope."

"I agree, Natalie," said Djuna. "But Kurt is explaining the operation of the mechanism."

"Yes," Kate agreed, "Kurt is saying that better social institutions can tame the demons and we can replace conflict with cooperation."

"Yes, *peut-etre*," said Natalie, somewhat brightened by the optimism of the younger women. Perhaps.

"Demons, that's a good word," said Kurt. "That was the start of the last war. All the old resentments, fanned by economic rivalries that benefit the fortunate few, sent a generation off to

Flanders Field and unprecedented slaughter. Imperialism, the coveting of other people's lands…" and Kurt's voice trailed off.

"And the generals?" asked Natalie.

"The generals?" and Kurt's voice turned to scorn. "You know what the German general staff said of the British army: 'lions led by donkeys.'"

Djuna clapped her hands, "Why it was a war of the *bons mots*!"

"Eight million people died, Djuna," Kate scolded.

Djuna turned a hawk-like glance at Kate and said derisively, "I was in New York in 1917. I saw the rising enthusiasm for the war. Seems to me a lot of people got exactly what they wanted."

I nodded my head sadly. I had been one of them. Mina smiled at me and said, "The only person I knew at the time who really swam against that tide was Cravan," referring to her now dead husband. I smiled in acknowledgement to her and turned back to Kurt.

"Yes," Kurt said. "But you don't realize it until the war is over. The self-important men, the ones with the grand theories, the moneyed voices."

"The hard-faced men who look as if they had done very well out of the war," I added, echoing words from 1919.

"Who said that?" asked Djuna.

"Stanley Baldwin, the current British prime minister."

"Oh, but the English have the gift for words," Djuna said.

Kurt looked out the window into the distance and said, "Then came the peace and all the cheap politicians who said the Germans could be made to pay, a promise that could never payoff in reality. They never learn."

"Kurt, what is the one practical thing to do to stop future wars?" asked Kate.

"One thing? Stop the leaders from telling lies to the people that are used to justify the wars. Mass delusion precedes the rush of events leading to war." Kurt looked sympathetically at Djuna, "By the time it gets to 1917, it's too late."

Djuna nodded. Then her eyes lit up, her head slightly nodding in agreement. Lies and delusion were old friends to her, as I knew from her writing. "I see a beautiful drama, a theater of the absurd, my chance for Surrealist immortality."

I smiled. The war was that.

Natalie watched and added her nod of approval. She pronounced her benediction, "If women cannot rule equally with men over the lives they together create, should not simple race preservation demand that the Matriarchal again dominate the Patriarchal?"

Kate and Mina, eyes sparkling, held their wine glasses up in salute to Natalie.

Kurt looked thoughtful and concluded, "More honesty, a commitment to build, not destroy. That would make a good start."

Djuna set her glass down and looked up at the ceiling and softly recited some lines of poetry:

While blue and khaki share the heroes' mud,
And women tend in white or weep in grey,

"Is that your poetry, Djuna?" asked Kurt.

"No, those lines are Natalie's. She wrote them during the war."

Natalie smiled at Djuna and said, "You remembered?"

"Of course," Djuna said.

Kurt came back in, "Well, my novel's heroine is a woman in white who tended the wounded. But it's the hero who ends up crying."

Kate spoke up, "Yes, Kurt. We need to speak about the woman in white. She needs to be a woman, not a luminous goddess in the sky."

"She was a luminous goddess to me."

Djuna looked at him sympathetically and then with a sarcastic smile spreading across her face said, "Let's see. The yellow gold hair, the angelic face described in words pure and virginal."

Kurt looked at her; he guessed what was coming.

"Let's see. Sexuality. A heaving bosom under the draped gown of a goddess."

Kate smirked and said, "Yes, Kurt wouldn't miss the heaving bosom."

Djuna's smile turned mischievous; she straightened her back and pushed her shoulders back and heaved her beautifully proportioned bosom up with a big breath and eased her chest back down with a long sigh and a delicious smile on her face. Kurt's eyebrows went straight up.

"See, I understand," said Djuna.

Kate laughed. Natalie looked playfully askance at Djuna.

Kurt smiled and said, "You sure do."

"Now Kurt, a woman's allure may be the sum expression of her whole body, but a woman's sexuality is below the waist. It starts damp and gets wet from there."

He laughed, "Just like in your book."

Djuna smiled at him and nodded her head sagely. I could see he was following the lesson Djuna was teaching. She moved on, "Let's see. In this story, the heroine gets pregnant. Right?"

Kurt nodded his head in agreement.

"Well, then someone wet bed somewhere. Right?"

"Well, yes…"

"Write about it."

"Yes, ma'am."

Kate added, "Kurt, death makes a woman a goddess, not life. So before the death, we write about a woman. After the death, a goddess—the beautifully remembered memory."

Kurt nodded his head in understanding. "Guess I got some rewriting to do."

Djuna looked at Kate and said, "See, this wasn't so hard. He's a good student."

I smiled and thought to myself that when Kurt saw that bosom heave he was a puppy. Just like Morrill with Margaret Anderson.

I looked at Natalie and said, "A good lesson on writing today." Natalie smiled. Djuna was always fun.

I looked at Djuna, "From one of our best writers." She smiled warmly at me.

Dinner was served and Natalie spoke to Kurt about the Women's Congress for Peace, an international convocation of mostly women speakers that was held at rue Jacob during the war. He was fascinated that there were so many voices speaking out for a peaceful solution to the war long before the Armistice. When you were in the trenches, it all seemed so inevitable, so foreordained. Choice was nowhere to be seen. But Natalie sadly concluded about the Women's Congress "that whatever my passions had been, they were no-wise political."

Djuna made a bitter point, "But Natalie, it is exactly that your antiwar and feminist views were political that gave them power. They will only listen to us when we have power."

Djuna lifted her wine glass and took a long draught. She thumped it down and pronounced, "A power is a power is a power. I think Gertrude gave us that wisdom."

We all laughed, but it was a rather brittle little laugh.

Natalie sighed, "Nevertheless, grand ideas seemed to dissolve into petty arguments at our Congress. With the Versailles Treaty, I had some hope for the League of Nations, but…"

She turned to Kurt, "So it's now time for literature to speak. We have distance now. Maybe new truths can come to the fore. Hemingway's book will sure shine a spotlight on your book as well. Bill and Kate will see to that."

"And so will I," said Djuna rather grandly. My plan was falling into place rather nicely.

After dinner we walked out into the garden and the gathering dusk of the late summer twilight. We thanked Natalie and walked out onto rue Jacob. I said, "Let's get a coffee at Deux Magots? Maybe a drink up at La Coupole?"

"Love to. But I can't," said Djuna. "I need to find where Thelma wandered off to."

She turned to Kate, "We'll be in touch about an article on this project."

Then she stepped forward and stood before Kurt and held out her hand, "I am delighted to have met you. It's been a fascinating day. You and your novel are in good hands," and she turned and smiled at Kate and me.

Kurt shook her hand, his left hand clasped on top of hers, "The delight has been all mine. I've never met a woman quite like you."

Djuna dipped her head at the compliment. She turned and walked briskly up rue Jacob. Kurt simply stood there and watched those hips move that tall carriage up the sidewalk. He turned towards me and let out a low whistle. She really had his attention.

We turned and walked down the street on our way to the Deux Magots. Kate turned and asked me, “What was Keynes’ conclusion in his book?”

“You really want to know?”

“Yes.”

“He said that vengeance would be swift, that there would be a final civil war between the forces of reaction and revolution…”

“No role for reason?” she asked. “Just war?”

“I think he felt reason was driven from the temple long before…”

“So we go back to something more primitive.” She looked up at me, “What else?”

I took a deep breath and continued, “…before which the horrors of the last war would pale…and destroy the civilization and progress of our generation.”

“Keynes wrote that in 1919?” asked Kate.

“Yes.”

“I see,” said Kate glumly. “We’re not dealing with small themes here, are we?”

20. Coffee at Les Deux Magots

We took a table in the evening shade overlooking the square and the church of Saint-Germain-des-Prés, its bell tower golden in the falling sunshine of summer twilight.

"It's too early for Montparnasse. Café crawling doesn't start 'til dark," I said.

"That's how Bill used to find his clients," joked Kate to Kurt.

"That's not what I meant," I said, correcting Kate. "That's where I could always find my clients. There's a difference."

Kurt laughed. A waiter came up and I ordered coffee all around.

"I have been working on the manuscript. Could I hear in your own words how you met Elsa?" asked Kate.

"Sure. After I had been in Koblenz a couple weeks, we had our service and supply operation humming and repairs to public facilities underway. Some Germans approached and asked if I would visit the hospital. It had been a church hospital taken over for military casualties. I shrugged my shoulders and said 'sure.'"

The waiter set small coffee cups down on the table. Kurt put some sugar in his cup and stirred it idly as he remembered, "There was an older lady, dressed in the habits of a mother superior, and next to her a younger woman in the gray smock and white blouse of the German nursing service. The older lady turned to the younger one and said, 'Frau Erdman, would you escort the major through the hospital?" So that is how I met Elsa."

"What was the hospital like?"

"This was about two months after the Armistice. It was the dead of the winter. Keeping the rooms warm was hard with not enough coal. The blankets were dirty and many were thin. The men that were going to die had already died. The men who got well after initial surgery had gotten well and left. What was left were men caught in a terrible limbo, disabled by horrible wounds but surviving."

Kate's face fell in pained realization.

"We started to walk the wards. Some of the men would recognize my uniform and shake a fist at me and try to struggle up from their beds. Frau Erdman would walk up and speak with them, reassure them. The response was always the same, 'Ja, Frau Erdman.' They obeyed her without question, their eyes deeply respectful."

"What was the basis of her authority?"

"Alleviation of pain, getting whatever supplies were to be gotten. In particular, getting antiseptics for treating the wounds. Infection is the killer in these hospitals."

Kate grimaced at the thought, the endless misery underlying the statement.

"And something else. A constant determination to get the job done, to keep her assistants going regardless of discouragement." Kurt laughed at a memory.

"What is it?" asked Kate.

"Oh, she was what the Germans admire, a real front-line leader who can set the example. Her husband had been a company commander; it was like she picked up that torch. That counted for a lot in early 1919; there was so little of it, anywhere," and Kurt gave a small bitter laugh.

"After we went through the wards, I simply asked what she needed. She looked at me and told me: it was some of everything, but in particular antiseptics and blankets."

Kate looked at him.

"I said I'd do what I could. When I got back to my headquarters, I got some supplies organized and arranged for a truck to drop something off every morning. I assigned a sergeant to this task and asked him to look after other things the hospital might need. He took some initiative here. Then I found a couple German-speaking medics and had them go over in the afternoons. They of course would grab some stuff from our dispensary. And so it went."

"You didn't go back?" Kate asked.

"No, I went back, after about a week I went over one afternoon to see how it was going. Frau Erhard came out to greet me, a big smile on her face, and held out both hands to me. Her smile just knocked me over. She took me for a tour of some of the wards. The soldiers smiled now; they all thanked her. She tried to send some it my way, but you could tell the soldiers felt that it was she who was the miracle worker. And she was.

"Afterwards, we stood by the nurses' quarters and it was late on a winter afternoon. Next to the quarters was a big garden, frozen in the winter frost, but I asked her if she would like to take a walk through it. She said yes—with some enthusiasm to my delight. We walked and talked; there was a happiness in her voice I hadn't heard before, a lightness to her manner."

"I returned her to the front door of the nurses quarters and took my leave. She invited me to come back, that she had never enjoyed a walk in a garden so much, and laughed as she looked over at the frozen expanse."

"And you?"

"Something came over me, a determination to see where this was going to go."

I laughed. Kate looked at me, "You were going to say something?"

I said, "Yes, Kurt had just met the only other person who could command an infantry battalion as well as he could."

Kurt laughed and said, "You know, in those months in 1919 we were all working to make things better, better for average people, the people who had borne the battle, suffered the consequences."

Kate smiled and her face turned to one of satisfaction and she said, "What a wonderful person to fall in love with."

Kurt looked at her with a pleased sense of affection.

We sat there and chatted in the gathering dusk. After coffee, we did a round of calvados, the fiery apple brandy. Then we stood up and walked up to Montparnasse.

21. Drinks at Café La Coupole

Kurt and I stepped aside and let Kate enter the brightly lit bar, which was thronged with Americans sitting at tables, standing at the bar, and clustered in groups in between. Kate made a beeline for Solita Solano and Janet Flanner. Kurt and I followed.

"So nice to see you," Kate gushed.

"We just got back from the Comédie-Française. Nightcap. We were at Natalie's today. Saw you at a distance. Fun."

Kate turned and introduced them, "Kurt, these are my friends Solita Solano and Janet Flanner."

"Pleased to meet you," Kurt said as he shook each of their hands in turn.

"They're Nip and Tuck in Djuna's book," I added.

"You're in the book?" Kurt asked, his eyes wide with open amazement.

"They're the Sisters in Heaven," Kate said, beaming with pride at her friends' inclusion into Djuna's *academie des femmes*.

"Great little book," Kurt said. "We were just discussing it last night and this afternoon."

Solita looked up at the ceiling and, mischievously like a schoolgirl, recited, "How am I to help it if I go astray when every Law of Love and Desire was long ago as mixed as a Contortion of Traffic? I do not know a blind Alley from a Boulevard—"

Janet cut in, "You would follow, all panting and blind with good Intentions—"

Solita put up a hand to stop the recitation, "But that's Djuna's book." Solita turned towards Kurt and me, "This afternoon everyone was talking about Kurt's new novel. It's the buzz here tonight."

"Really?" Kurt said with genuine astonishment as he looked around at the chattering crowd.

"We heard your talk today at Natalie's. Refreshing. A new look at the old war is really needed," Solita said. "And I heard you talk with Djuna about her book. You have the eye of a critic."

Kurt smiled, but behind the smile he was taking a full measure of Solita; she was a provocative beauty. She of course noticed and turned half sideways, did the vamp, and batted eyelashes.

Kurt laughed and looked at her wolfishly—he could do that rather well—"And you write, too?"

Now Janet laughed and said to Kurt, "Alas, she has friends—already."

As that sunk in, Kurt looked more than a little disappointed. He looked at Solita longingly.

Solita looked at him with that abashed look that the good looking have that always says sorry to disappoint you.

"Understand," he said.

Janet gave him a playful frown and moved the conversation on, "Next year, you come out with your book around the same time as Hemingway, and they'll be talking about the two books in these cafes for years."

"But will they buy the book?" asked Kurt.

"If they talk about the book in Paris, they'll be buying the book in the States by the thousands. That's how it works."

"And Janet's one of the big pipelines. She writes a regular column on Paris for *The New Yorker,*" Kate added.

Kurt was amazed and turned in a small circle looking at all the smartly dressed women staring across their drinks glasses and through the smoke of their cigarettes at the boisterous men talking about their grand schemes, the masterpieces soon to be started, the contracts almost signed. A piano started to play and Kurt looked over to one end of the bar, a look of surprise crossing his face as the rich quality of the music registered with him.

"Hey, the piano player's pretty good," said Kurt.

"That's Hilaire Hiler. He's a pretty good painter and he can put the melancholy into a jazz or blues piece like no one else in Paris," I said.

"Got the girls gathered around."

"So he does." Solita made a sweeping gesture with her hand at the chattering couples moving like a tide towards the piano.

Just then, a French voice bellowed, "Let me up there." The lusty French woman pushed her way past the women around Hiler and plopped her rear end on top of the piano.

Kurt said, “Look at that,” as he took in the full figure, the beautiful white face under the arched eyebrows, the smooth black bobbed hair—a living incarnation of the wild and beautiful side of Paris nightlife.

Kate said, “That’s Kiki of Montparnasse. She’s a living legend. Mistress of the Surrealist painter and photographer Man Ray.”

“A legend?” Kurt asked idly.

“Djuna described Kiki in one of her articles as the *diabolique* who softly complains that life is so limited, so robbed of new sins…”

“We need new sins?” asked Kurt incredulously.

We all laughed and turned our heads towards the piano. Hiler went up-tempo and Kiki looked up and stretched her neck out and the husky voice started singing one of her famous bawdy songs. The young women laughed and clapped.

Kiki sang and as she came to the end she leaned way over, her voluptuous body almost spilling out of the top of her too small dress as she crooned out the final syllables. Now the men joined the young women clapping and hollering—she was living the lyrics. She finished and smiled warmly.

“Not only are the women’s books naughty in Paris, but so are the songs,” exclaimed Kurt in something of amazement. “But Djuna’s book is way above a barroom *chanson* sung by a sultry *chanteuse*. Djuna strings words together into images in ways that I have never seen and would never have thought of.”

“New words to describe the old sins,” said Solita.

“She has the talent, that girl,” added Janet.

Kurt looked momentarily thoughtful. “No, the way she puts the words together is from some other world. Women see reality differently than men. Even I see that now,” Kurt said. “Djuna makes that point in striking ways. I never understood what originality really meant until now.” He laughed and said, “You really can see it on the dirty side of the street.”

Solita gave that sally a warm and invitingly provocative laugh. I wondered if she was warming him up for something. She said, “Underneath all that sensuality is some sort of raging Puritan.”

"It powers her writing. She, like Joyce, is the great Modernist writer. She's one novel away from greatness," said Kate.

I nodded my head in agreement. It was all there. Her current novel was solid, a real hit. Most thought she was capable of something even grander. It was all coming together for Djuna.

From out of the crowd on our left, Bob McAlmon came crashing into Kate, almost spilling her drink. "'Scuse me, Kate."

"Quite all right, Bob," Kate replied.

He looked at me, "Hi, Bill." Then he looked at Solita and Janet. "I know you two," he said rather unsteadily, "I think."

"Evening, Bob," Solita answered.

He spread his arms wide and incanted, "We're all survivors of another and far gayer company and of a wilder, more adventurous time."

Bob swept his arm out and encompassed the crowd, saying, "All these people now, they speak lines as flat as stale beer."

He looked at me and smiled sheepishly, "So there's nothing to do but have another drink." He held up his half-full glass in front of him and stared at it unevenly.

His face turned forlorn, a lost look crossing his brow, "If only Djuna Barnes and Mina Loy turned up, the evening might be saved." Bob looked at the empty door. No one was there. Then her jerked his head up and put his foot forward and headed towards the bar with a wobbly gait.

"He's a friend of Djuna's?" Kurt asked.

"He's a friend of everyone's," replied Kate.

"He's published a lot of authors on the Left Bank. He published Djuna's book *The Ladies Almanack*. But he's fading, I'm afraid," I said. "He's always calling out the names for whoever isn't here."

Just then I saw Djuna come through the door. She looked like she'd had a few. She scanned the entire room with her eyes, saw us, and then took another long sweep of the room. I could guess who she was looking for. Djuna came over.

"I'm looking for Thelma. Have you seen her?"

"No we haven't," I gently replied. "Not tonight." The evening search for Thelma was becoming a bitter ritual.

"What a lover! She says she wants me," and she looked imploringly at us, then she sighed, "along with the rest of the world." The bitterness of the remark would have tarnished gold. "I've been loved in a relationship strange, and now it is forgetting me…the accumulated dishonesty of it all..."

"Why not have a cup of coffee with me?" asked Kate gently. Djuna didn't hear her.

"The Squatter's got her and is trying to take her to New York," Djuna spit out, referring to the most recent and determined suitor of Thelma. The rumor was that this other woman was on her way to becoming the scheming predator in Djuna's next novel, a corrosively bitter romance, which of course was the basic gist to all of Djuna's writing.

Djuna remained quiet for a second, then saw Kurt and brightened. She said to him lightly, "We have something in common. My goddess seems to be deserting me. Yours was taken from you. You and I are left alone on the shore. Betrayed by life."

"Let me buy you a drink," Kurt said in a tone of sympathetic concern.

"I'd like that."

He reached out for her elbow and guided her over to a far corner while catching a waiter's attention.

I turned to Kate, "He really likes her."

"I think there's something in him she likes. I haven't seen her like that with a man since New York."

Solita added, "She used to have a penchant for men. Thelma was always something different, I think."

Janet laughed, "A penchant for something," and she paused, "but not a penchant for anything—there's always something there that grabs her interest."

I watched Kate as she seemed to look back into the recesses of her memory and said, "I always thought, at least back in New York, the blood ran hotter in Djuna when she was with a man. Thelma was always something of a surprise to me."

"The blood runs hot, the mind burns brightly—that's Djuna," said Solita, summing up.

I nodded me head absently but thought that was the magic to go with Kurt right now.

Kate and I chatted with Solita and Janet about the afternoon at Natalie's for a while. Out of the corner of my eye I saw Kurt and Djuna head for the door.

"There they go," I said.

"Some things are taking a turn here," said Solita.

We all stood and watched them walk down the sidewalk. After a moment, Kate turned to me, "Okay, handsome, I think maybe we should be heading back across the river." She looked over at the now vacant door, "I don't think we'll be seeing them anytime soon."

I put my arm out and guided her towards the door.

Janet said by way of goodbye, "Oh, Bill, I forgot to tell you best wishes on the sun rising on your new friendship." She smiled at Kate, "It must have been a nice lunch that day at La Quatrième." Behind her, Solita laughed and her eyes sparkled in agreement.

Kate's face broke out in a broad smile of satisfaction at the approval of her friends.

22. Luxembourg Gardens

Kate and I walked up boulevard Saint-Michel in the Sunday morning sunshine and through the iron gates into Luxembourg Gardens. I carried a basket in which Kate had packed a baguette, some croissants, and a bottle of wine. Underneath the spreading shade trees we found a table with some chairs off to the side. Kate spread an oilcloth across the tabletop while I walked over to a kiosk and bought a couple of coffees and brought them back.

"They said they'd meet us here *midi*," I said. "To review the rewrites."

"I can't believe they spent Saturday rewriting. They had something else on their minds when they barreled through the door of La Coupole Friday night."

I laughed, then looked out to one of the garden paths and saw Kurt and Djuna walking towards us. "Here they come."

"Hi, Bill, Kate," Kurt said.

"Such fun to picnic and talk about writing. I've the manuscript right here," and Djuna pulled it out of her handbag and plopped it on the table.

"Let me get you some coffee."

"With cream," said Djuna and smiled winningly at me. She was buoyant.

"Same for me," Kurt added.

I walked over to the kiosk and got a couple more coffees. As I came back I could see Kate and Djuna animatedly talking, Kurt listening. I put the coffees on the table and sat down.

"I got the goddess off her plinth and a woman into the bed," Djuna said, speaking about the heroine in Kurt's novel. She was picking up from where she had left off Friday afternoon at Natalie's dinner table. Turning serious, Djuna said, "I think we should go back and trace how their love story developed since it was intertwined with the history that went on that spring. The romance is the story."

"Yes, the winter and spring of 1919 anchors the tale," I said.

"Before turning to the romance," said Kate, "I'd like to know more about these food missions that were taking Kurt away from Elsa. And the role of Maynard Keynes." Kate turned to me, "Bill, when did you first meet Keynes?"

"At Trier in Germany. I went with Marshal Foch on his train to meet with the Germans. The marshal was meeting with the President of Germany, mostly about nothing. The French had kept the Armistice a military matter since the fighting stopped, so a French-speaking American officer was always detailed to go with them whenever they were meeting the Germans—or anybody else for that matter. This meeting was the first where American and British finance officials from the Versailles conference got a chance to meet the Germans."

"How about you, Kurt?" asked Kate.

"Same thing. I was at Trier. But Trier was right in the American zone, so I was already there. The American command wanted to get an informal word to the Germans that the Americans wanted to get Hoover's food relief off the docks of Rotterdam and up into Germany. The message was that cooperation would be rewarded."

"So they picked you?"

"Yes, if a general speaks, then it's official. If it's just a major, well, then it's just gossip."

"Devious," said Djuna.

"No. Just clever enough to get past the French."

Djuna laughed and took a sip of coffee. Kate's eyes twinkled and she too drank from her cup, but I could see she was thinking.

Setting down her cup, Kate asked, "So what happened in Trier?"

"I was in the railway car with Marshal Foch and the German presidential party," I said. "It was next to the car where the meeting with the Germans was scheduled.

Kurt broke in, "I walked over to that car, the car where the Allied finance officials were to meet the Germans, and climbed the steps into the carriage. I'd been told to get in touch with an American named Sheldon. He was our food guy."

"Did you?"

"Yes, Sheldon told me the deal turned on the Germans turning over their merchant ships to the Allies. Then the food would be released. The French were making all sorts of complications about the German's gold. The French wanted it. The Germans wanted something for it. So I was standing in the back of the carriage when the Germans came in."

"Did they march in dripping Hun arrogance?" asked Djuna playfully.

"No, they were a sad lot, beaten down, dejected. One of 'em looked like a broken umbrella. They stood at one end of the carriage, we were at the other end. A small bridge table separated the two shuffling groups. They bowed stiffly, some of the British returned the bow sort of nervously."

"No arrogance?" asked Djuna with a twinge of disappointment.

"No, but ultimately something better. A small man, well and neatly dressed with a high stiff collar, a shiny baldhead, eyes with extraordinary sorrow in them, stepped forward. He spoke almost perfect English. This was Dr. Melchior."

"This is where Keynes first started his friendship with Melchior?" I asked.

"Yes. Melchior wanted a loan with which to buy food. Keynes gently persuaded him that was not going to happen." Kurt looked reproachfully at Djuna, "All the Hun stuff was in the Congress and the House of Commons."

Then Kurt returned to his story, "But Keynes negotiated, right under the French noses, a small food for gold exchange. So on a small scale, the supply of food began at that moment. Keynes imparted a sense of fairness that Melchior quickly grasped."

Kate warmed to the story and smiled at me. Djuna broke in and asked, "Melchior was not much of an accountant?"

I laughed and said, "No, he was a banker for M.M. Warburg, Germany's biggest Jewish banking house." I turned serious and said to Kate, "I was in the railway carriage with Foch. I saw the Germans come out and start walking down the platform of the railway station. Then I saw Kurt come out of the railway car and casually saunter over to Melchior and speak with him, for, oh, thirty or forty paces. They walked along together talking. Then he looked at Kurt and nodded, almost smiled I think. Kurt veered off and went over to an open door and spoke with an American brigadier general. Then he came out and walked back towards the railway car where Keynes was."

"Yes, just after the Germans departed, Keynes and several others started a bridge game in the railway carriage. I left and went outside and caught up with Dr. Melchior. I spoke with him and the general just as Bill described and then headed back to the railway carriage. Bill came out of Foch's carriage and came over and spoke with me," said Kurt, remembering the day.

"There's more?" Kate asked.

"Yes," I said, "Keynes came out of his carriage and came up to us. He told Kurt that he was dummy at bridge and had a few minutes to talk. He looked at me and asked who I was. I told him, 'Major Lawrence, a military aide attached to the Foch party.'"

Kurt laughed and said to Djuna, "Maynard joked with Bill, 'That must be a barren duty with few intellectual rewards.' Bill laughed. Maynard liked him."

"Then Keynes turned to Kurt and asked him about Melchior," I said. "He was deeply interested. Kurt told him what he had said to Melchior. Keynes rubbed his hands together and said, 'Jolly good show. This is coming together. We must work together where we can.' Then he shook hands with both of us and said that he had better get back to his bridge game and he left."

"Kurt, what did you tell Dr. Melchior?" asked Kate.

"Just what I said earlier. I assured Dr. Melchior that the American command wanted to get the food moving into Germany on a large scale. That's what I told him, and then I went over and told the general that the message had been delivered and understood."

"I see," said Kate. "But the French kept making trouble?"

"The damn French wanted all the German gold to go to reparations, meaning to the French, and none of it for food," said Kurt with disdain.

"There was another complication," I said. "Hoover wanted money for all the food he had brought over from America. He had promised American farmers top dollar for bottom-of-the-barrel bacon."

"Yeah, and Congress forgot to pay for it," Kurt added with a bitter laugh.

"So what was the hang up?"

"The French. They wouldn't agree to anything. That's what I read in the papers. Later Maynard told me that when he was at the Treasury in London preparing for the conference, he wrote the prime minister that if Germany is to be 'milked,' she must not first of all be ruined. So the French deeply upset Maynard's sense of logic."

Kurt turned to me and said, "Hell, Bill was at Versailles. Tell us what happened."

"Nothing. That was the problem. Then some dominos toppled over. The American government told the British that aid was being cut off. The British told the French that they couldn't support the franc any longer. The franc plunged. Then the British pound followed."

"Yeah, right after that the army sent me on another food mission. I went to Spa, Belgium at the beginning of March for a meeting of the Armistice Commission. Maynard was there, so was Melchior. The British government had instructed Maynard to be clear that the merchant marine had to be handed over. The Germans wanted firm assurances that enough food would be delivered to Germany to feed the people until the August harvest."

"So the British were intransigent, too?"

"No, the British admiral just said that 'substantial progress' had to be made."

"Who would decide that?"

"Maynard simply took it upon himself. I watched as Maynard talked with Melchior. He said that the British and Americans would handle the French if Melchior could get Berlin to show some flexibility. Then he turned to an aide and said in an undertone that everyone could hear, 'Can't we break down the empty formalities and talk about truth and reality?'"

"So what did you do, Kurt?"

"The meeting broke up and Maynard went over to the small room where Melchior had an office. I followed. Maynard beckoned Melchior and they walked down a hall and into a vacant room and closed the door. I stood guard outside. Maynard worked it out with Melchior. The two men came out and stood in front of me, deeply emotional, and pressed hands and then Maynard turned and headed down the hall and into the street. I followed."

"Did he say anything to you, Kurt?"

"He said he was returning to Versailles and would attract the attention of the Great Ones."

"And you went back to Koblenz?" asked Djuna.

"Yes, I arrived back the following night. I went to the hospital to see Elsa.

"Yes, the heroine in the book."

"Yeah, right," Kurt continued, "The grounds were quiet. She let me into the quarters she shared with the mother superior."

"Let me pick it up here in your manuscript," said Djuna and she picked up the clump of papers. She turned to Kate and said, "I rewrote it."

"Good. It seemed too crude, blunt."

Djuna rolled her eyes in agreement and then started to read from the manuscript—

"The mother superior has been called to Cologne."

"Will she be back?"

"Possibly."

"Major Eckhart, do you like my new quarters?"

"Yes, very much so."

Looking around Elsa's new quarters, I asked, "You are alone. Won't the maid wonder about visitors?"

"Well, a colonel from our army, a major from your army, it's all the same to a maid."

"There've been German colonels here?"

"Here? Now, in 1919? No. I have that much respect," and she paused and slowly intoned, "now."

"Your husband was an officer."

"Yes, then I was a Frau Hauptman. His wife. The wedding ring separated me from the chase, and major, the chase starts right after the first battle, too many wives, too few men. Then widowhood comes to the community, one casualty notice at a time. Life starts to get hard. Life seems short."

She stood in front of me, eyes down, the soft words of memory burbling up. “Me, the wife of a company commander? Yes, at first I was respected, left at a distance.”

Then she gasped, sobbed a breath. “Then you become a widow. It changes. You are now in need of companionship, so it is believed, you are possibly missing some intimacy, it is thought. This is suggested to you. Then you see gallantry for what it is—an invitation. The war gets worse, life gets more insistent, the concern for your ‘needs’ more intense—the invitations more insistent. Then it is not for you, but for them, their needs.”

She laughed, ‘It is called a Fatherland, right? You lower your eyes and nod your head in acceptance. It is simple patriotism.’ And she looked up eyes sparkling, her smile laughing.”

“I see.”

“You do? It was hard in Germany in 1918. The women in the factories had it worse.”

“The room was warm and lit by candlelight and there was the faint scent of incense. In the hearth a fire was burning down to embers. She came up to me, lightly stroked the skin behind my ear with her fingers, kissed me right below the ear lobe, and said, “What would we do without our American major?”

She kissed me again and with her other arm pulled me into her and pushed her chest into mine. I caught my breath and whispered, ‘Elsa.’

She whispered, ‘Kurt.’ Then she pushed back from me and dropped to both of knees in front of me, she looked up me and then turned and started to fumble with the buttons on my fly.

It took a moment for me to figure out what she was doing. I quickly reached down and grabbed her arms and yanked her up, ‘No. Not this way.’”

I pulled her to me and she buried her face in my shoulder. I said, ‘I will be true to you to the last day. You must believe that.’”

She looked into my eyes and then buried her head in my shoulder again. I said, “I have to go away to Brussels for a few days. About the food. I will be back. We will begin our future, a future together.”

I kissed her on the forehead, then each cheek, and looked at her and said, “Smile.”

She smiled. I turned and walked out the door and went back to my quarters.—

Djuna laid the manuscript down and looked up. She turned to Kurt, "I had to add her perspective to the story. It is what brings dignity to what would otherwise be a tawdry tale."

"I know. There was something else there that night, that maybe I didn't love her, that my cooperation had to be bought, some sense of this was the way it was in the world..." There was a pain to Kurt's voice that I had never heard before. "But I walked out of there feeling like a man, a different kind of man for maybe the first time in my life. A new chapter was unfolding; I had just not imagined the happiness I felt with this woman."

"Yes," said Djuna with real sympathy and she smiled as she said with deep irony: "You reaching down and stopping a woman fumbling at your fly is so out of character for you, Kurt," and Djuna laughed, "that of course you wouldn't know how to write it." Djuna reached out with her hand and gave Kurt's cheek a good pinch and waggle like he was a schoolboy.

Kate and I laughed. Kurt smiled at Djuna with boylike affection.

"Djuna, you captured the story in its bittersweet beauty," said Kate.

Kurt nodded his head in silent agreement. I agreed. It was a beautifully written passage. And Djuna had brought an original sensitivity to the scene.

"Now we return to Versailles?" asked Kate and she looked at me.

"Yes." I set my wine glass down and said, "The logjam over delivering food to the Germans was broken at Versailles. David Lloyd George, the British prime minister, took down the French finance minister?"

"Who was he?" asked Djuna.

"Keynes described him in his book as a short, plump, heavy-moustached Jew, well-groomed, well kept, but with an unsteady, roving eye…"

"Well kept?" Djuna mused, a gleam in her eye. "By whom?"

"Wealthy and powerful interests in France."

"So he wasn't an accountant?" she asked.

"Trickier."

"Yes, the roving eye," she said. Suddenly, Djuna made a show of scanning the horizon of the park with her hand over her brow like a sea captain, just like she had done in Natalie's garden. Then she turned to Kurt, "Keynes being an upper-class Englishman, he didn't like Jews to start with. Right?"

"Actually, Melchior is a Jew. He is the only non-family partner at the merchant bank M.M. Warburg of Hamburg and Berlin. So unlike so many others in his class Maynard makes all kinds of distinctions about people. If you're mediocre…if you're good…if you're brilliant…Melchior is brilliant…his contribution to Germany immeasurable...he became one of Keynes' great friends."

"What did Keynes think of the French?"

"Not much, and he grew more exasperated with the French as time went on. Felt they were always missing the larger picture."

"Yes," I said and shrugged my shoulders in agreement and took a sip from my wine glass. "Back at Versailles, brilliance was lacking. The main event was a meeting of the Supreme War Council. Wilson was back in the States, but Colonel House, his top aide, was there. David Lloyd George ran the show. The British made the case for the ships-for-food exchange. Lloyd George said the French would be sowing the seeds of Bolshevism all across Europe if they objected. Said they'd start the next war. Really laid it on."

"You saw that?"

"Yes, I was a military aide all week."

"Maynard later told me about Lloyd George's performance. But I'd like to hear your side of it," Kurt said eagerly.

"Well, just after Lloyd George finished haranguing the French a messenger rushed in and delivered a telegram. Lloyd George read it and leaped up and said it was from General Plumer of the British Army on the Rhine. German women and children were dying from lack of food; the Germans felt that it would be better to die under a hail of bullets than starve to death. Revolution was in the air."

Kate's face turned grave.

"But French finance minister Klotz still objected," I added.

Kate's look turned to disgust.

"Lloyd George stood up and paraded before the audience like a lawyer before a jury. Then he shouted that women and children were starving and here was Monsieur Klotz prating and prating on about his 'goold'. Lloyd George leaned forward and with a gesture of his hand made like a hideous Jew clutching a moneybag. Poor Klotz sunk back in his chair visibly cowering."

Djuna straightened up like a shot, a delightful expression dancing on her face, and she cooed, "Goold." She bent over to mimic clutching a bag of gold. "Like Shylock and his pound of flesh. Right out of Shakespeare," said Djuna, referring to the play *The Merchant of Venice*.

Kate was enthralled. A broad smile broke across Kurt's face.

"Then the prime minister finished him off. He roared that three names would go down in history as the architects of Bolshevism: Lenin, Trotsky and…'Klotzky'."

"Great theater!" shouted Djuna clapping her hands together. She looked at Kate, "Don't you think so?"

"Yes," agreed Kate and then added, "but children were starving."

I broke in and said, "There's more. The French premier, Clemenceau, later whispered that he was saddled with a finance minister, Klotz, who was the only Jew he ever met that didn't know anything about money."

Kurt laughed, "Hadn't heard that." Then Kurt turned serious, "The reality was quite the opposite. Maynard wrote that Clemenceau wanted to crush Germany and that he did not trouble his head to understand Klotz's overwhelming financial difficulties."

"Yes, I would have dinner with French colleagues," I explained, "and talk about the impossibilities of a large reparation and they would always come back: 'But Germany must pay; for otherwise, what is to happen to France?' The vast suffering of the war overshadowed all other thoughts."

Kate nodded her head sympathetically. The French had suffered horribly.

"Clemenceau wanted a Carthaginian Peace," said Kurt. "Klotz just wanted some money to rebuild."

"Carthage!" exclaimed Djuna. She started to steer an imaginary plow across the oilcloth spread on the table, gritting her teeth and saying, "We'll plow salt into the fields." We all laughed at her mimicry of the great vindictive peace of Roman times.

"You laugh, but someone—me for example, since it will take a writer with a large talent—should write a play called *Versailles*," said Djuna rather immodestly, the absurdities of the Peace Conference stimulating her imagination to new levels.

"Satire or farce?" I asked.

She made a face, "What did Keynes say about Clemenceau?"

"Dry in soul and empty of hope."

"And David Lloyd George?"

"Cast in the role of the enchantress, the Welsh witch…watching the company with six or seven senses not available to ordinary men…"

"Uhm…lot of material to work with. I would say farce—the laughing face of tragedy."

"I agree. A trial of the principals in the theater of the round, the statesmen's words the evidence of the prosecution…" and my words trailed off.

"What is the charge?" asked Kate.

"The next war," I said.

"The crime is not yet committed," said Kate. "Maybe there's hope." She bore into me with an accusatory look; the next war was not going to slip past her on little cat feet. She shifted her tone, "I believe we are back at Versailles and the French have given way on the food issue. Where does the story go from here?"

"Let me see," I said. "Four days later an Allied delegation headed to Brussels to arrange the ships-for-food transaction. Mr. Hoover's food started moving to Germany."

Kate turned to Kurt, "So that was when you left Elsa the second time, to go to Brussels?"

"Yes, but there was one more hang up in Brussels. The Germans had to clearly give up the ships at the beginning of the negotiation. For the British it was all about ships. That was the deal. The British admiral asked Maynard to grease the wheels, make sure there was no hitch."

"Were you at that meeting, too?" Kate asked Kurt. The story was turning into a mystery for her, a journey up a dark political river to a place of an important, but little known, decision.

"Yes, as I mentioned before, I was again called away from Koblenz. The Allies were going to meet with the Germans to arrange the surrender of the German merchant marine. With the surrender of the ships, then Hoover and the Americans would start moving thousands of tons of food off the Rotterdam docks for Germany. The threat of starvation was starting to stalk the streets. There wasn't enough food in Germany to get to the August harvest."

"I met Maynard at the train near where the British were billeted. I had a motorcar and took Maynard and a Royal Navy captain to the hotel where the Germans were staying. We entered the lounge and Maynard pulled over a German secretary and said he wanted to see Dr. Melchior. Melchior came out and we took a lift up to some aide's bedroom."

Kurt looked at Kate, "The bed was unmade, there was an unemptied chamber pot on the floor, a chemise lay across the bed—it surely wasn't Melchior's room. Melchior took no notice. Maynard gave the chamber pot a brief pained expression and then launched right in. He explained that the German's first statement had to be they were giving up the ships. Then everything else would follow as had been agreed. Maynard asked him if he could deliver on this. Melchior looked over at the captain and me and said simply, 'Yes.'"

"We went back downstairs and drove back to the Hotel Britannique. We had dinner with the British delegation."

"Was that it?" asked Kate.

"Mostly, I stayed the entire next day and worked on technical details but the food trains were arriving in Germany by the time I got back to Koblenz."

"And you went out to the hospital and saw Elsa?"

"Yes."

"She knew you had something to do with the food trains?"

"She guessed. And I said 'yeah'."

Djuna picked up the manuscript and said, "Let me pick up the plot." She started to read—

"We can have dinner together. I have new quarters. The mother superior has left and I am taking her place."

"You are?"

"Yes. Aren't you pleased?"

"Of course I am. It's 1919. A new beginning?"

She came up to me, "For us?"

"For us. I will make it so."

"And whither thou goest?"

"You will follow. Always."

She stood up on tiptoe and kissed me. She reached up with her hands to the top of my tunic and started undoing the buttons and said, "Possibly last time I started with the wrong buttons?"

I stood there for a moment as she undid the buttons and then I reached across and undid the button on her shirtwaist at her throat and brushed the collars apart, then the second button and the third. I stopped at the top of her smock and let my hands fall down to my side.

"You let the top of one little dress stop you, major, or is there some subtlety to you that I haven't detected before?"

Kate laughed, Djuna looked up, eyes sparkling. She continued reading:

I looked into Elsa's eyes, "As you wish."

She took off my tunic and set it on a chair and then took me by the hand and led me back towards the bedroom, "We can begin here."—

Djuna set the manuscript down and looked up and smiled. Kate said, "It's beautiful, Djuna. You enveloped the seduction with the mood."

Kurt sat there caught in his own reverie of that memory, mumbling, "Djuna, you understand."

Djuna leaned over towards Kate, her smile cracking wise, "This is where they 'wet bed,' but that's another story."

Kate roared with laughter. Then she turned to Kurt, "So where did this go?"

"The next day I returned to my quarters, but now I had what I really wanted—a love with the woman I wanted more than anything else in the world. I started coming over to dinner several times a week, we spent pleasant time together, joked and dared to think about the future—in 1919 to think about the future was a wonderful feeling."

I nodded in rueful agreement—to have a future in 1919 was indeed a wonderful thing. I thought with Jenny that I had grabbed ahold of mine.

Kate stood up and stretched and looked at the afternoon sun now far over into the afternoon sky, "Maybe we better call it quits for the day?"

"Yes, I have to take Kurt over to the Gare du Nord for the night train to Berlin," Djuna said.

"You don't have to."

"I want to. I want to tuck you into your sleeper. Kiss you goodnight."

Kurt smiled warmly and looked at me with newfound satisfaction. We all stood up. Kurt and Djuna headed north up a gravel path towards her apartment. Kate and I turned and went through the big iron gates of the park and down boulevard Saint-Michele towards river and home.

23. Berlin Remembered

Towards the end of August on a Saturday morning, a messenger knocked on the door of what I now called "our" flat. Kate opened the door, took the little message—*un petit bleu*—and tipped the messenger. The messages were little slips of paper ingeniously blown around Paris in pneumatic tubes.

"It's from Djuna. Kurt's back; he has more manuscript with him."

"Do they want to meet?"

"Yes, late this afternoon. At the Closerie."

"Fine," I said.

With the sun falling in the western horizon, we walked up from the river in the summer sunshine and through the Luxembourg Gardens and along the tree-lined parkway past the fountains to boulevard Montparnasse. Coming to the entrance of La Closerie des Lilas, we entered and I spoke to the maître d'. Over his shoulder I saw Kurt and Djuna sitting at a table on the *terrasse.* I pointed out our friends to the maître d' and he smiled and held out his arm towards their table. We walked over and Kurt stood up; Kurt and I shook hands. Kate sat down next to Djuna and I took a seat next to her.

"Here's some more manuscript, Kate, I've read it through. Your turn," said Djuna, tapping her finger on top of the pile of typewritten pages.

"I'll read through it tonight," answered Kate. "I'm fascinated by the story of Kurt and Elsa." Turning to Kurt, Kate asked, "Could we hear in your words some more about life in Berlin?"

"Wonderful idea," exclaimed Djuna. "Can we, Kurt?"

"Yes," said Kurt. He pondered for a couple moments and then said, "Elsa and I left Koblenz in early September and arrived in Berlin; it was still warm with the last days of summer. I had all my army savings, in dollars, so we were almost rich. A dollar a day bought you the life of a millionaire in Berlin. That's been true ever since; dollars are gold in Berlin. We got a nice flat, second floor, on a side street a couple blocks from the Tiergarten. You could see the trees if you looked up the street."

"Berlin was now the capital of the Weimar Republic?" asked Kate.

"Yes, the constitution was approved by referendum in August. A coalition government under Ebert was in power."

"You were a reporter. What was the big news?" I asked.

"Yeah, I was working for the *Chicago News*. The big story was out on the steppes to the east of Germany. Poland was fighting with Ukrainian nationalists over Ukrainian oil fields. Czechoslovakia traded arms for oil with the Ukrainians. It was sort of like the Balkans before the war." Kurt shrugged his shoulders in fatal resignation and continued.

"Above the tangle of local conflicts was the larger war between Poland and Soviet Russia. As the Communists consolidated power, their military under the Red Army marched west into Poland. It was all very confused in late 1919."

"What did that have to do with the price of wheat in Chicago?" asked Djuna.

"The Ukraine is where a lot of wheat gets grown. A big question all across Europe that September was how large was the harvest going to be, what would food cost during the winter of 1920? Would people be able to eat?"

"Whoever thought Chicago was going to be the center of the world?" said Djuna.

Kurt looked at her like she was a slow child and said, "The price in Chicago puts wheat from the Great Plains on barges down the Mississippi River to New Orleans and then onto ships bound for Europe. A couple pennies in Chicago moves mountains of wheat out on the Plains."

"I thought economics was about billions and now you tell me pennies move mountains," said Djuna, laughing and preening behind her big smile. Her mind just seized on contrasts and absurdities.

Kurt smiled indulgently at her.

"Where did it go wrong, Kurt?" I asked.

He took a sip from his beer and let out a sigh and said, "This may sound incredible, but it may have already been lost by the time Elsa and I arrived in September."

"But the Peace Treaty was barely three months old," said Kate, shocked. "Didn't it settle anything?"

"The Germans hated, and still hate, the Versailles Peace Treaty. So you look at who signed the Treaty on behalf of Germany—a coalition led by the Social Democrats. They took the public relations fall for the Kaiser, the aristocracy, the militarists, the industrialists. The dissidents of the *ancien régime* were all in the background whispering about stabs in the back."

"They were plotting to regain power?" asked Kate.

"Not exactly. They were building a foundation of rottenness upon which some future reactionary government could come to power. Reactionaries first fan dissatisfaction with the existing regime."

"I see," I said. "In Paris, it always felt like we were dictating to the old regime, the militarists that had waged the war. But they were gone."

"Yes, the old regime was swept away in a matter of days after the Armistice," said Kurt. "A real republic took its place. The German people finally were able to assert themselves."

"So the Allies didn't grasp that they were dealing with a new Germany," I said.

Kurt nodded his head back and forth and said, "That was the dumbest thing the Allies did. Have the Social Democrats carry the can for the Peace Treaty."

I understood. Kate glanced at me, her eyes full of understanding at the opportunity lost. She turned to Kurt and asked, "Back to Paris, where were Keynes and the German banker?"

"Well, Keynes went back to England a couple weeks before the Treaty was signed. Dr. Melchior resigned and went back to Hamburg. More importantly, Max Warburg, the head of the Warburg Bank in Hamburg and Berlin, advised the German government not to sign the Treaty. He resigned from the German delegation in Paris and went back to Germany. If he would've stayed, you would've had a Jewish banker signing the Treaty, called the *Diktat* in Germany. Ugly. Who knows where the politics of a Jewish banker signing the Treaty would have gone?"

"A *Diktat,"* said Djuna, turning the word over on her tongue. "Sounds wonderfully sinister."

"Yes, you get the sense of one-sidedness," said Kate with an air of resignation. Then she looked directly at Kurt, "What do you mean about the politics, Kurt?"

"The leader of the right-wing National People's Party, an old-line Prussian nobleman named Graf von Posadowsky-Wehner, screamed in his speeches about robbery—robbery of wealth, robbery of sovereignty—and then asked 'Where are President Wilson's promises?'"

"They didn't like the Treaty?" deadpanned Djuna.

"They damned the republic and its supporters as the 'Jew-Republic' and called them traitors to the nation and 'stock market hyenas.'"

"Stock market hyenas," repeated Djuna and rolled the phrase around on her tongue. "We're not speaking about the Berlin Protestants here, are we?"

"No, in Germany there's banking and then there's money-changing…" and he let his words trail off.

"Money-changing?" repeated Djuna. She knew the answer; she drew the word out in a long hiss, "Jews."

"They called it the Shylock treaty, a vampire sucking the blood out of Germany," replied Kurt.

"Shylock?" mused Djuna. "All these statesmen reading Shakespeare, who would have known."

Kurt sighed and added, "The War Guilt clause of the Treaty was deeply resented by everyone."

We all nodded in agreement. The War Guilt clause had become a running sore in Germany.

"What went wrong, Kurt?" I asked.

"As I said, after the Armistice, the Social Democrats came to power, a republic was formed—the new coalition went about vigorously setting Germany on a positive path despite the chaos of everyday events stemming from the defeat. The Allies should have empowered this government through a peace treaty that promoted a democratic Germany organizing Eastern Europe. That would have been the bulwark against Bolshevism."

"That's a mighty big road not taken," I said.

"Yes, Keynes saw it clearly. He saw that the gamble on Germany had to be taken. Germany had to be given an eastern outlet for its organizing and wealth-creating energy."

"But the Big Three at Paris couldn't see it," said Kate, the singularity of the mistake again hitting home. The Big Three were Premier Clemenceau, Prime Minister Lloyd George, and President Wilson.

"Keynes explained it to them, often eloquently," Kurt said with the fervor of a disciple, "but it was economics talking to the stonewall of politics. Rational economics rarely makes headway against national political sentiment, particularly when the politics turn implacable."

"Implacable," said Djuna, putting another word away in her memory about the Treaty.

Kurt nodded at her and continued, "So they spent a lot of time in Paris fiddling with borders rather than the architecture of what a successful postwar prosperity might look like."

"Fiddling," said Djuna. She turned and looked at me, "Did you fiddle in Paris, Bill?"

"I'm not sure about fiddling, but I worked on a lot of borders," I replied.

"Let's go back to Berlin, Kurt," said Djuna. Kate nodded her head vigorously.

"Well, I met with Dr. Melchior—he was number two at the M. M. Warburg bank—because I had met him in the spring during the food negotiations with Keynes. He introduced me to Max Warburg, the head of the Warburg Bank, who provided me introductions all around Wilhelmstrasse," mentioning the street where all the government ministries are located in Berlin.

"When did you see Keynes again?" I asked.

"Almost immediately. I went with Dr. Melchior to Amsterdam for a conference on banking in October, an early effort to get the Americans to loan Europe money. Keynes was there. He read us a draft of his book, *The Economic Consequences of the Peace*. We were astounded. The insights. The might have been's…" and Kurt's voice trailed off.

"Yes, I remember the Peace Conference breaking up. President Wilson left to board his ship that night. I went to the dance the British had at the Hotel Majestic in Paris and drank with a couple junior British diplomats I had met. One said that the Big Three could not see the future, so how did they expect to control it?" and I shook my head yet again.

"What I saw in Berlin was that only Keynes saw what it was like east of the Rhine. The others were all in the grip of home-country politics; victory can have a dirty underbelly," said Kurt. "They never saw the opportunity in the defeat of Germany."

Kate's eyes opened up, her expression in complete agreement with Kurt's insight. She had never looked at 1918 that way. She had only seen the victory parades, some overall triumph that in a small way had been purchased with her loss.

"So how did the Treaty fix the price of wheat in Chicago?" asked Djuna.

"The price in Chicago simply adds up all the impacts from around the world."

"And if Kurt's impact gets there first…" and Djuna let the thought finish itself.

"That's what the *Chicago News* was paying me for."

"And Dr. Melchior and his friends were tipping you off about who controlled what wheat field in the Ukraine?" asked Djuna.

"No. The bankers didn't know anything much sooner than I did. But in those years, Berlin was where the information was. But it was the German newspaper guys who had it. The news came streaming in from all over Eastern Europe. Elsa was really able to help me here. She read the Berlin newspapers and the two of us would find out where the reporters and editors hung out, the bistros and bars, and I'd start to meet with them, buy them drinks."

"Why didn't we think that of that, Kate?" Djuna said. "Get paid to hang out in bars and bistros."

"We weren't interested in the price of wheat," replied Kate.

Kurt laughed and then continued, "Elsa and I made it a habit to hang out at the Café Josty every afternoon around five. The café overlooks Potsdamer Place, a beautiful place to sit and watch fashionable Berlin pass by. So the German reporters knew where to find me; good information was worth more than a drink. I wasn't in competition with them, so it was just a little something extra for them."

"So you became the best connected foreign correspondent in Berlin?" I said.

"At least on economics," replied Kurt

Kate stood up and took a couple of steps towards the entrance, holding both arms out in welcome. Mina and her daughter Fabienne were coming towards her. Cheeks were kissed and Kate bent down and repeated the ritual with Fabi. Kurt and I stood up, as did Djuna.

"Kurt, Mina is one of my oldest and closest friends in Paris," said Djuna.

"Yes, we met at Natalie Barney's I believe," said Kurt, and he held out his hand. Then he reached out his hand to Fabi and gave her a polite shake in the fashion of an adult to a child. Fabi smiled. I pulled up two more chairs and Mina and Fabi sat down.

"Djuna tells me you are based in Berlin?" asked Mina. Then she spoke to Kurt in German; it was one of her native languages.

"Have you been in Berlin?" asked Kurt.

"Yes, in the early 1920s," she answered. "Like everyone else in Paris."

"That's when Mina started one of her best prose works," said Djuna. "Mina, can I tell them about it; I love it so much."

Mina nodded her approval.

"It starts with a Victorian woman masquerading as a Christian. By metamorphosis, she becomes a caged bird. All the young women become birdlike creatures with rustling bustles and pouting bosoms."

"In their cage?" asked Kurt.

"Yes, the suitors dangle the sweets of marriage in front of them as their only means of escape."

Kate nodded in agreement with that statement. Marriage had seemed the only way out for young women in her generation.

"But in the middle of this birdlike paradise is a tree and in the tree is a serpent…"

Kurt nodded.

"If a maiden tastes the fruit of the tree, the serpent's hiss brings on the blight of impurity and she will disappear into the streets and onto the oblivion of life's dungeon."

"Yes, impurity," muttered Kate in remembered distaste. "The shackle."

"The way out?" asked Kurt.

"Oh, of course—marriage. But the imagined sweets lose their savor after the ceremony; they reap no harvest of promised ecstasy. The marble halls of marriage become another birdcage."

Mina politely clapped her hands, "Well done, Djuna." Kate nodded her head in agreement.

Mina turned to Kurt, "And Djuna reads to me from the manuscript of her new novel, just started, the intensely poetic love story."

My ears perked up, another novel by Djuna could be a commercial success. "Not to intrude, but what do you think of it, Mina," I asked.

"Oh, the love story pours over me with a sensation of beauty such as I never received from any unison of words…Djuna is the novelist who writes like a poet," said Mina.

I agreed with Mina and she would know. Djuna and Mina were possibly the two best writers at combining words into new images, new thoughts, a perspective never before gazed upon. In a literary market that prized originality, taking them to market always left me with a sense of being one short step away from real critical success.

Mina looked at Kurt and then turned to Djuna and said, "He's big, just like Cravan." Arthur Cravan was her long dead husband and Fabi's father. Mina looked back at Kurt and said, "Cravan also had that eloquence of direct statement that Djuna says you have."

Kurt nodded his head in polite agreement at the compliment.

Mina leaned over to Fabi and said, "Your father was like that."

I noticed that Fabi seemed only mildly interested. The never-seen and long-gone father was possibly something of a chimera in her mind. I was sure that once upon a time his absence had been a real hurt for this beautiful little girl.

We continued chatting into the setting afternoon sun, listening to Mina and Djuna talk about New York during and after the war.

The war had been liberating for women in New York. Then the talk turned to the Provincetown Players and the theater after the war and the colorful nightlife that went with it.

Kate laughed at a memory and Djuna asked what that was all about.

"You," answered Kate, grown mellow by the red wine in the warm sunshine.

"Me?"

"Remember that little speak' over on West Fourth Street?" asked Kate, referring to a speakeasy in Manhattan.

"Oh yeah, sort of," said Djuna, an uncomfortable look coming over her face.

Kate turned to the rest of us, "Everyone was drinking and this writer guy turns to everyone at the table and says men are so much superior to women because men can pee and write their name in the snow."

"Kate!" shouted Djuna.

Kate just kept going, "Djuna slams her glass right down and jumps into the conversation and shouts, 'I can make a period!' She all but brought the speak' down."

We all laughed, even little Fabi.

A little bit later we broke it up, Kate and I agreeing to meet Kurt and Djuna the following afternoon.

Kate and I walked back towards the river and I said to Kate, "Do you see how Djuna always picks out the end points of a contrast. She repeats a phrase and almost instantaneously you see the absurdity behind it. I watched her all afternoon volley one point after another back to Kurt, always with her unique twist."

"That's the engine of her creativity, I think," replied Kate.

"Yes, we're watching genius at work," I marveled.

24. Le Café Dome

Kate and I walked along the sidewalk of boulevard Montparnasse in the warm summer sun of early afternoon towards Le Café Dome. We scanned the *terrasse*, searching back into the deeply shaded shadows underneath the awnings, looking for Kurt and Djuna. I saw a boisterous group of Surrealists and waved to Man Ray and André Breton.

"There she is," Kate said, pointing to a wildly gesticulating Djuna, whose hands were going this way and that as Kurt leaned back in his chair laughing. We walked up and pulled chairs out and sat down. A waiter came over and we ordered a couple of beers. The shade felt good.

"Djuna's just been telling me about what her novel *Ryder* is about," said Kurt. "Or at least what she had to edit out."

"Oh, the bodily fluids," I soothed.

"The everyday effluences of our common biology, what makes us people. Urgh," gritted Djuna. She didn't like censorship.

"Let's go back to Berlin in 1920," said Kate. She got out her pad of paper and a pencil.

"Oh no, teacher's getting out her pad. This is going to be intellectual," joked Djuna.

Kate smiled and said, "Kurt, I understand the tragedy that befell you and Elsa in the winter of 1920. What I would like to ask today is how your career as an economics correspondent in Berlin in the 1920s got started. You seem to have been unusually successful at it."

"When Maynard Keynes' book *The Economic Consequences of the Peace* came out, we all read it avidly. It was quite popular in Germany. He felt that a successful peace had to be based on successful economics. The peace could never dictate the economics. Economics works by a different set of rules."

"What rules?" asked Kate.

"Ah, the little girl—teacher's pet—asking after the rules," chided Djuna.

"No Djuna, it's about rules being in conflict with rules. Just your cup of tea," replied Kate rather curtly. Djuna dipped her head at the compliment.

"Ladies," said Kurt. "Keynes was the one person in a position to be heard that argued that Europe could not prosper without an equitable, effective and integrated economic system. He was the only person looking at the whole."

"The peace didn't do that?" asked Kate.

"Hardly. Keynes argued the Treaty did the opposite."

"You say opposite. What do you mean?" asked Kate.

"The politics and the economics were in conflict with one another," answered Kurt. "That has been my overall framework for looking at the tangled economics of Europe throughout the 1920s—the vantage point if you will."

"So his book guided your journalism?" asked Kate.

'Yes, you analyzed the economics to understand the impact on the politics. And vice versa."

"When did you next see Keynes?"

"Often. Through my friendship with Dr. Melchior, Keynes invited me to write a series of in-depth articles on Germany and Eastern Europe for the Manchester *Guardian* in 1922."

I cut in, "Those were the famous *Guardian* supplements, Kate, and were printed in five languages. They were all the talk among the political circles in every European capital in 1922."

Kate looked at me, "So you've been following the argument all along, Bill?"

"Yeah, I followed the events because I had seen the Paris Peace Conference in person. I made a point of covering some of the economic conferences in the early 1920s to see what might change. There was a good market for magazine articles about the conferences—beautiful hotels, distinguished statesmen, serious business."

Kate of course understood the hooks for the magazine articles. "What did you see?" she asked.

"Always too little, too late," I replied.

Kurt jumped back into the conversation, "But I want to make a point, Kate, about the news before the era of the big conferences. I was hired in the fall of 1919 to report agricultural news out of

Central Europe back to Chicago, and later New York. What I saw at the end of Keynes' book was his statement that if agricultural trade was not reestablished with Russia, then the price of wheat in 1920-21 must be scarce and dear. That was a nuts and bolts prediction right where I was working. It told me what to look for. The news from Berlin would move the price of wheat on the Chicago exchanges. People think that the price of wheat has something to do with the harvest in the Dakotas. Actually it had a lot more to do with wheat coming off the steppes of the Ukraine."

"Communist wheat from Russia rocks the price in Chicago," marveled Djuna.

"Yes. Keynes said, 'the world markets are one.' It sounds simple, but he is the only one who really meant it."

"Not Germany, not France, not Monte Carlo?" asked Djuna.

"One market," answered Kurt. He looked at her quizzically, "Monte Carlo?"

Djuna shrugged her shoulders and said, "Just checking to see if you know your stuff."

"What did that mean for you?" asked Kate, getting the conversation back on track.

"Readers back in the States thought I was prescient. My career prospered."

"And what did it mean for Germany?" continued Kate.

"In the last pages of his book, Keynes said that Germany has to be the creator and organizer of wealth for her Eastern and Southern neighbors."

"And the Treaty didn't do that?" asked Kate.

"The Treaty hobbled the big draft horse of Central Europe."

"And bread costs more in New York as a result?" asked Djuna. "And Monte Carlo?"

"Yes. That is one of the consequences of the hidden economic currents."

"Ah, wonderful," marveled Djuna, "a hidden current—the best kind—changes the price of bread in New York."

Kate smirked at Djuna and continued, "So after Elsa died, you continued in Berlin, Kurt?"

"Yes, Dr. Melchior encouraged me. He read from Keynes' book—'We are at the dead season of our fortunes.' There was nowhere to go but on, he counseled."

"Did Maynard say anything more about Klotzky?" asked Djuna, eagerly.

"Klotz," corrected Kurt. "Keynes said if he were the Americans he would not give any money to those governments that engineered the Peace Treaty. He said the governments were just false idols which had survived the war. He said they'd just squander the money and he named Klotz in particular—'M. Klotz will use the money to put off the day of taxation a little longer.' And he went on about the other governments. Keynes was disillusioned with the Paris Treaty."

"How was Germany to rebuild Central Europe?" I asked.

"With a loan from America?" replied Kurt.

"A loan from America?" asked Kate a little skeptically.

"That's what the Americans thought," laughed Kurt.

"Yes, that came up again at Genoa in 1922, didn't it?" I said.

"Yes, but always with the same answer from the Americans; they were not going to be the lender of last resort." Kurt shook his head sadly.

"Where did the great German inflation come from?" asked Kate, referring to the hyperinflation of 1923.

"Once again, Maynard saw it coming. He quoted Lenin in *Economic Consequences* that the best way to destroy capitalism was to debauch the currency, that it engaged all the hidden forces of economic law on the side of destruction."

There was a rustle behind me as two men came up to our table. The larger one said, "Ah, a bourgeois quoting Lenin. I said I had to hear this myself." The new voice came from André Breton, who was now standing next to Djuna. Man Ray was standing next to him.

"You must join us," Djuna said.

Breton pulled up a chair and sat down next to Djuna. Man Ray sat down next to Kate.

Breton squinted at Kurt, "Maynard? Is that your friend Keynes?"

"Yes."

"The bourgeois married to the Diaghilev dancer?"

"Yes, that's him."

"What could such a great artist see in an economist? Like marrying a bank teller."

"Or Mina Loy being cooped up with a French accountant," laughed Kate.

André looked quizzically at her, "A poet with an accountant? The absurdity…"

I laughed and said to André, "Keynes is quite talented."

"He can really turn a striking phrase," Djuna added. "No telling what he could do if he took it up seriously. The writing that is," said Djuna.

"Degas did the ballet. How do we do the economics?" asked Man Ray.

"I see it," said Djuna rather excitedly, using her hands to frame a canvas. "We were talking about a disembodied tongue flickering away in an eternal flame—"

"Yes, your little book…" said Breton. He turned to Man Ray, 'I told you she was one of us."

"Yes, the beautiful metaphors that both hide and reveal the meaning," added Man Ray. He could speak Surrealism fluently.

"I thought of disembodied lips floating on a silvery sky—the incarnation of love floating by itself," said Djuna.

"That would be a beautiful image, Djuna," said Man Ray, stroking his chin in thought. You could see him file away the image in his photographic memory.

Djuna continued, "The title of the book *The Economic Consequences of the Peace* floats on a silvery sky above the message…"

"What's the message?" asked André.

"I don't know yet," said Djuna. "But there's a beautiful irony here because the word 'peace' is not about peace but really about war."

"Of course, a striking irony. I see the power of what you are saying, Djuna. We must speak of this some more at another time, another place," said Man Ray. "You have such a sense of image."

Kate watched this exchange with intense fascination, the real players were at work today.

"Where were we?" I asked. "I think Kurt was going to tell us about the Great Inflation in Germany."

"Yes," Kurt said. Then he spoke directly to Breton, "I was just telling Kate that Lenin said the best way to destroy the capitalist system was to debauch the currency."

"I come from a simpler time when only girls and women could be debauched," said Djuna.

"In Germany in 1923, first they debauched the currency, the women and girls came next."

"Oh, I think Kate and I saw the preview in 1921," said Djuna.

"There goes the sense of middle class identity," I said.

"Could this happen in American?" asked Djuna with an air of impish expectation.

"Inflation or debauchery?" asked Kurt.

"Well both. You can't get to the one without starting with the other, right?" Djuna said.

"All this anger just because the post office censored your book?" I asked.

"Yes," snapped Djuna and she smiled wickedly. She really didn't like them.

"Kurt, after 1924, stability and prosperity came back to Germany. How did that happen?" asked Kate. "What changed?"

Kurt looked thoughtful for a moment, and then he brightened and posed a question, "The big thing?" He took a sip from his beer, "The Americans finally came through with the Dawes Plan in 1924—sort of. Germany pledged national assets, money was loaned to Germany, and reparations were paid to France. New York had already poured a lot of money into Germany; it wanted to stabilize its prospects."

"So the peace hasn't completely failed?" said Kate, making the question a statement.

"Not yet. Now a lot of Europeans say that it's New York that is playing the international Shylock."

"My, how Shakespeare travels," said Djuna. "But I think the Episcopalians control the banks in New York."

"The reparations issue tarnishes everything it touches," said Kurt. "Even Episcopalians."

"Yes, that damned spot, the money spot," said Djuna. "Out, damned spot," she said mimicking the great line by Lady MacBeth.

"Nevertheless," said Kate with hard-edged insistency, "The present arrangements may allow for some state of peace and prosperity."

"Because of the Episcopalians?" asked Djuna incredulously.

Kurt laughed. "Yes. Today, Dawes bonds are trading above par in New York. New York is the source of German credit," said Kurt. "As long as New York holds up, Germany holds up," he added quietly.

"That worries you?" said Kate.

"Yes, everything is interconnected. If we could have started off in 1919 with a clean slate like Maynard proposed, then all these devilish interconnections based on a bad treaty and poor economics would be gone."

"Out, out—devilish interconnection," Djuna shouted gleefully. "See, I know some Shakespeare, too."

Kurt looked at her indulgently and said, "Just adding more money, more bonds to a bad structure…where does it go?"

"I see," said Kate. "Papering things over."

"Time to change the wallpaper," whispered Djuna to Breton.

Kurt took a long draught from his beer and explained, "The war loans never created any profitable assets which would generate the income to fund repayment. Therefore, payment can only be made by lowering living standards."

"So these are bad loans?" asked Kate.

"Real rotten apples. That's Maynard's key insight: demanding repayment is not serious politics. One country cannot go into another country and force repayment. The French tried that in 1923 when they occupied the Ruhr in Germany. The effort failed."

"So we wait, possibly at the edge of a volcano," said Kate.

I broke in, "One of the poets said we live in an age of dollars and no sense."

"That's an almost eternal condition," said Kurt with a laugh.

"Ah, a truth speaks," mused André Breton. Man Ray nodded his head in solemn agreement.

"That is the volcano," I said. "It's almost ten years later and they're still arguing about reparations, about war debts—it's like the war is trying to claw us back into the trenches."

"Well, Bill, I can at least understand what you're saying—clawed back into the trenches. We can get Man Ray to paint it," said Djuna, and she turned and said to Man Ray, "Terrible tentacles oozing out of the mud." Man Ray nodded his head.

"Yes, one labeled 'reparations,' another 'interwar loans,' and so on. They never let us go," said Kurt.

"Well, Man Ray can take this on," said Djuna. "The truth always needs painting."

"The German Expressionists already have," said Kurt glumly.

"Yes, but they are overwhelmed with sorrow and anger," said Man Ray.

Kate looked at Man Ray and said, "Yes, but that was the reality about the last war."

"Yes, but Surrealism will use irony to make a larger statement about all war," he said.

"I agree," I said. "Not only all war, but a warning about a next war.

Man Ray nodded his head in agreement.

"That's been Keynes' focus since 1919. Averting another war," said Kurt. "He feels only an uncompromising statement of the truth can avert catastrophe."

"Of course," said André. "That's in the Surrealism Manifesto. Only statesmen deal in falsehood, not artists. Can an economist be an artist? Or just married to one?"

I smiled and nodded my head wisely.

Kate took a breath and leaned back, "I see." She looked over at me and followed up on Keynes, "Bill, you said you hadn't seen Kurt since Genoa. That had something to do with Keynes, too, didn't it? What was that about?"

"There was a big international conference held at the Grand Hotel Miramare in Santa Margherita outside Genoa on the Italian Riviera in April 1922. A lot of the big conferences in those years were held in the sumptuous resorts of North Italy. I went to write a feature article about the final diner, the beauty of the resort, the personalities involved. Things like that. Thought I could shop it to *Vanity Fair*. And I did."

"Bill already knew they wouldn't decide anything," Kurt threw in.

"The French took the subject of reparations off the agenda—the only subject really worth talking about—and the French prime minister refused to attend…" I said.

"Was that Klotzky?" asked Djuna.

Kurt laughed, "No, it was Poincaré, a small minded provincial lawyer with the mind of an accountant."

"That bad?" joked Djuna. "Where do the French find all these accountants?"

Kurt rolled his eyes.

"With the French out, the Americans refused to attend since no 'business' could be done," I continued.

"Americans only do 'business,' never diplomacy," said Djuna turning to Kate in pseudo-explanation, just playing with the words for Kurt's benefit since she didn't give a hoot about any of it.

Kurt beamed at her. She batted those big eyelashes, jangled the bracelets.

"Why even have the conferences then?" asked Kate.

"Lloyd George, in one of his last gasps as prime minister, had the idea of reviving Europe's economy by rebuilding the Soviet Union. That would boost Britain's export trade."

"And Germany would have benefited for the first time from one of these international financial shenanigans," said Kurt.

"But Keynes was out of the British government, wasn't he?" asked Kate. "He was working for a British newspaper, you said."

"He was, but he brought an ingenious exchange rate scheme loosely based on a gold standard to the conference. Get the conversation rolling, he said."

"What would it do?"

"Finance the reconstruction of the Soviet Union among other things."

"It was a great idea," said Kurt with remembered satisfaction.

"What went wrong?" asked Kate.

"The United States refused to play—again—its role of lender of last resort."

Kate laughed, "Not part of Harding's 'Return to Normalcy' program."

"It's worse than that, Kate," I said. "America fought bravely in the war and then deserted on the peace."

"That's why the peace failed," added Kurt.

"There was an American counterrevolution in 1920 that gave power to the moral dictatorship of congressmen from rural districts…" I said. "The rural reactionaries."

"Political power went into the hands of businessmen with the narrowest of aims; they simply wanted profits," added Kurt.

Djuna pouted and said, "And they took over the post office, too."

We all laughed.

"What did the French accountants want?" asked Djuna.

Kurt rolled his eyes in disbelief.

"Bingo," said Djuna.

Kurt sat down his beer and said, incredulity in his voice, "You won't believe it. The French wanted the Reds to honor the Moscow streetcar bonds from the time of the Czars." He shook his head at the memory of the misguided obstinacy of the French.

"Ring-a-ding-ding," sang out Djuna, pulling on an imaginary streetcar bell rope. "Make those books balance."

Kate laughed and then looked directly at me, tapping her fingers on the tabletop to bring attention to her next question.

"You said you saw Kurt there. What was that about?"

I looked at Kurt and he nodded his head for me to continue. It had all been hush-hush.

"Kurt and I were talking out in the Grand Park behind the hotel at the end of the conference—standing on a walkway under a spreading palm tree in the warm spring sunshine. Suddenly Maynard Keynes came striding up the walkway looking for Kurt. He saw Kurt and then he saw me. He squinted at me searching for the remembrance and then he said, 'Yes, the railway car. Trier, 1919.' I nodded in agreement."

Kurt added, "Maynard said he wanted to see me after the conference and talk about the Soviet Commissar for Foreign Affairs, Georgi Chichirin, who he rather liked."

I added, "Keynes took both of us into his conversation. With good humor, he said, 'Chicherin is a rather amiable and agreeable snake but we could have made a start except for the French.'"

"An economist with wit," exclaimed Djuna. She looked at me, "Is that the end of the French accountants?"

I laughed, nodded yes, and continued, "Kurt said he agreed completely. Keynes continued, 'We act as high priests…the heretics must repeat our creed…instead of trying to disentangle the endless coil of impossible debt we merely propose to confuse it further with another heap of silly bonds. The belief that all this protects and maintains the sacredness of contract is the opposite of the truth.'"

These words sank in on Kate. She slowly nodded in understanding.

Kurt broke in, "But part of the reconstruction plan would have had Russia exporting wheat. The world price would have fallen. A lot of people in New York and Chicago would have liked to understand that—before the news, ahead of the crowd."

"And make a big profit?" asked Kate.

"Huge," replied Kurt.

"What happened?"

"Nothing. Then the Russians and Germans got together by themselves and cancelled each other's debts and started a program of cooperation, including military exercises. The German army now secretly maneuvers on the Russian steppe. When German boots march into France next time they will have Russian mud on them."

Kate was taken aback by the last statement. "Next time?" She looked at me.

"My endless anxiety. You know that," I said.

Kurt watched our dismay and then continued, "But then Keynes really said something striking: 'Both Lloyd George and I believe that Lenin is a supreme opportunist and he would have taken the bribe—the western credits. If only the French and Americans…'" and he let his words trail off.

Kate looked questioningly at Kurt, almost beseechingly.

"Once again history might have taken a better turn," said Kurt. "But the ghost of Versailles stalked every one of those postwar conferences. Yesterday's mistakes had an iron grip on the throat of any statesman proposing something new, something that might work."

"So, at Genoa, what did Keynes want you two to do?" asked Kate. She looked at me to continue.

"Keynes said to both of us, 'Write it up.' Remember, Kurt was also writing for the supplements rolling out from the Manchester *Guardian* under Keynes' editorship. I was freelancing. He wanted Kurt to carry the ideas forward in the articles he was writing."

"So you had your instructions. Was that all?"

I took a breath, "There was more. Keynes got ready to leave when suddenly he turned around and faced Kurt and said, in a rising voice almost like a barked command, 'Eckhart, you understand!' He paused and smiled—'Few do.'"

"And?"

"Keynes turned on his heel and walked back to the hotel, shoulders forward in that loopy stride he has."

Kate looked at Kurt with an appraising eye. You could see she understood that Kurt did understand and at a profound level.

Djuna broke in, "Did he go back to his ballet dancer?"

"Why yes, he married her." Kurt laughed, "The clever dog caught the wild duck."

"I didn't know economics could be such fun," said Djuna as she clapped her hands.

Breton now spoke up, "Djuna, we must talk about this. There needs to be a Surrealist understanding of what looks like crass bourgeois politics."

She laughed, "And we'll get Man Ray to do the painting."

"Yes," said Breton very thoughtfully. "But what message floats on the silvery sky…"

"Like love's lips," finished Man Ray.

"That is the question," pronounced Djuna very emphatically, pounding a fist into her open palm.

Kate laughed and then half-seriously asked, "Kurt, what happened to Dr. Melchior?"

"He's the German representative to the League of Nations finance committee. In fact, he's the chairman. Few men have done so much for Germany. He married his longtime mistress, the French romance novelist Marie de Molènes."

Again, Djuna clapped her hands and exclaimed, "Sounds like the dour dog caught the clever duck!"

We all laughed. A look of consternation crossed Breton's face and he said in a quizzical tone, "A banker marrying a novelist? An economist marrying a ballerina? Possibly it is more Bohemian at the very top than I had imagined."

We all laughed. I stood up and said, "Great fun. Kate and I need to be going or I will have a very tired duck on my hands. Isn't that what you say, honey?"

"No, sometimes I say I'm such a goose. It's entirely different."

"I see you as a swan," said Breton in the grand manner.

Kate blew him a kiss.

I looked at the group and said, "I was thinking of having a house party towards the end of September—we can celebrate the sales of your new novel, Djuna. If Kurt could come over from Berlin, we could finish editing his novel, or come close." I turned and looked over at him, "Kurt?"

"Sure, I don't see any problem," and he looked longingly at Djuna.

"Done," said Djuna in her snappy New York way. She returned Kurt's gaze with one of welcome expectation.

I turned to Breton, "You will bring the Surrealists?"

"*Bien sûr,*" he said. "And you will bring the swan?"

"Of course."

25. Fête

My drawing room was crammed with chattering guests, the housekeeper busily serving champagne from behind a little table. Mina's daughter Fabi was circulating with a tray of hors d'oeuvres. Djuna was standing next to a table where a stack of her new novel *Ryder* was displayed; she was chatting with Mina. The novel was a surprise bestseller in New York—a surprise at least to her publishers. They had not figured out that the first book published by an American woman to challenge American laws on obscenity would be a barnburner. The book was flying off the shelves. Djuna's drawings in the book were sexually subversive and the post office—great critics of both her art and writing—insisted two be pulled. Djuna lived to rattle the American bourgeoisie.

Across the room next to the tall windows Eugene Jolas and his wife Maria were holding forth with Elliot Paul, who was accompanied by a beautiful woman rumored to be a *Vogue* fashion model. Jolas was the founder and editor of the experimental literary journal *transition* that published Surrealist and Dada art and avant-garde writing pretending towards the revolutionary. Of course the revolutionary is a hard target to hit; too often you get cocktail party radicalism or champagne socialism. Nevertheless, a strength of the journal was its publication of translations from many of the foreign writers working in the Surrealist and Expressionist traditions. You could find a whole world in one small journal, and of course it was always on the shelf at Sylvia Beach's bookshop.

Jolas, his pretty wife on his arm, was pressing the big, jovial Elliot Paul on the power of art to transform politics. Elliot, one of the grand presences on the Left Bank, guffawed at the overreaching intellectual pretension of Jolas's statement and replied, "The question of the hour is who is the prime minister and whether his mistress is to be trusted?" Across the room, Djuna heard the barb and smiled; she moved to break away from her conversation partners.

Elliot was a long-time newspaperman on one of the English-language Paris dailies and a novelist unique from the hundreds of other expatriate American café writers in Paris—he had three published novels to his credit. Elliot also had an almost solitary distinction on the Left Bank—he was a great admirer of Gertrude Stein's writing, whose writing was not well appreciated and even less well read in Paris—and everywhere else. She could not understand why James Joyce stood on top of the Paris writing pantheon while her writing was consigned to the shadows.

Djuna strode across the room and took up position next to Elliot and I strained to hear the conversation. Djuna sallied forth, "I understand the prime minister and his mistress—his presence brings the powerful and the clever to her salon—for what is a Parisian salon but a mix of art, scandal, and politics."

"Yes, but it is scandal which transforms politics, not art," said Elliot, making a sidewise glance at Jolas as if he had stolen the table silver.

"But, Elliot, who cares? We're on a different continent from the Protestant Ethic."

"Thank the gods for that," said Elliott and he beamed a smile full of roguish anticipation at the *Vogue* fashion model.

"But tonight is about art," said Djuna. "What I don't understand is your enthusiasm for Gertrude. Do you weigh art by the pound?" Djuna was making fun of Gertrude's thousands and thousands of pages of impenetrable prose.

"Now, Djuna…"

"You understand Jim's greatness, Elliot, but standing his work next to Gertrude's?" Jim was James Joyce and Djuna was almost the only writer in Paris on a first-name basis with him, partially as a result of a great interview she did with him in 1922, which was published in New York. Hopefully she would do that for Kurt next year.

"Djuna," and Elliot launched in with great enthusiasm, "Gertrude's work has such a feeling for the continuous present…"

"You mean it's interminable. You can tell that just by thumbing the pages."

"Now, Djuna, just because…"

"She always parks me with Alice…"

"Have a little heart; your friend Mina gave her a great introduction at Nancy's salon last year…"

"No one's perfect," Djuna said tartly with a bright smile on her face, which she flashed towards Mina.

Elliot pressed his point, "Wait a minute, Djuna. Mina said Gertrude was a prophetess and that the younger writers had dug into her manuscripts for all sorts of riches. You jealous or something?"

"Me? Jealous of Gertrude?" and she looked down at Elliot with a frown. "Honest, that thought had never crossed my mind," and she laughed.

Elliot laughed and said, "I hear your novel is selling well in New York."

"Yes, thank God. I need the money."

Mina came walking over and stood next to Djuna and nodded at Elliot. She asked, "What's the question?"

Bob McAlmon, reed thin, handsome and cocky, perked up when he heard Mina's question; he was expert at having an answer for all unanswered questions. He sauntered over next to Mina, champagne glass in hand, and asked, "The question?" and he paused before continuing, "We're getting near the end. What Paris once offered is no longer here."

"The end?" asked Djuna. "I'm just beginning."

Janet Flanner came over and nudged into the circle. Looking at McAlmon she said, "*The Little Review* says the new world order has changed and that to reform the world-mind is too big a job for art."

"Well, the world is reasonable…but something's wrong," said McAlmon.

Janet let out one of her brittle laughs, "Well, I'm reasonable, it's the others who are mad."

"Let's see, now—the question… the end… something's wrong…the others are mad…so do I have everyone right?" asked Djuna. "I would think the subjects are too small for art."

"There's a sense in the air…" said Mina.

"Never mind the air; what do you think?" asked Djuna.

"I only fear fear itself," replied Mina, which got everyone else's head nodding in agreement.

"Fear?" asked Djuna.

"Too old for love, too young for death," sighed Mina.

"Oh, come now, Mina—too old for love? You, who have 'gentlemaned' with the handsomest of the handsome all these years," said Djuna, quoting 'gentlemaned' from *Ladies Almanack* in its ironic sense. Everyone laughed. Mina smiled enchantingly.

Elliot laughed, too, and, looking at Mina, quoted from the *Ladies Almanack*, "Delight is always a little running of the Blood in Channels astray!" It was Djuna's turn to beam at Elliot's recognition of her writing.

Djuna turned to the *Vogue* fashion model and said, "Are you going to run astray outside the channels? Tonight?"

"I always try to stay a private delight," she said with a sardonic smile under ironical eyebrows. She flashed a knowing glance at Elliot.

Djuna eyed the fashion model with a long look, took a speculative glance at Elliot, and replied, "Remember the best and most satisfying love is that of the other's bed."

The fashion model made an elaborate curtsey holding her skirt out and said, "Madame, your lesson will be my instruction."

Djuna's eyes flashed with good humor and she said coquettishly, "There was a time when I would crawl in your bed and show you…"

The fashion model smiled fetchingly, Elliot whispered to Djuna loudly, "It's my channel that's going astray tonight…find your own…"

As I listened to the repartee from across the room, I was interrupted with a greeting from over my shoulder. "Good evening, Bill," said a friendly voice, a pat on the shoulder by way of welcome.

I turned around, mildly startled, "Oh, hi, Ford. How are you tonight?" Ford Madox Ford was a best-selling English novelist; he had published Djuna in his highly regarded *Transatlantic Review* a couple years back, the best of the little magazines published in Paris in the 1920s until *transition* came along. Hemingway had guest edited one of the editions. Ford liked to misunderstand Djuna. With Ford was his current companion, the writer Jean Rhys.

Djuna saw Ford, looked around for Kurt, and stepped away from her circle. She walked over and dragged Kurt away from André Breton and a small group of gesticulating Surrealists. She came striding over pulling Kurt along behind her. "Oh, Fordie," she cooed—you knew the rapier was not too far away, "I've decided to follow your example. I've got a new roommate, too." Djuna pulled Kurt close to her and put her arm around his waist and hugged him.

Djuna turned to Jean and said, "Hi, Jean, tell me, did you teach Fordie those exotic sexual tricks?"

"No," drawled Jean. "He's too busy writing," she said with the sting of a wasp.

Djuna turned to Ford and behind the smile of a satyr said, "Oh, I so wanted you to give me some pointers."

Ford stumbled on his words, "Always a pleasure to speak with you, Djuna."

Kurt stuck out his right hand to shake Ford's hand, "I've just finished reading the last novel in your war series. Brilliantly done." Kurt looked at me, "Don't you think these are some of the best to come out of the war, Bill?"

"Why, yes. Dos Passos for the Americans and Ford for the British—of course." I felt I had to add Dos Passos; he was one of my writers.

Ford mumbled, "Thank you, what did you say your name was again?"

"Kurt, Kurt Eckhart. Here, let me get you some champagne," and Kurt led Ford away by the arm towards the champagne table, speaking to him animatedly about his four war novels, the tetralogy *Parade's End.*

Djuna pulled Jean over towards us, saying, "It's hard to put the naughty into that little boy. So serious."

Jean laughed. "Yes, he mostly admires my writing. But not always—sometimes me."

"The old boy has put out some of the great novels on the war," I said.

"You really mean that, Bill?" Djuna asked.

"Yes, his famous line from *Parade's End* sums up the war—'No more Hope, no more Glory, no more parades for you and me anymore. Nor for the country…nor for the world, I dare say…None…Gone.'"

Djuna nodded her head, pondering the words. They were good ones. She liked their arrangement.

I took a sip of champagne, "It's all there."

"None...Gone…of course," she said, savoring the words' bleakness. She looked around the room. "Oh, Kate has broken free. I want to talk with her. I'll leave you to be watchman of the night." She strode off across the drawing room, twisting around groups of talkers, nodding to friends.

"Your friend, he was in the war?" Jean asked.

"Yes, he was wounded just before the Armistice."

"Ah, yes—the wounded. They have stared into the abyss and come back to tell us. I want to hear what he says." She turned and looked at me and whispered, "You know, Bill, these words will be with us until the end of our days; they haunt Ford."

"Yes, probably far beyond our time, Jean. The consequences of the war are going to travel through time and will carry the literature with them." I sighed.

"Yes, a long time…" Jean turned and went across the room to where Kurt and Ford were talking.

Hearing a rustle behind me, I turned and there was Sylvia Beach and Adrienne Monnier coming through the door. Our Crowd was showing up in force tonight. Sylvia was smiling like a pixie, humor glistening from her bright eyes. Adrienne smiled from a handsome face framed by lush golden brown hair; she was a stout presence surrounded by a vast encircling gray satin skirt.

Sylvia looked around the room, saw Eugene Jolas and his wife, and said, "Oh, there's Jolas. I must speak with him. His magazine sells and sells. Always a bright spot."

Adrienne continued scanning the room, "Oh, and André Breton," she said, mentioning the leader of the Surrealists. "With Man Ray," mentioning the great American Surrealist painter and photographer. "And of course, Kiki." She patted my arm and said to me, "Breton's magazine *La Révolution surréaliste* has been a bestseller this year in both our bookshops. And Man Ray's postcards sell and sell."

I looked at her quizzically.

"Some of them have clothes on. The others—the ones you like—are with the *bouquinistes* down on the river," Adrienne said, laughing.

Sylvia laughed and said to me, "The Surrealists can always be counted on to stir a tempest in a teapot. One of them wrote last year that the Marquis de Sade simply wished to give back to civilized man the strength of his primitive instincts. That kicked off a two-year debate among the Surrealists. And of course everyone else wanted to follow it. So the magazine has sold and sold."

"I'm afraid primitivism is staging a big comeback…there are forces that want to throw Europe back into the dungeon," I said.

"Well, yes, but the subject of sex is a hardy perennial…inside or outside of a dungeon…and you combine it with primitivism and…" Sylvia said with laughing eyes. She nodded over at Kiki of Montparnasse to make her point. Kiki was standing next to Man Ray in a black dress a little too small with a rather large crowd of admirers around her. She was chatting like a magpie.

"We so like your singing," one of the admirers interrupted—to Adrienne's disbelieving amusement.

Adrienne smiled and said, "Now that Kiki's got everyone in her spell, I'm going to go sneak a talk with André."

Sylvia laughed and watched Adrienne walk away. She turned to me, "You have all the luck, Bill. I try to run a business and wind up babysitting the avant-garde."

"What happened?" I coyly asked. Actually, I'd been hearing boatloads of gossip all summer.

"Scott and Zelda came over for the summer. They were here for four months. Now Scott's a great pal, but he streaked across the rue de l'Odéon, dazzling us for the moment...but confusion attends his every activity…" and Sylvia let the words hang.

"Then the Joyce family came back from vacation…the demands of that family…" and her words trailed off dragging years of weariness and fatigue behind them. It was obvious that the passion had gone out of Sylvia's devotion to the Joyce cause.

"And our other great friend?" I asked while arching an eyebrow into a question.

"Oh, I got a letter from Ernest. He's in Sheridan, Wyoming. Pauline gave birth to a baby boy named Patrick. The fishing's wonderful and he finished his war novel. You remember, that's the one he was talking about all the time last winter before he left."

"Yes, of course. Do you know much about it?"

"It's a doomed romance, set during the war."

"The book ends during the war?"

"I believe so."

"What happens next?"

"He said he'd revise it over the winter and that *Scribner's Magazine* would serialize it in the spring. Publication will be in the fall."

"Well, that really fits my timetable. I'm going to try to get Kurt's novel sold by the end of the year. It's really about the failure of the peace more than the tragedy of the war. So it should complement the discussion surrounding Hemingway's book."

"Shrewd. But then you always are, Bill." She looked across the room and said, "Oh, there's Djuna. I want to talk to her about getting some copies of her little chapbook. I'm getting lots of inquiries."

Word about Djuna's *Ladies Almanack* had spread across the Left Bank. Sylvia turned and started across the room to where Djuna and Kate were chatting.

Kurt came up to me and said, "Ford's a fascinating guy. Really has an eye for how the war twisted British society out of shape, how it undercut the foundations of the whole country. You don't see that from the trenches."

"Yes, you kill enough young men and people start to ask why?"

"Yeah. Or rail against the sky, howl at the moon. That's what they're doing in Germany." Kurt sighed, "You don't get the peace right and…" The thought hung in the air.

"I know," I said.

He nodded in conclusion and then he looked over at the circle of women around Kate and Djuna that now included Sylvia, Mina, Janet and Solita Solano. His expression changed and he playfully said to me, "I still think maybe you kept her from going across the river."

"Kate?"

"Yeah, she's comfortable with women on the other side of the river. You could see that in Berlin and here…in the cafes…"

"I think she's simply learned how to move comfortably in the society of all women. They really support each other. Important for a writer. This era on the Left Bank of Paris is something special…maybe it will always be something special."

"Yeah, they all seem to get along so well," he said looking over at the group of chattering women, "but I still think I saw something in Berlin…"

I laughed, "I think little girls, girls much younger than Fabi, preen in front of the mirror, with a scarf, or the veil from their mother's wedding dress, or something, and imagine themselves with Prince Charming. They define their future against the destiny of some handsome prince."

"You think so?"

"Their longings are set before they have longings."

Kurt laughed, "You're probably right." He took a sip of champagne and asked, "Are we going to that jazz joint you mentioned later tonight?"

"You bet," and I nodded across the room towards André Breton, "The Surrealists will lead the way. André will give us a nod when he's ready. It's not a place you get to too early. Like Bricktop's."

Fabi came walking over with her tray of hors d'oeuvres. She stopped, looked at Kurt, cocked her head sidewise, and then came forward. "I just wanted to see," she said to Kurt. "You do look a little like my father's pictures."

"Yes, he does," I said.

"You're with Djuna. I'm glad. She's been unhappy. Thelma. Now she's happy."

Kurt smiled and said, "Thank you, that's a real compliment."

"My mother and I are leaving for New York. My sister's there. She just had a baby. My sister tells me things," and she looked at me brightly.

"I'm sure she does," said Kurt good-naturedly.

"She's told me about men. But I don't know about some of my mother's women friends…" and she let the words trail off, her face covered with a mild look of perplexity. She brightened, "But I'll learn."

"I'm sure you will," I said reassuringly. She turned and walked away. I said to Kurt, "Before Joella hit courting age, there was little that Mina had not told her about men…and women."

"Well, in Paris…"

"Interestingly, Joella took away from that knowledge a sophistication and realism beyond that of almost all the women she knew in Paris."

Kurt laughed, "Not hard to do."

"She felt too many of them were shallow and narcissistic."

"The women in the cafes, at the salons?" laughed Kurt. "And Kate?" he asked, a little more seriously.

"No, I don't think so. Both girls always liked Kate, she was closer to Joella in age."

"And Kate told her things, too?"

"Probably," and I laughed.

"Seriously?"

"Yes, I think Kate has looked back at 1918 every year since, each year seeing it differently, drawing some new insight."

"Yes," said Kurt wistfully. "You look back. For me, there has always been a growing beauty in the memory. Hope it has been that way for Kate."

"Yes," I said. I had never thought of it that way. But that was possibly what a beautiful life was about—getting the memories right.

26. Le Boeuf Sur le Toit

The taxi passed the massive marble Madeleine church in the darkness, its stolid Greek columns a light gray set off from black shadows behind. The taxi careened around the corner and headed down rue Boissy d'Anglas towards the river, swerving to a stop in front of the cabaret improbably named Le Boeuf sur le Toit—The Ox on the Roof. The gang piled out and pushed past the obliging doorman—he knew everyone by sight—and left overcoats and hats with hatcheck. The sweet sounds of Cole Porter were coming from Clément Doucet's piano; on the small bandstand some musicians were setting up, a couple black guys and three or four white guys.

"We're in luck. A *faire un Boeuf* tonight," cried one of the Surrealists, using the Paris patois for an after-hours jam session.

The piano melody faded away and the pianist looked over at the musicians and asked, "*Maintenant?*" The saxophone player riffed a few bars, the pianist nodded his head, and brought his left hand down to set a resounding chord and then tickled the ivories with his right as the melody took off. The other musicians jumped in after a couple more bars in some stuttered sort of order.

For almost half an hour, jazz rocked around the crowded club, champagne was poured, and conversations were shouted across the din. Then the jazz faded away and the musicians lit up cigarettes and stood to take a break. Djuna tapped her glass and Kurt reached into the ice bucket and pulled out a bottle of champagne and filled her glass.

"Oh, Kurt, I so want to write a play about *The Economic Consequences of the Peace*. A Surrealist Epic," said Djuna.

"A play?"

"Yes, the material is so right. The Dadists saw its true potential."

"They did?"

"Yes," and she pointed to the Dadist painting on the far wall, a solitary eye staring out from what looked like a collage of dirty gray newspaper headlines. "It's looking at me, telling me to seize the opportunity."

André Breton followed Djuna's glance to the Picabia painting on the wall and nodded his head in agreement. That the painting would speak to you made perfect sense to Breton. He reached over and waggled Djuna's knee, "How will you open your play?"

"It's all in my head. Let me explain."

"Of course it is in your head. Where else would it be?"

"A British army colonel will come out on the stage by himself and address the audience: 'This is the story of the peace to end all peace.' Then he will execute a right face and march off the stage."

"What is the first scene?" Eugene Jolas asked.

"We start with the Heavenly Twins. We will dress them as angels and suspend them on wires from the ceiling. One on each side of the stage."

"They were devils," said Kurt, speaking of the two British representatives at the Paris Peace Conference who led the Allies to demand ever higher levels of reparations .

"That's why we'll dress them as angels. In the first act they will be suspended just off the floor. The chorus will shout 'How high the reparations?' and the twins will hold out their hands and shout 'This high.'"

Djuna paused and thought for a moment, "We'll have a master of ceremonies on the stage. He will be dressed as a court jester. He will direct the play from the stage and he will bring the audience in as participants. The Jester will now turn to the chorus and ask, 'How high?' The chorus will chant 'Higher.' The Jester will turn to the audience and again ask how high and they will chant the answer. "Higher." We'll crank the Heavenly Twins a couple feet higher."

"Why include the audience?"

"Because all are guilty."

Kate laughed and I roared. Djuna was smack on the truth.

"In the second act, the Heavenly Twins will start a little higher and we will repeat the call and response. By the end of the third act, we'll practically have the Twins in the rafters."

"So we have taken care of reparations?" Kurt said.

"Yes, you're catching on," Djuna said. She turned towards Kurt and asked, "Tell me again why you're going back to Berlin just now?"

"I have to write an article on the hot money going back to New York."

"Yes, the hot money!" cried Djuna. Her eyes lit up, her expression came alive. "Please tell me, Kurt, please, that the hot money has something to do with the Heavenly Twins."

"Sort of. The hot money is short-term money that flows where the interest rates are highest."

"Why is it in Berlin?"

"It earns seven percent in Berlin and only five percent in New York."

"Yes, the Money Power! And now the Money Power in New York wants its money back? Why?"

"The stocks on Wall Street are going straight up. The hot money wants in on the action. The Money Power calls the hot money back home."

"Cooo…" moaned Djuna, trying to mimic the call to the hot money. She shook her head, "It doesn't work." Her face brightened and she said, "No, we'll have a French horn call from the forest." Djuna again clapped her hands with glee and said, "We will dress a flapper up and name her the Hot Money."

Djuna's face fell and she stopped and looked thoughtful, "But I need two." She asked Kurt, "What goes with hot money?"

"Well, easy money," he answered.

Djuna again clapped her hands in glee and shouted, "That's it. The other flapper will be Easy Money."

Djuna turned to the rest of us, "We'll dress the two flappers in shimmering gold dresses, one with a big scarlet H and M on her bosom, one on each side, and the other with a big scarlet E and M on her bosom. Every time we say 'hot money' or 'easy money,' the two Money girls will rush across the stage from different directions, do the Charleston in the middle, shake the bosoms, bend forward and give the audience the money shot, and then exit stage right and left."

"Brilliant idea," Elliot Paul exclaimed.

"What about the second act?" asked someone else.

"Oh, that's easy. We'll have Prime Minister Lloyd George come out and address the chorus—they're now the jury—and he will say that there are woman and children starving in Germany but no food can be sent because French Finance Minister Klotz wants 'his goold.' The chorus will echo, 'the goold.' The Jester will step forward to the audience and lift his palm and they will chant 'the goold.'"

I sipped my champagne and said to Kate, "She's brilliant."

"Who is French Finance Minister Klotz?" asked Breton, his face clouding over.

"He's the leader of the French accountants?" gaily replied Djuna.

"The French accountants?" asked Breton quizzically, confused by Djuna's answer.

"Those French statesmen in the grip of small-minded calculation," I added in an effort to be helpful.

Breton rolled his eyes and sighed, "Is there any other kind of calculation? Any other kind of statesmen?"

I laughed but saw his point and nodded my approval at Kate.

Djuna looked at Breton and said, "Accountants will not a drama make."

"*Bien sûr.*" Of course.

Djuna continued, "Then a beautifully robed actress—*très volupté*—dressed as the goddess Europa will enter from stage left and slowly walk across the stage. The Jester will throw rose petals in her path and call out, 'Oh fair and beautiful Europa.' Stealthily behind Europa will follow two sinister figures—Lenin and Trotsky—plotting to do evil deeds to her. Every time they get close, Europa stops and then they stop in mid-stride—their right legs frozen at right angles in front of them. The two Bolsheviks turn towards the audience and hold up solitary fingers in front of their mouths and say, "Shush." The two Money girls and the Jester repeat the "Shush" to the audience. Then Europa starts her stroll again. We do this three times and then Europa exits stage right, the two Bolsheviks following with big leers on their faces."

"What happens?"

"The Jester steps forward and asks the audience—'What happens to Europa when she is deep in the dark woods and the Bolshevik villains catch her?"

Djuna stood silent and looked at us and then said, "The two Money girls shriek out 'Oh No!'"

Djuna leaned over and crept forward a couple of steps while holding her hands up like a threatening zombie. Djuna continued, "Now Lloyd George comes forward in front of the chorus and says, 'When the Bolsheviks ravish Europe, then forever after history will chant out the names 'Lenin, Trotsky, and,' he pauses building suspense, 'Klotzky!"

Djuna straightened up and stretched her arms up towards the ceiling, "The chorus will shout, 'Lenin, Trotsky, and Klotzky'."

She reached over and picked up her champagne glass off the table and took a sip, "Then the Jester will approach the audience and lift his palm upwards and lead them in the chant, 'Lenin, Trotsky, and Klotzky.'"

"We'll have Man Ray film it!" added Elliot playfully.

Djuna stopped dead still and struck a pose of thoughtful contemplation, her chin resting on the palm of her hand propped up by the other arm and intoned, "In that case, the actresses can't wear clothes. Later I think for that. In the second act, we're still deep in serious economics."

"Yes, quite true," agreed Elliot.

Man Ray looked over at the beautiful blond behind the long cigarette holder, a fashion model for *Vogue*, sitting next to Elliot. She had been tagging along all night, "Do you want to be in the film? Possibly later? Very Bohemian."

"Oh, no, not me," she said. "I only remove clothes for an audition, when shall we say winning the job requires something extra, but before the camera I always wear clothes. Fashion photographs sell clothes, not skin. Don't want anyone to get the wrong idea."

Man Ray clapped his hands, "You should model for me. I do it completely the other way. You only take your clothes off before the camera's eye. Everyone gets the idea."

"What are you selling?" the fashion model asked.

"Beauty, of course."

"I'm selling clothes."

Man Ray handed her a slip of paper, "My address in case you decide on beauty in the future."

The model took the piece of paper and slipped it into her clutch bag and said, "Yes, of course, sometimes there is the question of the rent."

"Yes, the rent," said Man Ray. His face took on a saturnine expression and he said, "The rent refers most of my models to me."

Kiki wrapped herself around Man Ray's arm and said, "I came for the food and stayed for the fun." Man Ray beamed.

Elliot laughed and said, "I think Djuna's off talking about the truth tonight, not beauty."

"The truth can only be seen through the lens of the absurd," proclaimed Andre Breton rather grandly.

"Exactly," said Djuna.

"Dada was the true and correct response to the war," Breton said.

"Yes, but Kurt, and probably Hemingway, keep trying to use the metaphor of a doomed romance to describe the futility of war, some sort of rational and reasoned response to what is objectively mad."

"But Djuna, the tragedy was real, it happened to me," Kurt protested.

Djuna patted him on the knee and said to Kurt as if he were a slow-witted schoolboy, "Yes, dear. Someday you'll see that truth is on a higher plane than simple reality seen through the eyes of everyday life."

Breton leaned forward and looked into Kurt's eyes with fierce determination, "Yes, and your art is confined within the narrow walls of conventional thinking, like a statesman's," he spat out. "To get to truth, you have to break free of the chains of reason and other bourgeois crutches and indulgences." He turned to Jolas, "Right Eugene?"

"Absolutely. The writer expresses; he does not communicate in the bourgeois sense," replied Jolas.

Djuna nodded her head vigorously and said, "Exactly what I was going to say—I think?" She took a gulp from her champagne glass to make her point. Then she straightened up with a triumphant look on her face and said, “My play will do that.”

“How will it end?” asked Elliot.

“At the end of the third act, the final scenery will lower down showing a blue sky over a countryside of crosses. The crosses will emanate out in single-point perspective from the center of the stage up the sloping hills painted on the scenery. Over the crosses in the sky in silver letters will be emblazoned ‘The Economic Consequences of the Peace’.”

“Shouldn’t we have a closing song or something?”

“Yes, a final skit. Then a song.”

“Skit?”

“Yes, but first French Marshal Foch comes out and addresses the audience—‘The peace? It’s only a truce for twenty years.’ He executes a left face and marches off the stage. Then a British Tommy will come out and present arms. A British field marshal will come out and take a deep bow. A German general staff officer will come and stand between them. The German will pat the Tommy on the back and then tell the audience, ‘The British army? Lions led by donkeys.’ Then he will turn and kick the field marshal in the pants and push him off the stage with one boot kick after another.”

I laughed.

“The song?” asked Kate.

“The German officer will come out and lead the chorus in *Deutschland Uber Alles*. The Jester will hold his arms out and keep the audience quiet. Then Marshal Foch will come out and lead the chorus in *Mademoiselle from Armentières*. The Jester will again keep the audience silent. Then the British Tommy will come out, and with the Jester, lead the audience in *It’s a Long Way to Tipperary*. The field marshal and all the other cast will come out.”

“Bravo!” shouted Man Ray.

Djuna held out her hands palm down to quiet the group.

“Then the actresses come forward and start to disrobe. When they get down to their undergarments, the band strikes up a burlesque tune. Then—Kiki comes out in the altogether,” and she paused and looked at Elliot, “How much do we have to pay the Prefect to have the police raid the show?”

"Not much."

"Good. Then the police rush in and arrest and carry off the cast."

Man Ray jumped up and shouted, "A Surrealist triumph. We will establish Surrealism as the dominant revolutionary art form of the age, the anti-art of our time. You're inspirational, Djuna. How can we thank you?"

Djuna stood up and turned and faced him and bowed from the waist. Then she stood straight and stretched her arms wide and looked up, "I can see the headlines in the New York dailies now—'Jazz Age Ends in Paris, Police Raid Surrealistic Play for Public Indecency—Djuna Barnes Stages Modernist Triumph'."

Kate looked at me with a face of blazing happiness—the originality was striking. I almost fell out of my chair laughing. Kurt looked up at Djuna with awestruck admiration, the power of her talent hitting him right between the eyes.

André Breton stood up and said, "From you, Djuna, economics is always clear." He lifted his champagne glass in salute. "As to the experts," and he scowled at Kurt and me, "I'm not so sure."

Kate laughed and said, "Mr. Expert, I think it's getting late and we better be getting on home."

Djuna leaned over and wrapped herself around Kurt's arm, "She's right. We have work tomorrow before we can send you back to Berlin." And then she sighed, "All the economics tired me out."

Kurt laughed. We all stood up, settled the bill, and walked out into the cold early morning night. Kurt stepped off the curb and hailed a taxi, which swerved in and Kurt opened the rear door and guided Djuna into the back seat. Kate moved to follow and I held her back. She looked up at me with mock consternation and said, "I know. He'll have his hand up her dress before they hit the river. Does your mind always go to the carnal?"

"Mostly late at night," and I laughed as I watched Kurt follow Djuna into the rear of the taxi. I hailed another taxi. As it swerved in towards the curb, I said lightly, "I'll play with your garter as we cross the bridge."

The cabby came around and opened the door. I ushered Kate in and followed. She leaned over and kissed me on the cheek. I leaned over and kissed her behind her ear, "You're my sole carnal thought."

"How gallant."

She leaned back into the seat and said, looking back on the evening, "Oh, Djuna's play is all a dream, the breaking of reality down into its surreal pieces. Beautifully imagined."

"Except for the crosses."

"What do you mean?"

"The crosses are a vision. Nothing dreamlike about them."

"A vision?"

"A mental image we form in our present mind of what the future might look like."

"The crosses are a future reality? But it hasn't happened yet," she said with some insistence. "It might not. To do all that—again?" Her voice trailed off.

Kate always seemed to feel that her loss in the last war was going to be the last loss, that she had somehow borne the loss for the benefit for all women to come.

My turn to sigh, "Yes, that has been my fear since the last exercise at cross-making by our great statesmen. You know that. The victory in 1918 solved the problems presented by 1914; it was not a base for a peaceful future, 1919 saw to that."

"Where does it go?" whispered Kate.

"How much is endurable? By which route will men at last seek to escape their misfortunes? I don't know," I said as I recollected words from Keynes's book.

Kate sighed and nodded her head; yes, she knew that. Weary, she leaned her head against my shoulder.

"Okay, mister, it's Saturday night. Other visions? Women?"

"Women are objects, and then one of them becomes your personal vision."

"Objects?"

"Well, they are not men; they are something else. Damn close to the first distinction you make in life. The difference stays with you forever. Sure, women are persons, but the word 'person' is an abstraction. Better to say a woman is something simply different from you, like the freelance writer I saw last spring in the lobby of the theater with her friends."

"Yes, I think I know her. Nice looking, I think."

"Yes…I had been working with her off and on for years—a nice pleasant acquaintanceship. Then something happens and that 'object' starts to become a vision, an image in your mind. And it becomes very real and you see her as a vision in your future, in the world of tomorrow's potential."

"I'm not just another carnal thought?"

I laughed, "No, it's the beauty of the image, its potential to make your happiness—that takes over. The woman is in some filmy gown beckoning you forward—you know, come hither."

Kate smirked.

I laughed again, "That's why women have all the power. Only they hold that magic."

"Is this where romance starts?"

"Yes, the acquaintance becomes a romance. That marks the boundary line, I think, when the image moves front and center."

"In your heart or in your mind?"

"Both."

"And when she crawls into bed with you?"

"You go through a gate."

"When do I take off my filmy gown and become the carnal thought?"

I looked at her, into her eyes, and said, "The carnal? That is how you realize the beauty. You go through one to get to the other—it's the only way."

"The only way?"

"Yes, I think so. The little girl cannot realize her vision as the beautiful princess without prince charming. She knows this when she is little…from the time of her first doll…that this is what she hopes to become—the princess, that object of some prince's love."

She sat there for a minute, silent, the dark buildings of the Right Bank passing by the taxi window in the night. She said quietly, almost to herself, "When I saw the chance for love, its beauty, I always went through the gate…sometimes a golden gate."

"That is to live a beautiful life…"

"Yes, every once in a while…sometimes in Paris…" and she looked out the window. I guessed there must have been other memories.

I hugged her to me and remembered *yes, every once in a while…in Paris…*

She smiled with some satisfaction, contentment spreading across her face, and asked, "What brings on all this philosophizing? Besides the champagne."

"Tonight. Kurt said that he thought I saved you from going across the river, to the other side, to live a life with the ladies. I said no, I didn't think so."

"You sure of that," and she laughed.

"When you hold a woman in your arms and listen to the sounds of love, the breath heaving from deep inside…the romance with the prince…you know…you just hope you're the right guy."

"The bridge is coming up. Are you going to play with my garter?" And she looked up at me and whispered softly, "Mister Right Guy."

"*Avec plaisir, madame.*"

27. Café de Flore

Outside, beyond the windows of our flat, the air was crisp with the autumn chill, the leaves golden in the morning sunlight. Across the river, the sun bathed the façades of the buildings with light reflecting off the water. Kate lay curled up beside me, her dark hair spilled across the pillow in delightful disarray. She stirred, an eye opened, she turned her head and looked out the window. She let her head fall back. She reached over and grabbed my hand and held it close.

"We're almost done with the book project," she said.

"Yes."

"Mina'll be back from New York soon," she added.

"Right you are. Are you still going to sell her the lease on your apartment?"

"Maybe."

"What else could you do with it?"

"Well, it's the middle of October. I thought by springtime I would either be an editor in New York," and she paused and looked at me with dark eyes twinkling, "or a married woman in Paris. If I were married I would not need an apartment."

"Very practical."

She turned her head and looked directly into my eyes, twisting her head inquisitively like a small kitten.

"November is not a good month for marriage. The bells will be tolling another anniversary, for those gone and those still here," I said. All of Paris was going to stop for a minute of silence at eleven minutes after eleven on the morning of November 11; black crepe not white satin would be the color of the day.

"Yes," she said, nodding her head in slow agreement. "November is out. What might you suggest?"

"I think you could get married in a cathedral in Paris, say the first week in December. Do you have a groom picked out?"

"I was wondering whether the groom had picked out a bride? That is the question this morning."

"But can the bride give up that New York editorship? Think of the pearl necklaces, the soft mink stoles—the ecstasies of enthusiasm."

"Urgh. I have," she growled and buried her head into my neck. "I'm not Madeleine."

"Then Paris it is."

"Okay, mister All-About-Town. Someone has to say 'yes' here."

I pursed my lips and softly said, "Yes." I paused and looked into her eyes, "Are you happy?"

She buried her head into my neck again and grabbed me across the chest, "Yes, I want to be with you—here. You're only a big girl when you know you're a little girl. New York's not a little girl place."

"New York? A place to be from?" I whispered the question in her ear.

"Yes. From," she said in a little girl voice filled with determination, her face burrowed behind my ear and buried in the pillow.

I lay silent and wrapped an arm around her back and squeezed her to me. I looked up at the ceiling, thinking back to nine years ago and that walk back to my flat late at night down the deserted Paris streets. That was after my final coffee with Jenny—a lonely walk all alone. Yes, another nice place to be from. I turned my head towards Kate and said, "I never really felt that I would see someone like you again."

"I guess you never do until it happens," she mumbled into the pillow.

I lay there and simply let the contentment wash over me. Then I said, "Now for the big question—which church?"

She pulled her head back like a shot and propped herself up on her elbow, looking at me, and said, "Djuna loves Saint-Germain-des-Prés."

"So the bridesmaid gets to pick the church?"

"She knows the churches. She visits them a lot. They're temples of solitude to her."

"So Saint-Germain-des-Prés it is. Maybe there will be snow on the ground?"

"My dress will be white."

"We'll have such a lovely time together."

"Yes, isn't it nice to think so," and she leaned over and kissed me.

We took our morning coffee at the table in front of the French windows in the drawing room. Afterwards Kate sat at the work table and edited Kurt's manuscript. He had returned from Berlin last night with a raft of changes suggested by Djuna and Kate from the last trip. He had brought with him what we all hoped was the final draft of the manuscript. Djuna had been pining for him ever since he left. They took off together almost as soon as Kate stuffed the manuscript in her handbag. We all agreed to meet at the Café de Flore early this evening.

Kate and I walked arm-and-arm up the sidewalk from the river, Kate as gay and cheerful as a sparrow on a spring day. A woman's wedding day takes over her whole personality—the church, the friends, the day looked forward to from earliest girlhood, the beautiful white dress—the central ritual of our life.

We walked into the foyer of the Café de Flore and I spoke with the maître d' and told him another couple would be joining us. I asked if we could have a quiet place to talk for dinner since it was a business meeting. He pointed up the stairway, "*Monsieur*," and he turned to Kate and said, "*Madame*."

Kate walked up the twisting stairwell ahead of me to the second floor of the café. Reaching the landing I pointed to a table over by the window, the late afternoon light of a gray fall day putting a soft glow on the tablecloth. We sat down and Kate got out some typewritten pages of Kurt's manuscript and spread them on the table.

"I think the last pages ran out of gas. What's he driving at?"

"I'm not sure," I said.

Just then Kurt and Djuna came up. Kurt held Djuna's chair as she sat down. Then he took a seat and asked, "Well?"

"Yes, what do the editors have to say?" Djuna asked rather airily. "Where has our talent gone astray?"

"We think the end needs a sharper focus," I said.

"Yeah, I agree. I just sort of walk into a swamp of sadness when I think what happened in Berlin that winter," Kurt said.

"I have an idea," said Kate. "Kurt, why don't you tell us what happened in Berlin during the Kapp putsch. In your own words."

"Yes, confuse our minds with real facts," said Djuna.

Kurt laughed and started in, "Facts? In the winter of 1920? In Berlin?" Kurt took a sip from his beer. "Well, Berlin was getting back to normal under President Ebert's coalition government. The coalition was dominated by the Social Democrats but also included bourgeois parties and some from the Left. There had been rumors—Berlin teemed with rumors in those years—that the Junkers and militarists were planning a coup against the republic. Some thought they wanted to restore a monarchy, others an authoritarian regime dominated by the industrialists and given muscle by the militarists."

"Weren't the Junkers and the militarists the same people?" asked Kate.

"Almost. The Junkers are the old aristocracy, the Prussians living out on those vast estates in Eastern Germany. The militarists come from that caste but also from other parts of the German upper class."

"And the industrialists?" I asked.

"They're from the western industrial part of Germany around the Ruhr and along the Rhine River. The industrialists like to sell armaments to the militarists and appreciate a well-fortified system of privilege enshrined in the state to protect the wealth."

"Sounds so German," said Djuna. "Why did the putsch fail?"

"The war destroyed the prestige and legitimacy of German elites in the eyes of both the bourgeois and the working classes. The putsch ultimately proved that."

"What set it off?" asked Kate.

"The Ebert government moved to dissolve a large Freikorps brigade bivouacked to the west of Berlin, a brigade that had fought to free the ports of Bremen and Wilhelmshaven from the Communist forces after the Armistice and then battled Polish nationalists in Silesia. The Freikorps marched on Berlin with the support of a monarchist general and its public leader, Wolfgang Kapp, the reactionary Hotspur from East Prussia."

"All these Germans know Shakespeare—Shylock, Hotspur—who else?" marveled Djuna.

"The Freikorps marched on Berlin Friday night arriving at dawn."

"Then there was blood in the streets?" asked Djuna, rather expectantly.

"No, the Freikorps advanced from the west, the regular army marched out to the east, and the government abandoned the capital."

"Without a fight?" asked Kate, rather puzzled.

"Ebert and his government figured that the putsch would fall of its own weight. But just to make sure they called for a general strike to start on Sunday."

"So the sullen Berliners were under the iron heel of the militarists Saturday?" asked Djuna.

"Not exactly. At seven o'clock Saturday morning, the Freikorps started marching through the Brandenburg Gate from the west and down Unter den Linden, the soldiers singing, and the bands playing. The troops and the onlookers were all in the best of humor."

"Oh, what a wonderful revolution," said Djuna drily.

"Yes, Berliners treated it like a holiday and went around in large numbers and gawked at the Freikorps soldiers. The imperial colors—black, white and red—flew over Berlin again. Saturday night the restaurants were full, the theaters well attended. Everything was open but the dance palaces."

"Those hotbeds of subversion. Wise, those reactionaries," said Djuna, and she took a long sip from her martini.

"That was part of the problem. Correspondents started wiring dispatches that the coup d'etat was really just an Italian opera buffa—a comic opera. Everyone took it too lightly."

I saw the danger. The general strike would put the workers into a collision with the soldiers. That would ignite the violence.

"Where did the Ebert government go?" asked Kate.

"They went to Stuttgart. The rest of Germany stayed with the Ebert government, as did the army."

"What happened in Berlin?" Kate continued.

"I and the other foreign correspondents watched the troops march in from the roof of the Adlon Hotel where most of us had offices. Kapp sent a uniformed officer on a horse, who brought up to a halt in front of the steps of the hotel. He read out a proclamation to the journalists that the new government would liberate Germany from the misery, corruption and crime fostered by the old Government."

"They all say that, but do they mean it in the morning?" mocked Djuna.

Kurt took a draught from his beer and then organized his recollections, "The proclamation said that Bolshevism threatened Germany's eastern frontier. Only a strong Government would be able to ward off all dangers. German honor must be restored. No offense against the Constitution could be tolerated. Only a Government of deeds could save Germany."

"Ah, the Bolshevik bear!" exclaimed Djuna. "The rest is mush. But, hey, it would play in Peoria. Right, Kate?" said Djuna.

"Yes, the Red Menace plays well in the heartland, maybe in every country's heartland," said Kate with a smile.

"But worse than the Red Menace was the dark side. The Freikorps troops marched in with bizarre little emblems on their helmets—what we now call the swastika. We hadn't seen that before. And anti-Semitic leaflets were strewn over the streets and sidewalks saying that the defeat in 1918 came from a stab-in-the-back on the home front and that the Jews are to blame. Most people laughed this off, but some of it stuck."

"Why did people believe this?" asked Kate.

"Because the Allies said that Germany was solely responsible for starting the war, a statement that all Germany felt was a lie. So pair something false with something true and both seem true to the listener."

"So Lloyd George's little farce on Finance Minister Klotz in Versailles takes on a sinister tone," said Djuna.

"Not really. The Germans never heard of Finance Minister Klotz. Hatred for Jews comes out of the tortured psyche of a Central Europe that has been rubbed raw by a defeat in war that many still can't accept."

"What broke the back of the coup d'etat?" I asked.

"The general strike. It started Sunday. It brought Berlin to a standstill. And the rest of Germany rallied to the Ebert government in Stuttgart. No one wanted to go back to the Kaiser. By Wednesday the game was up. Early Thursday afternoon, the Freikorps lined up almost the entire length of the Wilhelmstrasse to march out."

"Still no violence?" asked Kate.

"Almost none. The column of troops started marching out right in front of the Adlon Hotel. The troops tramped across Pariserplatz, singing their marching songs in some good humor, and through the Brandenburg Gate. The Berlin crowds started to shout and give the soldiers catcalls and jeers."

Kurt paused, took a sip of beer, and then started in again, "Elsa, who was quite pregnant by now, was watching from the glassed-in terrace of a nearby restaurant. I returned to be with her to watch the final march out. Suddenly, some of the soldiers turned on the jeering crowd and fired shots into the sky. There was a stampede, but then the crowd sort of stopped and reorganized. Then came volley after volley of rifle fire. People rushed in panic down the street, others fell face downward on the street. Another reporter later told me these were minutes when almost anything might happen."

Kurt's face twisted in memory of what he was about to say. "Then, bullets shattered the glass of the terrace where we sat. Elsa caught the full force of shards of glass splaying across the room. She went down, blood coming out of her clothes in numerous places. Some other people helped me and we carried her to the hall of the Adlon Hotel where a first aid center had been set up. Some were dead, about a dozen more wounded. A nurse and a doctor looked at Elsa," Kurt stopped and looked at me, "You know the routine, triage."

I nodded my head sadly.

"The doctor worked with the nurse to stanch the bleeding and then said, 'Get her to a hospital. There are hotel trucks out back. Use them.' He told the nurse to accompany Elsa and we carried her out back and put her in the rear of a linen truck and got in and hurried off to the hospital. It was quite close."

Kate and Djuna looked at Kurt with their undivided attention.

"Elsa was rushed into the surgery room. Doctors came running. A nurse came out, crestfallen and told me the baby—a boy—was stillborn. I asked about my wife, pleaded…the nurse said the doctor was trying. She returned to the surgery. Some minutes later the nurse came out again… 'the hemorrhage could not be stopped…the doctors did everything they could…I'm sorry.'"

I watched a shiver go down Kate's back; her shoulders shook. Djuna was spellbound.

Kurt continued, "I was simply shattered. I sat down. The nurse from the Adlon tried to comfort me. After a while the doctor came out and walked over to me and said maybe I should take a walk with him…he would explain what he could…I stood up and went with the doctor down the hall."

Kurt was simply drained.

Kate said, "I'm sorry. I just wanted to know."

"I'm not good at this," said Djuna and took a big gulp from her martini.

Djuna leaned over and caressed Kurt's neck and patted him on the shoulder and then looked at Kate and me, "Love. So many search for it, so few find it."

I let everyone settle down and then said, "Getting back to the novel. When the protagonist comes out of the hospital room after seeing his dead wife and walks down the hall with the doctor, there needs to be just one emotion."

Kate nodded her head in sad agreement.

"Yeah, I know," Kurt said. "I didn't get it right. I was overcome by so many emotions." Kurt always spoke about the protagonist of the novel as himself of course. "But which emotion?"

"Rage," Kate said. "The doctor should say the operation failed because of lack of adequate supplies."

Kurt listened.

"The doctor spoke bitterly of the Allied quarantine, the British blockade, holding health supplies hostage to financial payments."

"Yeah, all that happened," Kurt said simply. "And the putsch."

"The promise of a peaceful future was stillborn in Berlin in 1920," I said.

"Yeah, the peace did not deliver its promise," said Kurt, eyes down. Then he looked up and I sensed a revelation was hiding behind his eyes. He said, "It was worse than that. Keynes predicted it in his book. I was forewarned; I should have been more vigilant to the possibility of danger."

"What did Keynes say?" asked Kate.

"He said that those who sign the Treaty will sign the death sentence of many millions of German men, women and children."

"I didn't know that," said Kate in a tone of reflection.

I remembered reading the words. I said to Kurt, "The conversation with the doctor while walking down the hall needs to drive home the point of the failed peace—the anger results from a terrible loss having come in a time of peace."

"Yes, we want to stay in step with the novel's theme of a brave war and failed peace," added Kate.

"Sylvia said at the house party that Hemingway's book is set in the war. Our tragedy after the war will make not only a nice complement but a powerful juxtaposition," I said.

Djuna's head swiveled as she followed the argument from me to Kate to Kurt and she added, "Yes, the drama of the juxtaposition. Tragedy is always strengthened by the 'might have been.'"

"Yes, the long look back," said Kate.

Djuna took a final sip from her martini and said, "Kurt, I can help with the ending. I know anger. I know how to write it."

Kurt looked up and nodded his head in approval.

Djuna turned to Kate and said, "Let Kurt and me work on the ending tonight and tomorrow. We'll meet you at the train station tomorrow night and give it a last look. Kurt can sharpen it up back in Berlin and he can bring the finished manuscript back early in November."

"We can celebrate the Armistice on a high note," I said.

"Yes, the bells…" and Kate let the words trail off.

The waiter came up and we ordered dinner. I suggested a good bottle of wine and everyone agreed. Dinner was served, we spoke about Germany in 1928—"okay unless the bottom falls out…there's a real dark side"—said Kurt.

Coffee was served. Kurt added a cognac to his, pouring it out of the snifter into the cup and giving the snifter a disdainful look, which caused Djuna and Kate to laugh.

"Not much of an aristocrat, is he?" said Djuna.

I said that New York was going to be a great book market next year; lots of new books were coming out as prosperity broadened its reach almost everywhere.

"Yeah, the easy money will do that every time," Kurt said.

"Ah, yes, the easy money," said Djuna with a twinkle in her eye. Then she changed the subject, "I'm going to Berlin for Christmas. Right, Kurt?"

"Yes."

"Haven't been there since 1921," Djuna said with a dreamy look on her face.

Kurt looked at her appraisingly and took a drink from his coffee. He looked at Kate with a wink and playfully leered at Djuna, "Kate was with you then?"

"Yes, she was," Djuna said and she looked off into the distance of her memories. "We almost became the very best of friends."

Startled, I looked up—someone had made a pass those many years ago in Berlin. Kurt glanced at Kate, his face not quite ready to make the question.

Kate nonchalantly looked across the table at Djuna and reached out with both hands and took Djuna's hands in hers and softly said, "Yes, almost. We've been good friends ever since."

Djuna's face turned soft and her eyes glowed with affection as she gazed at Kate. She squeezed Kate's hands and murmured, "Yes. Friends."

Kurt let the silence settle in, then said, "Yeah, we better be going."

Djuna dropped Kate's hands and looked over at Kurt and whispered, "Yes."

I stood up and held Kate's chair. Kurt had almost been right.

28. Gare du Nord

A waiter brought two cups of coffee over to the table in the station café. Kate stared at the entrance, "They should be here by now."

"Oh, they'll get here on time. Kurt wants to be on the train to Berlin."

"There he is." Kate waved. Kurt saw her and started walking over. He came up and sat down.

"Djuna will be here in a minute. She stopped off to speak with Janet. She wants to know the gossip from New York. You know..."

Yes we did. She was still broken up over Thelma Wood, who was now in New York with another woman, another patroness. A more indulgent one, I gathered.

Kurt reached into his briefcase and pulled out some typescript pages, "Here's the rewrite of the ending."

Kate took it and read through the lines quickly, with her pencil now and again landing on the paper. "Yes, hmm, good…well done." She looked at me, "It's great, Bill."

"Djuna knows how to put the words next to each other to create the sense of anger," Kurt said.

"Yes, she does. But this still has your stamp all over it."

Kurt nodded with a certain sense of satisfaction.

"Are we still on theme: brave war, failed peace?" I asked.

"Yes," Kate replied. "The doctor and Kurt walk down the hall, a long lonely walk for Kurt as the reality of the loss sinks in. The doctor explains that lack of medical supplies in the operating room is the cause of Elsa's death."

Kate paused: "Kurt asks why?"

She looked at me and continued, "The doctor says that the British blockade and Allied foot dragging on relief supplies for almost half a year after the Armistice are the cause. Yes, too few supplies for too long repeats Kurt."

"Is this some right-wing explanation? Part of the stab-in-the-back myth?" I asked.

"No. The doctor explains that he is a Social Democrat. The Social Democrats were the key to turning the victory into a prosperous peace, the doctor feels, but the Allies let the Social Democrats go down the drain in 1919."

"So what is the final emotion of the ending?"

"Kurt shakes the doctor's hand and walks through the door outside into the winter cold. He pulls up his collar and starts walking down the deserted streets in a sleeting storm, the molten anger in his head contrasting with cold grayness outside, the two clashing factors unable to resolve themselves."

"The gray cold of defeat and the hot anger of a cruel death?"

"Yes, that's the imagery. Up ahead Kurt sees an open door to a workingman's pub, warm and inviting, the poignant melody of a soldiers' song wafting across the evening stillness, the bittersweet desolation of the defeated soldiers inside haunting the harmony. Looking through the door, Kurt sees comrades sitting at the bar and tables in melancholy fellowship, the veterans left behind by the stillborn peace, sad in their subdued camaraderie."

"Another consequence of the failed peace?"

"Exactly. The last sentence has Kurt walking across the street towards the open door in the rain."

"Good." I looked up; Djuna was walking over. She came up.

"What d'ya think?" she said in that snappy New York way.

Kate answered, "Very good. A fine resolution of both the ideas and the emotions."

"I don't do ideas. Kurt does," Djuna said as she sat down. "But I helped him with the emotions, that slow-burning anger that goes with the great hurt. Kurt's going to do a little more work back in Berlin. Then we're done."

"I agree," I said. "By the way, Djuna, what's the news from New York?"

"I guess she's gone," Djuna said. "Losing her to that woman…" and Djuna's voice dripped scorn. She looked at Kurt, "I can't help it. It hurts."

"Don't worry," said Kurt soothingly. Then he teased, "Another dolly will show up down the road." He winked at me.

Djuna's eyes darted between Kurt and Kate and she blurted, "I'm not a lesbian. I was just in love with Thelma Wood."

Kurt smiled; she was like a kitten in his hands. “I know,” he soothed.

“I was always faithful to her. You know that. She left me.” She looked beseechingly at Kurt.

Kurt reached across the table and took her hands in his. Kurt had that fine understanding. I watched as that understanding lit up his eyes and he whispered to Djuna, “I know that.” I sensed that Kurt had found something that had been missing in him for a long time.

“I know you do,” Djuna said, with a little girl pout, the bond between her and Kurt deep and intimate, visible for us to see at the small table in the cavernous railroad station. I had never really seen Djuna like this. I glanced over at Kate. A look of happiness for Djuna was written across her face as the simple truths about her friend tumbled out.

Kurt took his right hand and put Djuna’s hands on top of his left hand. He patted her hands with his free hand, “You and I. We’re constant on these things. That’s the way we are. Together.”

“Together,” intoned Djuna like a little girl. She looked up and smiled at Kurt. You could see that “together” was an overarching goal in her life, the keystone that had been robbed from her when Thelma left for New York with the other woman. I now saw clearly that this was the solid brick Kurt was putting back into her life.

Kurt nodded at her, his calm sense of reassurance like a transfusion of spirit into her.

Kurt looked at his watch, “We better walk down to the train. I have a sleeper up front.” He stood up and turned to me, “Thank you for everything. You and Kate have been great friends.” He said it by way of goodbye.

I pulled Kate over to my side, reached out my hand and shook Kurt’s goodbye.

He reached out to Djuna and said, “Let’s go, sugar.”

Djuna rolled her eyes playfully and gave a warm goodbye look to Kate. Djuna turned and put her head against Kurt’s shoulder and the two of them started walking down the platform to the front of the train, so strikingly handsome together.

Kate and I turned and went outside into the gathering cold of an approaching winter storm and took a cab back to Île Saint-Louis.

29. The Bridge

I woke up and looked outside to a gray drizzly morning. The fine autumn weather of early October was gone. Beyond the windows the sullen river flowed timelessly down its channel, framed by the barren limbs of elm trees stripped bare by the cold of approaching winter. On the far bank, mist shrouded the dull façades of riverfront buildings.

Kate had kissed me goodbye when she left. The warmth of her was still in the bed. She was meeting Djuna for coffee at Les Deux Magots.

I got up, shaved, pulled on wool pants, tucked in a clean shirt, and pulled over my head a big wool sweater. I put on a thick overcoat, wrapped a muffler around my neck, and plopped a wide-brimmed slouch hat on my head. I was ready for a newspaper and coffee at the corner bistro down by the bridge. Then the morning's work.

I walked down the sidewalk towards the little square by the bridge. There was a crowd around the newspaper kiosk, pushing and jostling. An old truck drove up and people crowded around it, a young man stood up in the bed and heaved a bundle of papers off into the arms of the owner of the kiosk. The man hurried back inside his little shelter and started handing out papers to the outstretched hands of the thronging crowd outside, who were tossing coins into tin cans nailed to the frames at the side of the counter.

"Train Crash" was emblazoned in giant type across the top of the newspaper. I pushed to the front, pitched a coin into one of the cans, and grabbed a paper. I stepped back to the edge of the crowd and scanned the subheads: "Berlin Express Collides with Freight in Eastern France in Snow Blizzard Darkness."

I read down through the story: a freight train had crashed head-on into the express roaring through the fog-bound night for Berlin. The express was derailed and much of it was consumed in flames from overturned stoves. Scores were dead. Further on came the words "well-known Berlin correspondent Kurt Eckhart was among the dead, killed in the conflagration which consumed the first-class carriages."

Slowly I read through the story, the shock settling in, a sense of dismay spreading across my consciousness. Kurt dead.

I looked across the channel to Notre Dame sitting solid and eternal on Île de la Cité. I started walking across the bridge. As I came near the edge of the island I stopped and leaned across the bridge's balustrade watching the gray water flow by. My eyes followed the water coursing along the edge of the stone-lined channel until it met the larger branch of the river flowing down the far side of Île Saint-Louis. Little eddies formed and the water rippled where the two rain-swollen streams merged.

Ever since the war I had felt like a small child looking through one side of a glass door at people enjoying a party on the other side. Try as I might I could never attract their attention, I could never get my message through to the people on the other side. Kurt was the ablest man I knew. He had the story; he had the message down in an understandable way. Surely he could deliver it, break through to the broader public consciousness on the other side of the glass window. But now even Kurt Eckhart was stopped. Dead. The message did not want to be heard.

Out of the corner of my eye I saw Kate walk up. She came and stood beside me; she wrapped her arms around my left arm and leaned her head against my shoulder.

"I'm sorry," she said.

"Yes, it's tragic."

"The novel?"

"He had the only manuscript. The first-class carriages were consumed by fire."

"Maybe someone else will tell the story."

"Not his story."

"I suppose you're right."

"Were you with Djuna?"

"Yes."

"What did she say?"

"Oh, something about 'the good ones always leave…Kurt didn't have to go that far...'"

"Wit like a stiletto."

Kate gave me a wan smile, then looked down the channel: "I asked her—you were going to Berlin with him at Christmas—were you going to stay?" Kate caught her breath, choked up and held back her tears. Collecting herself, Kate continued, "She said, 'Maybe. I hoped so—everything seemed right.'" Kate wiped a tear from the corner of her eye.

"He understood her. Not many do."

Kate nodded: "She said…I wrote a poem about this…long ago…about the final moment...—

For you, for me? Why then the striking hour,
The wind among the curtains, and the tread
Of some late gardener pulling at the flower
They'll lay between our hearts when we are dead.—

"Djuna's eyes were soft and dark, tear-filled," murmured Kate.

I reached around and patted Kate's shoulder and looked across the water, the bittersweet beauty of the words lingering in my mind.

Kate looked up into my face. In a voice full of consolation, eyes flashing behind a sheen of tears, she said, "We're together…it's all we have…it's so much." I leaned over and kissed her upturned lips, the raindrops lightly sprinkling her tear-streaked cheeks.

I stepped back and reached around Kate's waist with my arm and guided her up the sidewalk towards the crown of the bridge. At the top, we stopped and looked down the channel to where its current merged with the larger stream. Sea birds, blown up river from the Channel by the winter storm, wheeled and dived into the wind-ruffled waters. We continued across the bridge in the rain.

End

Afterword on Hemingway's *A Farewell to Arms*

Ernest Hemingway's second novel *A Farewell to Arms* was serialized in Scribner's Magazine from May to October 1929. The book was published in September 1929 to excellent reviews. Some excerpts follow:

Excerpts from Reviews

To this reviewer…it is his greatest work. It is that rarest of all literary achievements—a glowing modern love story, the story of an emotion so profound and true that it is like reading the record of an overwhelming personal experience.

Mr. Hemingway's story has the war for its background…As the war grows in intensity and grimness, so does the love affair progress to a desperate, tragic emotion.

A.W.S., *The New Yorker*, October 12, 1929.

But, unlike the earlier novel [*The Sun Also Rises*], he is not concerned with the aftermath of the war, but with certain years and phases of the war itself…the war, however, is but a background for the real story.

The love of Lieutenant Henry for the nurse Catherine Barkley, a love so great that Henry eventually deserts, as he puts it, "declares separate peace," could only have come in the war and out of the war. The story of this attachment is poetic, idyllic, tragic.

Percy Hutchison, *New York Times*, September 29, 1929

Seventy times he rewrote the concluding pages of "A Farewell to Arms." He had no idea of ever being completely satisfied with them; he merely hoped that the words would eventually come nearer to his meaning. The pile of scribbled-out sheets made a formidable manuscript. Seventy times… "Now I suppose," he remarked, "they'll say that the ending is hurried."

Dorothy Parker, "Profiles: The Artist's Reward," *The New Yorker*, November 30, 1929.

The profile written by Dorothy Parker was intended as a humorous piece about Hemingway, the new celebrity writer. A re-issue of the novel in 2012 included copies of forty-seven different endings that Hemingway wrote. So Parker's humorous comment about seventy rewrites is an exaggeration rooted in reality.

SOURCES – BOOKS

Baker, Carlos. *Hemingway. The Writer as Artist*. 4th edition. Princeton: Princeton University Press, 1980.

Barnes, Djuna. *Ladies Almanack*. Normal, IL: Dalkey Archive Press, 1992.

——. *Ryder*. Elmwood, IL: Dalkey Archive Press, 1990.

Burke, Carolyn. *Becoming Modern: The Life of Mina Loy*. New York: Farrar, Straus and Giroux, 1996. (Loy's poetry quoted is all from this book.)

Cody, Morrill with Hugh Ford. *The Women of Montparnasse*. New York: Cornwall Books, 1984.

Cowley, Malcolm. *A Second Flowering: Works and Days of the Lost Generation*. New York: The Viking Press, 1973.

Farrer, David. *The Warburgs: The Story of a Family*. New York: Stein and Day, 1975.

Field, Andrew. *Djuna: The Life and Times of Djuna Barnes*. New York: G.P. Putnam's Sons. 1983. (Including line "This night I've been one hour in paradise.")

Fitch, Noel Riley. *Sylvia Beach and the Lost Generation*. New York: W.W. Norton & Company, 1983.

Ford, Hugh. *Published in Paris*. New York: Macmillan Publishing Company, 1975.

Hemingway, Ernest. *A Farewell to Arms*. New York: Charles Scribner's Sons, 1929.

——*The Complete Short Stories of Ernest Hemingway: The Finca Vigia Edition*. New York: Quality Paperback Book Club, 1987.

Herring, Phillip. *Djuna: The Life and Work of Djuna Barnes*. New York: Viking, 1995. (Including quote "I was never a lesbian—I only loved Thelma Wood.")

Keynes, John Maynard. *The Economic Consequences of the Peace*. London: Macmillan and Co., Limited, 1920.

——. *Two Memoirs: Dr. Melchior: A Defeated Enemy and My Early Beliefs.* New York: Augustus M. Kelley, 1949. (from Questia.com)

MacMillan, Margaret. *Paris 1919: Six Months That Changed the World.* New York: Random House Trade Paperbacks, 2001.

McAlmon, Robert and Kay Boyle. *Being Geniuses Together: 1920-1930.* London: Hogarth Press, 1984.

Morton, Brian N. *Americans in Paris: An Anecdotal Street Guide.* New York: The Olivia & Hill Press, 1984. (The flat on Île Saint-Louis with entrance at 2 rue Budé overlooking Quai d'Orléans was owned by American writer James Jones after WW II. American literary agent William Aspenwall Bradley lived on an interior street on the famed isle.)

Reynolds, Bruce. *Paris with the Lid Lifted.* New York: George Sully & Company, 1927.

Rodriguez, Suzanne. *Wild Heart: A Life of Natalie Clifford Barney.* New York: HarperCollins, 2002.

Seldes, George. *Witness to a Century.* New York: Ballantine Books, 1987.

Skidelsky, Robert. *John Maynard Keynes: Hopes Betrayed 1883-1920.* New York: Penguin Books, 1983.

——. *John Maynard Keynes: The Economist as Savior 1920-1937.* New York: The Penguin Press, 1992. (Skidelsky is the source of the wonderful line: "The clever dog caught the wild duck" and many others.)

Weitz, Eric D. *Weimar Germany.* Princeton: Princeton University Press, 2007.

Wineapple, Brenda. *Genêt: A Biography of Janet Flanner.* Lincoln NB: University of Nebraska Press, 1989. (Including the line that Jane and her fiancé Lane "were to be in love and he was to go to war.")

SOURCES – PERIODICALS

Flanner, Janet. "That Was Paris: The Greatest Refreshment," *The New Yorker*, 1974.

Flanner, Janet. "Letter from Paris," *The New Yorker,* February 9, 1929. With reference to: "Leading agent and prophet here on transatlantic affairs." The reference is to William Aspenwall Bradley, the American literary agent living on Île Saint-Louis, from whom the novel's protagonist Bill Lawrence is derived. (Bradley was happily married to the daughter of a prominent French politician.)

SOURCES – NEW YORK TIMES ARCHIVES

Birkhead, May. "Couturier Rivalry is Intense in Paris," February 12, 1928. With reference to: "Chanel now stands in a class by herself…a distinctive place in the world of couturiers."

Carr, Phillip. "Three New Plays by the Seine," March 4, 1928. With reference to Comédians de la Croix Nivert.

Renwick, George. "Berlin Upset Was Tame," March 15, 1920. Kapp Putsch.

Renwick, George. "Berlin Received Rebels Amicably," March 16, 1920. Kapp Putsch.

Associated Press. "Seek to Restore Order," March 19, 1920. Kapp Putsch.

Renwick, George. "Kapp's Rebellion Ended in Farce," March 19, 1920. Kapp Putsch.

Renwick, George. "Junker Farewell: A Berlin Tragedy," March 20, 1920. Kapp Putsch.

Associated Press. "Scores Are Killed in Berlin Clashes," March 20, 1920. Kapp Putsch.

Special Cable. "Berlin in Grave Straits," March 20, 1920. Kapp Putsch.

Associated Press. "Anti-Semitic Wave Accompanies Revolt," March 20, 1920. Kapp Putsch.

SOURCES – OTHER

History of the U.S. 30th Infantry Regiment. Internet: ww2f.com

Legendary Sin Cities: Paris, Berlin, and Shanghai. Docmentary: Ted Remerowski, Marrin Cannell, directors. Dvd and streaming version available at Netflix.

Barnes, Djuna. *The Book of Repulsive Women: 8 Rhythms and 5 Drawings*. New York: Bruno chap Books, 1915. Sourced from

Internet: digital.library.upenn.edu/women/barnes/repulsive/repulsive.html

Barnes, Djuna. *Finis*. The four-line poem quoted in the final chapter of the book is from Hering (cited above) on 312 (fittingly the last lines of his biography). Hering felt the poem was "perhaps written for Mary Pyne," her lover in New York who died of tuberculosis soon after World War I.

Millay, Edna St. Vincent. *Recuerdo*. RPO: Representative Poetry Online. University of Toronto Libraries. Sourced from Internet: rpo.library.utoronto.ca/poems/recuerdo

Sappho. *The Poems of Sappho Part I: Hymn to Aphrodite*. (*The Poems of Sappho*, translator E.M.Cox, 1925 translation) Sourced from Internet: www.sacred-texts.com/da/sappho/sappho).htm

Illustrations

Cover image: Café LaFayette (Portrait of Kay Laurel) by William J. Blackens, 1914. Image is in the public domain due to copyright expiration per WikiCommons.

Figure 1. Solita Solano and Djuna Barnes in Paris 1922. Public domain. WikiCommons.

Figure 2. Mina Loy and Djuna Barnes. Image from Beinecke Rare Book & Manuscript Library, Yale University. Fair use claimed for low resolution, cropped image.

Figure 3. Margaret Anderson. Image from *Little Review* webpage on internet. Public domain, low resolution image printed prior to 1923.

Figure 4. James Joyce with Sylvia Beach at Shakespeare & Co 1920, Beinecke Rare Book & Manuscript Library, Yale University. Public domain. WikiCommons.

Figure 5. Natalie in Fur Cape c 1905. Portrait of Natalie Clifford Barney, Smithsonian Institution. Public domain. WikiCommons.

Figure 6. Janet Flanner. Public domain. WikiCommons.

Figure 7. Cover art. Ladies Almanack by Djuna Barnes. Public domain. WikiCommons.